A Body To Bones

First Skeleton Series Mystery

Donan Berg

DOTDON Personalized Services
Rock Island, IL

Skeleton Series Mystery
DOTDON Books are published by

DOTDON Personalized Services
1800 Third Avenue, Ste 415
Rock Island, IL 61201-8019

Orders: mystery@abodytobones.com

Printed in United States of America
First U.S. Edition 2008

Library of Congress Control Number: 2008905533

Paperback
ISBN: 978-0-615-21458-0
Hardcover
ISBN: 978-0-9820855-0-9
Ebook
ISBN: 978-0-9820855-1-6

This is a work of fiction. The places, characters, and events only
exist in this book and the author's mind. Any resemblance to any
person, living or dead, is unintentional and purely coincidental.

For my parents, Milo and Veronica. They gave me life, love, and an inner compass to find my way, for which I will be eternally grateful.

Their spirits will find comfort in that their lives have not been drawn upon or combined to bring life to any character in this novel.

Their legacy is a happiness and great pleasure that grows with each morning sunrise in my life.

We all have special people, be they parents, grandparents, brothers, sisters, sons, daughters, spouses, cousins, nieces, nephews, or friends.

In meaningful little ways, remember to say thank you to each of them, and if you find my fictional story triggers a recollection of happiness, I dedicate the resulting discovered joy to you and yours.

Prologue

Spring of 1954

The quiet is broken by the slide of the wooden door to open the portal of St. Mary's confessional. A thin, unlined, purple velvet cloth hides the female penitent's identity from the priest, each in their own private space, permitting only voices to be heard. A hint of hair spray scents the air.

"Bless me, Father Murphy, for I have sinned."

"Yes, go on."

"I don't know what to say … where to start. I felt new life growing within me. At first, there was denial. I am married, but my husband was not the father. I did not tell anyone, not even the father. I suspect the real father does not even know what he created. I worry that my secret will be exposed, and many close to me will be subject to community disrepute, disgrace, scorn, and scandal. I have failed in other ways to live by what my mother believed in and taught me. I fretted that I was not worthy to be her daughter. Then I was consumed with the anguish of knowing that God will let this baby grow to be born, with the magnitude of all the consequences that I cannot hide. I have been drowning in guilt. I had to make a decision. I had to act somehow. Then God intervened. For my sin, God took two young lives, including my innocent daughter, my own flesh and blood. He cut out my ability to conceive more children."

"As humans, we never fully understand God's great plan. As God's family, we must believe He's compassionate. There is a sacred trust. For your—"

Before the priest can end this confession, he hears:

"One life extinguished was the result of an unholy union. Its death does not unburden me. My failure to be morally strong and my failure to honor my mother do not go away. I feel ashamed, conflicted. I cannot be truthful. To speak out will only bring shame, chastisement, and hurt the persons I love who live, or the memory of those departed. It's hard to hold it all inside, to not let the lies be seen, to bear all the pain in secret behind an accepted facade."

"Yes," the priest coughs before continuing. "We all, including me, have secrets from other humans but not from God. We must believe in Him, seek His forgiveness, and above all, pray to Him and believe in His everlasting life. Now, for strength and your penance, say three Our Fathers and three Hail Marys after saying your prayer of contrition."

The confessional portal sliding door is unexpectedly pulled closed the only way it can be—from the inside.

Ten years later....

"Oscar ... Where are you? I can't see you." Oscar hears his friend's voice echo behind him. Cobwebs stick to Oscar's hands and face as he creeps forward into the darkness. He feels an insect crawl across his forehead; he shakes his head. "Ouch," he yells, his head now hurts.

"Oscar, I'm scared. Let's go home. Where are you?" shouts Jim.

"I found something. It feels weird."

Oscar does not comprehend the magnitude of what he discovers, its potential to bring a killer out of hiding to strike again, or a past connection to the penitent and her confession ten years prior.

Chapter One

T hat's my jack. That's mine—gimme it."

"No, it ain't. You cheated."

The eight-year-old boy, in a bright yellow-and-brown-striped T-shirt and blue jeans with a hole in the left knee, stares at his friend sitting on the lowest of three concrete steps leading into Clinton's main and only bank. Oscar (oh, how he hates that name) wants Jim to give him the jack. Oscar is skinny for his age. Jim, a year older, outweighs Oscar by thirty pounds, not including the oversized black glasses he wears. Oscar is winning. He sees himself on the way to his first grand-slam victory. Always playing to win, Oscar isn't a cheater.

"I'll give you your stupid jack," retorts Jim. "Now you go git your ball." With a quick swipe of his right hand, Jim grabs Oscar's small, red, lucky rubber ball and flings it over his left shoulder. After thirty or so feet, it bounces once, twice, three times, ever slower, lower and lower each time until it's rolling down the block's concrete street gutter.

Slowly, oblivious to the ball in the gutter, a familiar solitary figure slowly pedals his blue-and-white fat-tire bike in the direction of the bank.

This man of average, regular build, in his early fifties, wears a railroad signalman's cap, which shows graying hair at the temples; black slacks; and a short-sleeve, white dress shirt with one button unfastened at the neck.

He will never arrive at the bank. Today's destination, as every other workday, is also on Main Street, but it is in the block before the bank.

The painted gold letters on the double front window panels proclaim in foot-high letters to all that pass this is the *Pioneer Ledger*, the chronicler of the town's life and death, mostly the latter. Nevertheless, the great majority of readers, claimed to be 1,059, use the *Pioneer Ledger* to keep track of family history or genealogy, social teas, school lunch menus, and create coffee shop and barbershop gossip.

Afternoon humidity is unseasonably high for a spring day. The sun in a cloudless sky bakes the emerging crops and softens street-tar joints. Vault locks turn automatically at three-thirty p.m., ending another regular bank business day.

1

Thomas Hamilton, a thrifty fourth-generation Scot, lets his bike slowly glide to a stop in front of the large gold letters of the *Pioneer Ledger*, where he lazily props up his bike next to the front door. He is in front of his newspaper office—the dream of many a journeyman printer. By any standard, the paper is small. Many weeks it is a struggle to publish its one edition at a minimum of eight broadsheet pages. Yet every Tuesday, a one-cylinder press in the basement creaks and groans from the exertion required of it. It sometimes balks, sometimes purrs, but always, to Hamilton's amazement, fulfills its printing task.

Today is Tuesday. At three-thirty p.m., Hamilton normally would be in the frenzy of the last-minute details of planning, brushing, and locking the chase forms that are bulging with lead type and made up into full pages, eight to twelve in number. It is always a chore for Hamilton to mechanically operate the small pulley to lower the lead pages down to the basement and into their proper position, ready for the press. Behind schedule this day, he is not one to give up or be hurried. For seventeen years now, he has never missed a deadline, and today will not break his streak.

The outside screen door slams.

A woman inside the front office jumps.

"I'm sorry, doll," apologizes Hamilton in quiet, loving, reassuring tones. "I'll remember next time."

The woman smiles knowingly. If sixteen years of marriage to Thomas Hamilton has taught her anything it's that he'll never learn to quit banging the door until it's nailed shut. At five-foot-five and forty-nine years old, she is always dieting to lose ten pounds, but the scale needle each week never budges from 145. She is wearing her Tuesday wardrobe of an ink-smudged dress, with her everyday wig pushed slightly behind the recommended frontal hairline. Her fingernails are painted dark blue—almost black—to match the ink. The darkish brunette wig matches the thinning hair it is trying to camouflage. A little hairspray keeps stray strands in place. Glasses, used for reading countless columns of the printed word, dangle in front of her neck with each bow attached to the silver chain around her neck.

"I'm sorry if I startled you, Sarah," repeats Thomas.

"Tom, George Windhurst was just on the phone. He … he wants to talk with you before he leaves town today."

"Why? What's he want? Any time I talk to him I stand to lose money. He always puts off buying a bigger ad."

"He didn't say why. He was ... ah ... sort of close-mouthed. Like always." Sarah bites her tongue. She doesn't like to take messages, even for Thomas. It always makes her feel inadequate when she fails to anticipate questions or isn't given enough details. Her mother only trusted her with housework; all other work is a man's job she was told.

"Did he say when he was leaving?"

"I think about five."

"Good, good. I've got a couple of things to get ready for tonight. Why does Windhurst always want to bother me on the day I've got the most work to do? He always says time is money—someone else's time and his money. I've got to live, too, you know. I'm going downstairs."

"Yes, dear—"

Hamilton, by title both publisher and editor-in-chief of the *Pioneer Ledger*, loses the rest of his wife's sentence. Halfway down the basement stairs, the smell of molten lead fills his nostrils. Quickly over his head and tied at the waist, a somewhat new leather apron protects his clothes. He is back in his element—relishing the challenge of creating words in lead.

Chapter Two

Opened books are piled high; sheaths filled with papers are on the verge of sliding off wall shelves. A single book precariously teeters on the crest of the brownish-red leather judge's high-backed chair. The chair, the room's most prominent feature, hints at the occupant's foolish state-court judicial aspirations.

George Windhurst cherishes the four-year-old second-hand chair. Its lack of legal pedigree matches his shortcoming of failing to get into the state's lower tier university law school and squeaking through an out-of-state night law school. He needed three tries to pass the state bar exam. Seldom hired for intricate legal matters, his practice of law revolves around smoothing out land disputes, creating matrimonial separations, defending petty theft and/or traffic driving charges, and automobile insurance claims.

His temples, sprinkled with gray, and the furrows in his forehead and chin inaccurately give the impression of a hard life of sixty-two years. Only the most perceptive of his farmer clients, with faces as hard as his, notice that Windhurst's face does not have the bronzed tint gained from day-to-day exposure to the sun, wind, and other outdoor elements common in a farming community. The one window in his office rarely lets in the sun; its brown-stained slats are always shuttered.

Tuesday is Windhurst's day to visit Clinton and its 842 residents. The rest of the week he spends his time in Winterville, twenty-five miles to the north, the county seat and three times the size of Clinton. In Lake County, Iowa, the two communities make up half of the county's population. In the summer, corn tassels and soybean pods dominate the landscape. Non-cash crop fields are either alfalfa or a pasture home to grazing dairy or beef cattle, chickens, and/or hogs, but never, never a ram, ewe, or lamb.

Clinton couldn't support a full-time lawyer, not even one of Windhurst's lackluster caliber. So Windhurst talked his two law partners into spending one day in Clinton. This saves his client a trip to Winterville, as legal documents have to be filed there in the Lake County courthouse. Collecting signatures in Clinton keeps Windhurst's Clinton clients away from visiting other Winterville lawyers, a definite competitive advantage he wants to keep.

Windhurst unlocks his office door and enters leaving the door ajar. Striding over to his desk, he reaches for the book on his chair—

but misses it. The resulting thud creates a sonorous echo on the parquet wood floor. Hamilton jumps, startled. He stands alone at Windhurst's open door.

"Come on in, Tom. Nice day, isn't it?" Windhurst slumps his broad shoulders and ample, protruding stomach into his chair. His five-foot-ten-inch frame does little to stretch out his 245 pounds. His rumpled tan suit, wrinkled shirt, and a tie, loose at the collar, contrasts sharply with Thomas Hamilton, who is neat and trim, wearing a white shirt and black slacks. Only his ink-stained moccasin is a clue that he has come from his newspaper. Thomas sits down facing Windhurst and crosses his legs at the ankle. Windhurst looks at the fallen book but leaves it on the office floor.

"Thanks. Sarah said you wanted to speak with me."

"Yes sir, I did. You know, it's nice to be able to talk with someone this afternoon. It's nearly five, and it has been the dullest day in two months. You know, having an office in a bank is supposed to be good for business. But then, being in the back doesn't seem to help. If it was you, you'd be happy to know the rent is cheaper here in the back."

"I try to consider my costs, but you didn't call me to talk about rent. You can talk to Godfrey about that."

"You're a hard man to waste time with, Tom. Sometime, we're going to sit down, just the two of us, and solve the world's problems. You and I could do that, you know."

"Sure, I know," replies Thomas without any conviction in his voice but with a hint of irritation at the dilly-dallying.

"There was one thing I was wanting to get your opinion on," Windhurst continues, "off the record. There's that rather large lot next door to you, owned by Old Man Peterson. The ramshackle house on it appears about ready to fall down. It is such a sight. It puts your nicely painted *Pioneer Ledger* building to shame."

"Yes, but I can talk only so often to Mr. Peterson, and half the time he doesn't hear me. I don't know if it's his hearing or he doesn't want to hear what I'm saying."

"Probably some of both, but maybe we can do something to help us both out. I know some people who want to buy that piece of property. Would pay a good price. More than it's probably worth or than it would go for at a sheriff's sale."

"Peterson won't sell," Thomas insists. "He's lived in that house for some seventy years; he was born there. Where else could he sit on the front porch and watch whatever is happening on Main

Street? So what if he doesn't mow the grass too often or own a paint brush?"

"Let's look at this with an open mind. Maybe he hasn't been offered a good price. Maybe nobody has talked to him lately. He may have changed his mind, like anybody else. I need your help. Talk to him this week. He knows you. I also know he won't talk to me. I tried last week. I was real nice and friendly, but he said I don't belong here, and he won't sell his house to no stranger."

"You want me to talk to him?"

"Yes." Windhurst moves a pen caddy to the side of his desk.

"And you think he'll listen to me? One thing I should know— who wants to buy his house so bad, anyway?"

"I really don't want to tell you, and really I can't. All I'm asking is that you find out if Peterson will sell his house. Your asking will hurt nobody. In fact, I reckon you've had your eye on that lot yourself. About time you stopped living all cramped up in the same building that your newspaper is in. You need to get into a house, and I would bet that you've saved a good many pennies to build yourself a new house big enough to entertain in. As mayor of this town, it would be fitting that you have a large parlor for all those meetings and get-togethers."

"I'm not the mayor, and I don't have any intention of becoming the mayor. I don't know where you get rumors and talk like that." Hamilton is becoming uneasier now. His ankles uncross. He looks at his watch.

The telephone rings. Windhurst lifts the receiver on the third ring.

"Hello. George Windhurst speaking. Just a moment." Windhurst looks right at Tom. "Excuse me, please?"

Hamilton nods. "I'll think about what you said." He rises and leaves, briskly closing Windhurst's office door.

"Sorry about the delay, Mr. Peterson. Yes. I've been working on trying to sell your property. Your neighbor, Mr. Hamilton, may have an interest in your residence, which I have been trying to kindle to get you the best price. If he comes to you asking if you are trying to sell your property, play hard to get. He thinks he is helping me buy it for someone else. If we play our cards right, he will end up buying it himself at a price most suitable to you, and of course, I think it only fair that my commission be adjusted upward also. Don't you think?"

6

Windhurst listens, his ear pressed to the phone's receiver. Then he continues, "Good, good. It's nice doing business with you, Mr. Peterson. I think we can realize our common goal by next Tuesday when I'm back in Clinton. Then we can start working on finding a well-qualified buyer for your industrial factory out by the highway to Winterville." Windhurst pauses again to listen, doodling as he waits. "Nice talking with you, Mr. Peterson. I'll be in touch. Bye now."

Windhurst clicks the phone receiver into place, takes a glance at the wall clock (it's now five-thirteen p.m.), and begins placing his scattered papers back into his brown leather briefcase. The solitary four-drawer file cabinet in the corner is locked. A smaller cabinet, containing only stationery and writing pads, is always unlocked. With a few measured steps, he turns and places the key in the door, gives the doorknob a twist, and closes the office for another week. Down the corridor past the bolted bank lobby doors, he pushes open the single opaque-glass exterior door and steps outside.

His foot almost crushes a jack on the bank step.

"Watch out, Mr. Windhurst!" screams Oscar.

"You still here? Don't you ever give up playing jacks? Go home for supper. You know, someday I'll step on and break every jack you got. Wanna bet?"

"Nope." Oscar's hand covers all of his jacks.

"Nope to you, too."

Windhurst turns to stride around the bank's corner. It is only a short walk to his station wagon, and in two minutes he is on the blacktop two-lane highway, first built by the WPA in 1936 and resurfaced between Clinton and Winterville in 1960 by the county. He is headed north for home, twenty-five miles away.

Once past the Clinton village limits, Windhurst sees to his left the silhouetted hunk of an old factory. Owner Arnold Peterson ("Old Man Peterson") is very anxious to sell it, along with his Clinton house.

The only shine from the factory that Windhurst sees is the gleam of the silver coin he could make if he finds a willing buyer. The task he assumes is very difficult. He has few prospects for the old factory, especially since he has no budget for advertising.

Without a real estate license he has to trust that Old Man Peterson will reward him with a gratuity that would equal a commission, as if he had a real estate license. Clinton does not have even one realty office. Someone must be the go-between, he rationalizes to himself, as he reverts back to watching for oncoming traffic.

Out of his view, a lone woman genuflects before the small gravestone as she places two single-stem red roses across the granite stone. It is a ritual, an act of tribute she has done each year for the past ten years. She needs no calendar reminder, for the constant guilt she bears is enough. No one in Clinton, she hopes, knows why there are two roses when there is only one name—Melissa—on the headstone. Her tribute must be to two lives, both young and innocent. One rose, an undying symbol of love, for each. Sarah Hamilton genuflects a second time.

Chapter Three

The old factory is a shrine to yesterday's failed grandiose schemes—schemes that dot its history with remembrances, etched into weather-beaten clapboard that's covered with layers of paint, one layer never the same color as the next. The two-story structure is an imposing sixty feet by one hundred feet, and each floor has twelve-foot ceilings. A rail spur was to be its link to faraway markets, laborers, and customers willing to spend big money. Standard gauge rails in good condition still exist, but the dollars never rolled over them. The land the factory sits on is best suited for grain farming, not manufacturing, and the local population is small, never having attracted the workers from the large cities 150 miles away. Eventually, the factory's equipment was auctioned off.

Arnold Peterson inherited the building three years ago through his family's second cousin to a great-something-or-other. He has no plans for renovation or demolition. The local Farmers' Cooperative Elevator Company willingly rents the building for seventy-five dollars a month to store fertilizer, seed corn, and other supplies the Elevator Co-op buys to get quantity discounts. Peterson has been thankful for this rental income lessens his ownership burden by paying the annual property taxes.

Each spring the Elevator has exclusive second-floor use, primarily to keep its seed corn inventory from becoming a local restaurant for field mice, even though the corn is packaged in fifty- or seventy-pound, multi-layered, heavy-duty paper bags. With Peterson's permission, the Elevator lined the second floor with galvanized tin panels to protect its stores. Peterson denied the suggestion of one member of the Elevator's board of directors to nest a cooper hawk in the rafters to keep mice away. Birds were clever enough to get inside the unattended building where sparrows, small songbirds like the eastern goldfinch, and an occasional pair of grackles built nests and left more droppings than anyone desired. After the spring seed-corn-selling season, the Elevator utilized the second floor to store unsold seed corn, plus a variety of hog and cattle feed supplements, bagged fertilizer, and even fifty-pound bags of dry dog food.

Occasionally, the first floor is used to store farm machinery for two different purposes. During the winter months, the lower level is a garage for used equipment kept on hand and ready for resale. This protects the equipment from weather-caused rust and corrosion. In addition, some smaller, new equipment that the Elevator sells would be parked on the first floor at almost any time of year. At first, Peterson personally controlled who and what machinery was put into the building, but after one winter of trudging through snow-banks and its spring melt creating a muddy, slippery entry road, he gladly gave the task to the Elevator manager, who also had a key.

It's unlikely Peterson was informed that the first floor has become the home hangar for the Cloud IX, not yet built but eventually expected to be the best sailplane glider in the nation.

The expectations belong to and are felt most intensely by Myron Goostree, Jr. Myron is twenty-two years old, but looks nineteen. His five-foot-ten-inch frame easily carries his 150 pounds of well-toned muscle, gained through six-day-a-week physical labor at the Elevator Co-op. He was graduated from the local high school without academic distinction before completing two semesters at a community college in neighboring Winterville, but he has yet to decide upon a permanent vocation. His father talked him into taking the open position at the Farmers' Cooperative Elevator Company three years earlier. Conscientious and always willing to put in an extra hour of overtime, Myron really needs the extra money to help pay the bill for the sailplane. He tried to get a loan at the local bank to buy a sailplane but was turned down. Too risky, Godfrey Klempler at the bank said. Undaunted, Myron convinced himself that he could build as good a sailplane as he could buy. No one else thought so, but Myron knew determination paid off. As a twelve-year-old, he had built a winning soapbox derby car after his first two efforts fell apart. He has never given up his dream of flying free for hours—catching the earth's next upward-lifting shaft of supporting air, all without the expense of gasoline required for single-engine aircraft flight—will be his if he keeps striving for he has experience in achieving his goals.

With one full year plus extra months of frugality, he attained his aim of a $700.00 down payment for a sailplane kit. He sent the money to the factory in Elmira, New York, and they shipped him one complete kit for a sailplane, a magnificent Schweitzer 1-26-E. Myron's research found it to be a model designed for—and already a proven winner of—championship races from coast to coast. His Elevator boss granted Myron one-year free use of the old factory, including no charge for utilities, as a sailplane construction hangar.

Myron took a week to read through all the directions. Having learned the flying terminology he was not, even on his best day, the equal of professional sailplane builders, though he has already put in countless hours studying for his first flight license.

For two months, Myron spent every spare moment separating, identifying, and assembling component parts. This Tuesday was to be no exception. The factory was the only town building expansive enough to build a sailplane with a wingspan of forty feet and a length of twenty-one feet, six inches.

Working on the glider was solitary work. Myron's two male friends from high school deserted him to play amateur town team baseball. The beer he gave up for his sailplane dream also lost him friends, but it also strengthened his resolve.

On this late afternoon, Myron is re-sanding a wing rib of its excess glue when he notices vehicle headlights flash briefly through a high first-floor factory window.

"Now what?" mumbles Myron?

Light shines briefly through the partly open sliding factory door and reflects off the partially built fuselage and into Myron's eyes before it disappears. A car door slams. Six sixty-watt incandescent lights strung on cords cast a dim glow in Myron's first-floor work area.

"Wanna hamburger?" a shrill female voice echoes throughout the factory.

"Sure!" Myron shouts back.

"When are you going to get this bird to fly? In 1984?" quizzes Wanda, holding a sandwich in a white-paper wrapper.

"Sure. How much you wanna bet it'll fly before then?"

"Nothing. Even you should be able to build a simple little airplane in twenty years. That is, of course, if you don't glue your fingers together."

Myron grins. "I'm going to do that just for you, so you can win the bet. What do you say—$1,000.00?"

"Oh, be quiet and eat the hamburger."

Myron tosses aside the sandpaper he'd been using and finds a chair for Wanda. He brushes a fine layer of spring fertilizer dust from its wood seat and sets it down in front of her. She straddles the chair, facing Myron.

Wanda and Myron met in junior/senior high school. Three grades apart meant little at the small regional school ten miles from Clinton. They lost touch when Myron goes off to college for a year,

11

but renewed their acquaintance once Myron moved back to work full-time at the Elevator. Slowly, over the last year, the two spend more and more time with each other, although much of it is in the old factory. What began, as a coy, teasing friendship has gradually become more serious.

"I must be going. I told my parents I would be home for supper," explains Wanda. Although she works full-time as a file clerk/receptionist for an insurance agent in Clinton, living at home was helping her save money for her dreams, not yet completely defined, but which she knows will include stylish clothes.

"It's after suppertime now," Myron responds.

"Not for my parents. They print the newspaper today, and they always eat late on Tuesdays."

Chapter Four

The newspaper front screen door slams shut.

"Wanda, slow down!" barks Thomas. "You want to spoil the cake your mother's baking?" Thomas is half-smiling to himself as he remembers his own penchant for letting the same door slam, but that was no reason to spoil his daughter.

He and Sarah had been married for six years when they adopted Wanda, a nine-year-old orphan, nearly ten years ago. Now, Thomas' thoughts wander back to the first time he saw the child—small for her age, even then; blue eyes full of wonder; blonde hair done up in a ponytail with a large polka dot ribbon; yellow frilly dress. The hair ribbons and frilly dresses have gone the way of early adolescence. Shrunk, flared blue jeans are the fashion and Wanda's in style. She stands barely five feet tall and usually wears high heels to increase her height when sneakers are inappropriate. High school gymnastics toned her muscles and added small, appealing silhouette curves.

Initially, Sarah voiced objections to Wanda's adoption: the child was too old; little was known of her natural mother; there would be no siblings for her to play with. The adoption agency helped Thomas convince Sarah that they could offer Wanda a wonderful home, but Thomas could not convince himself Sarah had fully expressed her opposition to the adoption and he still believes Sarah then wanted no child.

"Supper's ready," calls Sarah. It is simple fare—meatloaf, baked potato, salad, and green beans. The aroma of fresh-baked, cooling, angel food cake fills the air. Sarah's mother, if still alive, would be proud. Space is tight in the kitchen, squeezed as it is in the living quarters in the rear of the newspaper office building.

Thomas gives Sarah a peck on the cheek. "Paper's ready for addressing and mailing," he whispers.

"After supper, huh? Betty Friedan eats, too, you know."

"Okay, I was only teasing; you know that, Sarah."

Addressing issues for mailing the newspaper each week was not hard. An individual newspaper would be run through a stencil machine, which imprints the subscriber's name and address. Papers going to the same city are bundled together. Clinton, naturally, has the most bundles, twenty-five copies in each.

Later, Sarah performs this task alone, as she often has done. Thomas stops to inspect an issue. He worries over the obvious lack of advertising this week.

His eye catches this week's version of the popular column titled "From the Files." Each week, Sarah would go back to find the stories printed five, ten, and twenty years before and condense them for reprinting. Longtime town families enjoy recalling the highlights of the past or to find their names mentioned. Old-timers visualize where they were when the storm with ping-pong-ball–sized hail shredded the local corn crop. The recollections are often grander than what really happened, but Thomas is aware that was only human nature.

"Sarah, you're slipping this week."

"Why, why do you say that?"

"You've forgotten to include the biggest story event this village ever knew in this week's 'From the Files.' You must remember Father Cornelius Murphy, don't you?"

"Well … well, yes." Sarah grips a stencil machine support.

"You must remember that it was ten years ago that Father Murphy, without explanation or notice, left town. One day he was here, and by the next day he was gone." Thomas shakes his head. "To this day, no one knows what happened to him."

Sarah is speechless. Both of her eyes tilt upwards to the ceiling in a blank stare at the mention of Father Murphy. The color slowly ebbs from her face. She deliberately turns away from Thomas to pick up a refill for a half-empty glue pot.

Sarah's column omission was not a willful one. Two days earlier she had found some old photographs of her parents, taken in the Forties at a family reunion. Distracted, she rushed through her history column research as well as other newspaper tasks. Her father died in 1950; her mother in 1951. Both passing before they reach sixty years. Sarah's two older brothers now both live in California.

It was her mother who left the most indelible impression on Sarah, as her father was usually at work. Sarah was always told that a woman's place was in the home—raising children, cooking, washing, and caring for a husband. Now, the Sixties culture is giving her a different message. Dr. Martin Luther King in Washington D.C. pronounced his dreams for equal rights. Betty Friedan wrote a book on the feminine mystique and added her voice to the cry for liberating women to be the societal equal of men. Sarah tries to honor her mother, as she attempts to understand the evolving societal culture.

Thomas sidesteps past Sarah and takes five steps into the next room, where he reaches for a large bound book that contains a copy of the newspaper edition printed ten years ago that week. There on the front page of the *Pioneer Ledger* was the story that gripped the community for several weeks and spawned gossip and rumors. It reads:

Father Murphy Missing

Village Voices Concern

For Absent Priest

There was mystery in town this past week as every citizen wondered about the disappearance of Father Cornelius Murphy, pastor of St. Mary's Catholic Church of Clinton.

He has been St. Mary's pastor for the past five years.

Local grocery store owner, Myron Goostree, Sr., was the last person to see Father Murphy a week ago Tuesday as the priest walked towards the parish rectory at about 4:30 p.m.

No one in town has said they have seen the priest since then. Citizens are really puzzled as to what had happened. No one in town had ever heard anything bad about the priest, said one resident at the café this morning. He really liked kids and was always willing to help, said another resident.

Sheriff Ed Hendricks has been investigating and his office said he had no comment until additional persons were interviewed.

His office had no further comment.

At press time on Tuesday, the whereabouts of the priest was still a mystery.
Mass will be at normal 10 a.m. time this
Sunday with a substitute priest from Winterville traveling to St. Mary's.

"If you want, I can save this page here and put the story in next week's history column," offers Sarah.

"I think we should. You know the trouble we caught last year when we forgot to put in the silly story about the goat having four kids that happened ten years before," replies Thomas.

"Some days I think we should just forget this. Some weeks it's hard to find anything, and then all those petty jealous things arise."

"Ah, Sarah, you know we can't get rid of the history column. It's a struggle every week to make a dollar, and people read those old stories. We should try to keep everybody happy—at least most of the time. I've seen your smile turn the most ornery subscriber into a happy customer. Okay, doll? And, save a few of the smiles for me."

Thomas winks at her.

Sarah frowns, but she can't keep the sad look on her face. Her infectious smile creeps back.

"Where's Wanda?" Thomas asks. " I thought I heard her leave a little while ago."

"She, I think, went out to see Myron. Something about that air-plane. Oh, I'm not sure," answers Sarah.

"There's something I don't like about that boy," says Thomas. "Why I was rereading that story on Father Murphy, and the boy's father was the last person to see the priest before he disappeared."

"Why don't we leave the story alone? Put it away until next week's history file column. It seems that all you got on your mind tonight is old stories. I don't want to hear anything more. I've fin-ished the addressing."

"All right, all right. I'll close the book and put it back on the shelf for next week. Is that better?"

Chapter Five

Dark clouds begin to obscure the twinkle of the few stars out this night. The absence of a moon adds to the foreboding darkness along with a gusting west wind.

Wanda's two-door dark-green Fairlane heads back to the old factory. She has a sense of expectation. A few drops of rain hit the windshield as she turns off the highway and toward the factory entrance road. Small puddles begin to form in the dirt depressions directly in front of the sliding factory door, and the front tire of Wanda's car comes to a stop in one of them. Jacketless, she hurries into the dryness of the factory interior, squeezing sideways through its sliding door.

Myron pretends not to notice her—that is, until Wanda runs her finger down the nape of his neck.

"Time for dessert," says Wanda, playfully.

"Are you sure it isn't fattening?" asks Myron. He drops the sandpaper in his hands, pivots, and gently kisses Wanda's waiting lips. "I think I'll have seconds," he whispers and kisses her again, only this time he presses their lips together longer.

Slowly, very slowly, she opens her eyes, as the gentle patter of raindrops ping on the tin sheeting of the factory roof. A thunderclap startles her; Myron's arms reassure her.

"Hey, you didn't even eat the hamburger I brought," she says, looking to Myron's right side and pointing to it.

"I can live on love. Besides, I took one bite."

"Oh, be quiet."

The couple stands holding each other tightly as the rain intensifies. Myron feels the rhythm of Wanda's breathing.

"Next time, you need to bring your umbrella for the rain or at least some kind of jacket."

"Damn it, Myron!" Wanda claps her right hand over her mouth. "Look, you made me say it again, and I don't want to, but sometimes you say the stupidest things at our most touching of moments."

"Shush."

He kisses her lightly. The hint of an argument disappears in the tenderness of their embrace. Myron understood the argument now sidestepped was because Wanda needed to feel independent, and he realized that his rain advice was exactly what his mother said to him as a young boy.

"When are you going to get this thing done?" asks Wanda for the umpteenth time, changing the subject.

Myron grins. "Oh, I don't know. It's so much more fun doing other things." Wanda blushes.

"As long as you think I'm more important than some airplane, how can I get mad?" She rests her head against his chest.

Torrents of rain driven by the wind are now pounding against the factory clapboards.

"If I say something, Wanda, will you promise not to get mad? I really don't want you to misunderstand." He looks into her eyes.

"O-ka-a-a-y," she says slowly. "You're not going to be mean and say something ugly about my clothes, are you? This factory is not the cleanest place to come to, you know."

"No, it's not your clothes. I need to explain that my suggesting that you have a jacket for the rain was not a suggestion that you should be treated as a child who needs constant supervision. I care about you and I don't want you to get sick; that's all. I hope you can respect that."

Wanda gazes up into his eyes. "Myron, I'm not mad. I'm sorry if I overreacted."

"You want to watch the master at work?" asks Myron, letting go of Wanda and retrieving his makeshift sanding block from the floor.

"Sure, okay." Wanda finds the lone chair from her earlier visit this day, straddles it, and smiles impishly at Myron as she rests her pretty chin on her overlapping hands.

Chapter Six

"UNIDENTIFIED

BODY FOUND

IN OLD FACTORY"

C ried out the page one banner headline in the *Pioneer Ledger*. The whole town was pulsating with gossip. The café became so crammed with townspeople it ran out of coffee. Clinton was the talk of the entire county.

Earlier, Thomas had clumsily written the front-page story with Sarah's help—for they only had two hours on the Tuesday press day to gather the information, cast text type, set a headline, and squeeze the type together into a page chase.

Hamilton's phone is ringing off the hook this Wednesday morning. Everyone wants to know more, and everyone seems to have a question:

"Has the sheriff from Winterville said who it was yet?"

"Come on, Tom, you didn't tell everything in your story. Do you want an exclusive for next week?"

"Did you know that my aunt Stella has the answer to who the person was? You wanna know, too?"

"Is there a reward?"

The page-one story is short. Tossed aside in a box of previously used printing "cuts," Thomas finds an old zinc engraving of the factory at the time it was first built and presses that into service as a front-page story illustration.

In his very best journalistic attempt, Hamilton writes:

> An unidentified body was found early to-day in the old factory, owned by Arnold Peterson, outside Clinton near the two-lane highway to neighboring Winterville. County Sheriff Jonathan O'Day was called. He would only confirm that a

skeleton had been found in the factory and would be moved to Winterville for examination and safekeeping.

The identity of the body was causing huge amounts of speculation in Clinton. An unnamed woman was quoted in the cafe as saying the bones were of a man and must have been some tramp who had used the factory for shelter. That's why nobody knows who the man is, she said.

Sheriff O'Day said he was checking the list of missing persons to ascertain if there might be some lead there to determine whom the person might be.

"We're working on this as fast and efficiently as we can," said the sheriff. No person was allowed into the factory on orders of the sheriff. Before the sheriff left he put his lock on the building and posted a deputy.

Gordon Oswald, elevator manager for the Clinton Farmers' Co-op Elevator, said he was both surprised and angry. He said he was angry because the sheriff closed and sealed the factory without allowing the elevator access to machinery for sale stored in there. The sheriff said nothing in the factory could be moved or touched until state crime lab technicians dusted for fingerprints.

Everyone at the café was talking about the finding of the body. To most it's a big mystery. The *Pioneer Ledger* had no more information at press time.

"How's everything going today, Sheriff?" asks Attorney Windhurst as he pokes his head into the Sheriff's office. The office is small and contains a marred oak wood desk and old vinyl sofa to one side. An ashtray with a very used pipe sits on an end table next to the sofa.

Marksmanship and police federation certificates and plaques decorate the dark paneled walls. The desk is clean and clear, except for a double-decker in-and-out box, a penholder, and a group picture of the sheriff's family. And, added today is one open case folder, manila with bendable prongs for papers.

"Working on the skeleton found in Clinton yesterday, but you'd not have interest in that since the bones wouldn't be a paying client, now would they?" the sheriff snaps back.

"Could be. Does the skeleton have any gold fillings?"

"Shut up. I'm busy. Now git on out of here."

"That's no way to treat a friend of justice and officer of the court, Jonathan."

"Git, I said. I've not the time to sit and bullshit with you, George." Windhurst hunkers up his huge body, senses a losing battle, and backs out of the Sheriff's office. He winks to the comely matron on duty at the dispatcher's desk and walks directly to his car. For a few seconds he sits behind the steering wheel, and then the decision is made. He'll be in Clinton in half an hour.

The wooden steps to the porch squeak under Windhurst's weight. Old Man Peterson is in his familiar porch rocking chair, sitting and watching. The radio is on, and an announcer is recapping the latest Major League baseball scores from Arizona and Florida.

"Top of the day to you, Arnie," Windhurst greets him. "How's everything?"

The creased wrinkles on Peterson's face take on new dimensions as he turns toward Windhurst.

His voice quivers and creaks a little; the words are audible. "I'd have a better day if your hand had some money to buy this house," grouses Peterson.

"You know I'm trying, consider I'm here in Clinton today, on a Wednesday, when I was just here yesterday."

"I don't think you're here to help me. Everybody knows about the bones. Maybe that's why you're here today."

"No, no, I just—"

"Well, you've must have heard the latest rumor." Peterson fastens a button on his shirtsleeve cuff and reaches for a half-full glass of iced water.

"No, no," Windhurst repeats. "I just got here, and this was the first place I stopped, to see you."

"Well, it's all sort of silly what these townspeople are saying. They say it behind my back, but my ears ain't dead yet."

"What's that?" Windhurst steps closer.

"Oh, it's them old ladies in town gossiping about my wife. Fill the café with wild accusations, they do."

"Your wife?" asks Windhurst with a puzzled look.

"Yes, sir, my wife. It was in … let me remember now … 19 and 53 when my wife left me … just up and left. She said to me that week, she's going back to Montana to be with her sister. Said she can't put up with caring for me no more. I got one postcard from her. Said she was sorry and was coming home. That's it for the past dozen years."

"Didn't the authorities investigate that your wife was gone, that she was missing?"

Peterson shakes his head. "At first, I don't say anything. I think she'll come back once she calms down. I don't want anybody saying she left because I beat her or any similar hogwash. I wrote a letter to her sister, who scribbled a note on the back of my letter that my wife isn't … wasn't there. I figured she was on her way home."

"Was she?" Windhurst moves and a board creaks.

"I don't know. She never came." Peterson sips his water.

"Didn't her sister get concerned?" asks Windhurst.

"I don't know. It's hard to recall, but I seem to remember that her sister was ill. I know her sister was older than my wife. The sister passed back then, but I don't remember when that was. It was so long ago. After a couple of months, I talked to Sheriff Hendricks when he came to town."

"What did he say?" Windhurst rubs his forehead.

"He was not much help. He said I could go try to find my wife; that was the best thing I could do. He said he'd keep his eyes and ears open but that, sooner or later, she would come back. It was not like she was eighteen years old, he said. That was, like I said 19 and 53, and when people in town did not see my wife, they asked me about her. I said she was on a family trip, and after a while, people forgot and went on with other things. Now, she's being talked about again."

"I don't understand," says Windhurst.

"Them gossiping women in this town say I made that all up, that I've killed her and hid her in the old factory. I could easily do that, they're saying, since my family relations owned the factory. The bones are my wife's, they say. They say the sheriff needs to look for a woman's ring or a broken and healed little finger."

"Why?" asks Windhurst.

"They say they remember that she broke her little finger in the kitchen at St. Mary's Catholic Church about nine months before she disappears. I know she was spending a lot of time at St. Mary's. I remember her two fingers being taped together."

"I wouldn't pay no heed to the women," Windhurst advises. "You know they all talk for sake of talking, to try to be important."

"I heard," says Peterson, "that one woman said I broke my wife's arm, another that I would often beat her. It's all hogwash. We were married forty years. With all the talk I don't enjoy going to the café now to play euchre. People stop talking when I walk past the door."

"You can't stop all the gossip. That I do know."

"Yeah, I know, but you won't tell anyone about this, me telling you, will you?" Peterson stares at Windhurst. "I don't want anybody spreading lies like these town women do."

"No, no. You're my client, Arnold. Well, I think I'd better be getting about the business of trying—damn fly—to sell your house here. I'm happy you cut the grass. That will help it sell."

"You do that, you hear. I still want $7,000.00 for this here sturdy house. It could be worth lots more with a little paint and stuff. I just can't do it myself. Remember: that's $7,000.00 after you get your share. And, don't forget about getting me an offer for the factory. It could be special to someone."

Windhurst nods affirmatively in response to his client. He sucks in his more-than-ample stomach as he squeezes behind the steering wheel of his car, and in no time at all his tires are creating a dust cloud on the dirt road that leads to the old factory.

A sheriff's car is parked sideways in front of the factory door. A lone, bored, sleepy-looking deputy is in the car, sipping coffee from a metal cup. Gordon Oswald, manager of the Farmers' Co-operative Elevator Company, angrily paces back and forth behind the sheriff department car. He stops to glance at the approaching Windhurst.

Oswald's looks are typical Scandinavian. He's in his mid-fifties, never married, six feet tall, and his muscles are taut from tossing fertilizer and feed sacks for thirty years. His avocation of fishing is reflected in his tanned complexion. A solitary fishhook has become a permanent addition to his faded white yachting cap, a gift from good-natured fishing buddies who highly praise his fourteen-foot, single-propeller Fish-Craft with mock adulation.

"Say, George, help me get this dumb deputy to let me get into the factory," Oswald calls out. "I got a couple of cultivators in there for customers. Hell, I won't be long or disturb nothing."

"You talk with that deputy here?" asks Windhurst.

"Yeah, sure. He says he got orders, strong orders from O'Day himself that nobody is to go into that factory. Official business, he says. It could be a day or two before the sheriff decides to get his ass out of Winterville and get over here."

"Gordie, you hold your tongue a moment. Let me walk over and talk real polite with this here deputy."

The visit was quick. Windhurst returns to Oswald.

"He's as stubborn as a walleye hiding under a rock ledge on the opening day of the season," says Windhurst in language Oswald understands. "He told me about the orders from the sheriff, same as you. Won't budge."

"Come on, George, there must be a law that says they can't keep my machinery locked in there. I own every nut, bolt, and washer on all of them cultivators."

"I think the only way would be to talk with O'Day. I'll stop by his office in Winterville—I'm headed that way now. I'll see what I can do for you. I'll try my best and give you a call back at the Elevator in an hour if I'm successful. How's that?"

Oswald kicks a stone.

"What have I to lose?" a resigned Oswald says. "I'm stuck now. What gets me mad is that there are people who don't believe in cemeteries like the rest of us. I'd sure like to get my bare hands on the man that's causing all this trouble."

Oswald kicks at another stone but this time misses.

Back at the Elevator, Oswald waits by the phone. He tries to check some outgoing grain shipping reports, but his mind does not register the figures. A phone ring interrupts his mind's wanderings.

"Hello? Yeah, sure, I've got that cultivator. No, I can't get it to you today. I've got to check it over. Make sure you get your money's worth. How about tomorrow morning? Sure, first thing. First thing in the morning, I'll have it for you. We can settle then, okay? Damn good deal you're getting, you know."

"Excuse me, Mr. Oswald. Sorry—I didn't know you were on the telephone." Myron steps through the doorway into the main office of the Farmers' Co-op. As elevator manager, Oswald is and has been his only boss.

"That's okay, Myron. I was just finished, and I'll be finished in trying to sell that cultivator I got stored at the old factory if that s.o.b. of a sheriff doesn't let me get it out of there by tomorrow morning."

"I don't understand." Myron stops dusting himself off.

"Oh, it's that bunch of bones they found in the factory. The sheriff closed the place so he could have his investigation. Probably bringing down the state crime boys, like it was an election year, to show us how well he's regarded at the state level."

"Everybody in town is talking about them bones," Myron says. "I was going to go to the factory tonight myself, but I read that short story in the paper today—especially where it says the sheriff closed the place. I've got my sailplane in there, with no chance to work on it. I was going to go there after supper tonight. I hoped they would have them old bones out of there by now."

"Well, they haven't. They ... or I guess I should say the Sheriff is probably being ornery—his giving orders."

"Anybody say who used those bones while living?" asks Myron.

"No, but I hear tell that most people think it was some bum years ago riding the rails, lost a serious fight with another bum, got killed, and the winner didn't believe in Christian burials. To me, it's stupid to believe a story like that. Doesn't make sense. Neither does listening to the names of runaway lovers mentioned at the café." Oswald stops talking to pour himself a cup of coffee.

"Oscar Anderson—the kid that's always playing jacks—told me it was no man, but a woman because he saw a ring."

"How'd Claus Anderson's boy know?" asks Oswald. "He's just a little boy, after all."

"He knows," says Myron with a serious look. "Because he was the one who found the bones."

"What!" exclaims Oswald.

"I thought you knew. It was Oscar and that other kid, Jim something. Yesterday morning I'm told."

"For heaven's sake, Myron. How'd they get in the factory yesterday morning?" Oswald's eyes widen and his eyebrows rise. "It must have been because you forgot to lock the door again; was that it? Was that why you didn't mention them boys to me all day? You tell me the honest truth now."

"Honest, Mr. Oswald. I did close the padlock on the factory door. Wanda saw me."

"I don't know how much to believe from either one of you starry-eyed kids or what you would have seen or remembered. It being a full moon and all."

"Aw, come on. There was no moon. I was working on my sailplane. Wanda brings me food, and she likes to sit and watch."

"I get up pretty early to go fishing these days, but you'll have to get up earlier than I do to make me believe that you and Wanda are only interested in that piece of wood, that may someday, if the Good Lord allows, fly." Oswald glances distractedly at the silent telephone.

"Honest, Mr. Oswald," Myron repeats.

"Well, okay. You get going now, and I'll see you bright and early tomorrow. We need to change that grain auger from the south bin before noon." Oswald disconnects the office coffee pot.

Myron heads home. He hopes his mother will have supper ready by the time he arrives. One day soon, he tells himself, he's going to have to get his own place to live. It's great not to have to cook or wash clothes, but he has no privacy. He had to hide the pink birthday card with little hearts that Wanda gave him in a stack of flying magazines or else it would have become dinner table conversation. When he attended the wedding of his friend Erik three months ago without Wanda, he was asked so many times: "When are you going to settle down, get married, and start a family." Grandparents, aunts, uncles, and cousins at the wedding seemed so attentive to and enamored of and by all the little children running around the church reception hall.

I could learn to cook. Everything is now in a can or jar. I don't need to have a garden or to learn how to pull on a cow's udder to get milk.

Wanda is more than a good friend but she hasn't said anything about their getting married. His sailplane needs to be completed first with a location found to permanently store it.

Back at the Elevator, Oswald continues to watch a silent telephone. Windhurst had said more than two hours ago he'd call in an hour; Oswald gives up the wait, locks his office, and walks three blocks to the café for supper.

Chapter Seven

The *Pioneer Ledger* telephone extension in the Hamilton kitchen had been keeping Sarah from completing her weekly household chores with its incessant ringing all day long.

"Yes, he's here, Mr. Windhurst. Just a minute." Sarah cups her hand over the mouthpiece as she calls out, "Thomas, it's for you! George Windhurst."

Thomas turns off the bathroom sink faucet, grabs a hand towel, and steps into the kitchen.

He is puzzled. Why would Windhurst disturb him again? The office phone has been ringing all day, even now after the newspaper office was closed. "I have telephonitis," he had told his Sarah.

His mind reminds him he had better things to do. *I should have been out trying to collect some past-due bills for advertising—Goostree at the grocery is three weeks behind. Although I like the two pages of grocery advertising from him every week, I'd like it even better when he's paid me for it.*

He sees Sarah dutifully pick up his used towel from the kitchen floor as he lifts the receiver off the counter.

"Thomas Hamilton speaking."

"Tom, this here is George Windhurst. I'm at home in Winterville. Need your help with Sheriff O'Day. He's got the factory closed, and I'm trying to help Oswald over at the Elevator get some old cultivator or planter or something out. He wants to sell it, and the Sheriff has left his deputy there to guard the old place. Don't see much sense in it, not much at all—" Windhurst's words strike Thomas as needless idle chatter. Thomas waits for Windhurst to breathe.

"Well, what can I do?" Thomas is perplexed; everyone knows he is a good friend of the Sheriff's. He has to stay friends, its good business. Sometimes, it's his making the Sheriff look good at election time, and the Sheriff in return letting Hamilton in on hush-hush information. Nothing too confidential, but Thomas knows that he must live and let live. It's like one brother confiding in another brother—a family thing.

"Can't you talk to the Sheriff and convince him to let Oswald get that one piece of machinery out? Won't hurt anything."

"Why don't you ask him? You see him more often in Winterville than I do," suggests Thomas.

"Oh, you know, it has to do with interfering with justice. Puts me in a pickle so to speak. I tried to talk to Sheriff O'Day this afternoon after I talked with the deputy at the factory. Seems the deputy called the Sheriff on the car radio and told him to watch out for me. The Sheriff gave me the brush-off. I thought you'd help me out, unofficially. You know, let me owe you one. I'm not asking you, mind you, to break the law. What do you say?" asks Windhurst.

"I'll have to think what to say. Give Jonathan a call in the morning. Nobody's going to work any fields tonight in the dark anyway."

"That'll be fine. Remember, don't mention me to the Sheriff. To show you my good faith, I'll talk with Arnold Peterson, and I think I can get him to reconsider his asking price of $10,000.00 for that house of his. You're smart to realize it could be worth more with a coat of paint and a little work here and there. Think of the advantages. It's right next door to you. There'll be room to entertain."

"As I told you before, $10,000.00 is way too high. I think my $6,000.00 is more reasonable. Who knows what's wrong with it?"

"You drive a hard bargain, Thomas. Think again about what the land itself would be worth to you. It's a way to get one of the better lots. Let's find a way to get together on this. I'll try to get Arnold to knock a few hundred off the asking price."

"If you want me for a buyer, you'd better—and then some."

"Consider it a *try*. Now, you'll call O'Day?" repeats Windhurst.

"Like you say, I'll give it a try, but don't expect me to call O'Day before morning." He hears Windhurst wish him well.

Thomas places the telephone receiver back in its cradle. "Now you stay quiet," Thomas whispers to the phone. He unbuttons his perspiration-stained shirt, pulls his arms from its sleeves, and holds it in his right hand.

"You'd better get a clean shirt on, dear, that's if you want to eat at this table." Sarah's eyes twinkle, and Thomas grabs her about the waist, squeezing tight.

Sarah speaks very low and softly into his ear. "If you want to eat, it still means you have to put on a clean shirt."

He gently pulls her with his left arm as he walks backward out of the cramped kitchen to their bedroom.

Hugging Sarah, the sleeves of his soiled shirt dangle above the floor behind her. Thomas opens his right hand; the shirt floats in a meandering flow to pile on the floor. The bedroom floor carpet never lets the world know when the shirt lands. The only light comes from a forty-watt bulb in a porcelain base on the nightstand. The soft glow filters through the lacey lampshade, creating an intricate pattern on the plastered bedroom ceiling.

Thomas eases into bed. He is a right-side sleeper, having been so since childhood when growing up meant sharing a double bed with a younger brother. Adulthood and marriage brought a queen-size bed and no longer having to read comic books by flashlight under the covers to avoid his mother's wrath and commands to go to sleep. His childhood friends tell him that there are better things to read than *Superman* and *Little Orphan Annie*. Thomas does not care; he enjoys the stories in his favorite comics. His boyhood pals taunt him as a sissy. His memory flashes back to the fleeting glimpses they'd show him of voluptuous, naked female flesh, barely covered in strategic spots. He was always teased—doesn't he want to see more? Many a time the only thing that saved him was the bell to resume class.

As an adult he has read author upon author glorifying and idolizing the carefree days of youth, the inquisitiveness, the impulsiveness, and yet, all that remains most vivid to him is the teasing he endured.

The sensation of a touch on his shoulder brings him back to the present. Sarah's forefinger traces concentric circles on his shoulder. A moment without spoken words passes, seems to pause, and then flits into history.

Thomas closes his eyes, reaches for Sarah's hand with his left, and twists his body toward his wife. Unwanted blankets give way, up, and over. Supper can wait. They hold each other; the growing warmth of their bodies becomes a substitute for the blankets.

Unnecessary clothes join the unwanted blankets. The light switch clicks—off.

The awkwardness of first love, long since gone, has been replaced by gentle, predictable tenderness, neither dramatic nor adventuresome, but kind, soft, enduring love, and everlasting respect.

"What's wrong, dear?" Sarah almost smothers the words into Thomas' ear. Her lips kiss an earlobe.

"Oh, nothing. Let's just enjoy these moments away from the world," comes Thomas' quiet answer.

"Dear, you forget that I know you, and sometimes I get so frustrated when I know you're keeping something to yourself and do not let me into your world. We've tried too hard, loved too long, not to know the outward telltale signs, even if the inner truth is still hidden. I can think back to the first time we met other than passing on the street. Our destiny together was never apparent from that meeting." She settles comfortably into his arms as she reminisces. "It's a church auction, where we ladies prepare picnic baskets and you men bid on them while we stand backlit behind a white sheet that is the curtain to hide our identities."

"I remember," says Thomas as he wiggles his toes.

"I went home and cried because you hardly ate anything as we sat in the church hall to eat. I thought I was a failure. I had tried to make everything in the basket from scratch, following my mother's recipes and what she taught me. I lied to her that you ate the whole basket, when in reality my neighbor's dog chomped it down."

"Sarah, you must tell the whole story. I had two wisdom teeth pulled the day before. I couldn't eat much. How many times have we laughed about it since? Huh, tell me, ten, a hundred times. You know by now that I can be stoic, as I was for the basket auction. The way you keep telling the story, focusing on one little part and not the whole, is how you perceive a lot of things. I'm not trying to be overly critical, but you need to forget the details and see the whole." He kisses the top of her forehead. "Do you recall the story of the different blind men who touch the elephant? Because each one only senses a small part of the elephant, each fails to realize there is an elephant standing before them."

"I'll never know why my father opens a grocery store when there was already an established grocery in town," says Sarah, unexpectedly. "Then six months later, he sells it and becomes a traveling salesman, but that's neither here nor there, is it? You didn't have family in this town. You were an adult in your mid-thirties when you came here to buy the *Pioneer Ledger*."

"I don't know what you're getting at. We're here now. That's what's important." Thomas feels Sarah's body change position.

"I should mimic what you often say 'Oh, nothing' but then you'd say the same thing I said to you. We know each other too well."

"I still don't—"

"Shush," Sarah interrupts and presses her finger to his lips. "We do not hide the physical tricks of how to kindle the body senses, and our bodies react by instinct to often exhaust both of us, satisfying a need, at least, until the next time. I understand that, and I'm not foolish enough now to believe that we should give up that wonderful part of our life. We're real people, the two of us. Our life is not one of those wildly passionate ones where the heroine waits, as in the romance novel, for a shining knight on horseback clad in armor to gallop in and speak idyllically of amore."

Thomas stares silently into the darkness, still holding his wife, and is more confused than ever. He's heard the auction basket story many times. The conversational shift to Sarah's parents is new. He knew them when they were alive. Both were good, hard-working people. Sarah's mom stayed at home, raised the family, and tended to the household chores. Her father was not a business manager but could he sell. All the traveling required to call on his customers had to be difficult for him and the rest of the family.

Thomas remembers that nearly twelve years ago he thought he was then losing Sarah to another man. There was a period of many months without intimacy, close to a year. At first, he believed it was Sarah's reaction to the pain of childbirth.

Before she became pregnant, he had asked her to help out with the newspaper. She knew people, especially other women who would call in with social items to be printed. He could spend more time trying to increase advertising, especially finding Winterville businesses wanting Clinton customers. They frequently argued over inconsequential things, like if a cake was moist or dry, always with no resolution. Sarah would fret her hair was thinning for no reason. She becomes enthralled with an unquenchable need to immerse herself in church work at St. Mary's. She's always there. Her friends, all married women raising kids while their husbands worked, except one, stop calling after multiple times of being told she was not home.

Finally, she had agreed to help, but only on Mondays and Tuesdays when the work necessary to get the newspaper out was most intense.

Sarah's voice breaks the bedroom stillness and halts the memory wanderings that had taken hold of Thomas.

"I've thought often recently about asking you this, but somehow, I always fail to get the words out."

"I don't understand," replies Thomas, squeezing Sarah's hand.

"We were young and alive, so much in love. We could go on for hours in ecstasy, wild and passionate, all-consuming. Then, that all changes around the time of my accident." Sarah's body tenses.

"Nothing changed, Sarah. I've never blamed you for what happened. I know your mind harbors painful memories—our lovely daughter in the wreckage of our car—but Melissa's death was an accident. That's all. She was flesh of our flesh, bone of our bone." Thomas rubs the back of Sarah's shoulder.

"The pain of being told she died in my arms on the way to the hospital still clings to me. I was responsible for all that happened. I was the only one to blame. I was the one ... I was the one."

"Sarah, if I had been driving, and not you, there would be no one who could say that there would not have been an accident." Thomas, who cannot see clearly in the darkness, senses that she's crying and by touch wipes away the first of several tears sliding across Sarah's cheek. Thomas feels his own tears welling behind his eyeballs.

"Come on, doll; please don't punish yourself any more than you already have. We both know there was no way for you to avoid that drunk driving towards you from the side road onto the Winterville highway. You did the best you could, steering for the ditch. God knows I could have lost you, too. Our baby Melissa ... our Melissa, the baby girl we gave life to—" Thomas loses the battle against his own tears. Their tears join, each with the other, to dampen the shared pillow.

"It's not only that," says Sarah. "It's that we can never have another child, another Melissa of our own. I've taken something from you that we can never have again. I sense that, even after all these years. My mother always told me the greatest fulfillment a woman can have was a roomful of children, to have a large family. A family a mother can be proud of and children who can be there when parents get old and are unable to take care of themselves."

"You've made your mother proud. You've told me you turned down a marriage proposal to honor your mother's wish to be ready to care for your parents when they were old or ill. I'm sure even I would not have worked as hard or been as selfishly dedicated as you were, and without complaining, at least not to the God Almighty."

"How do you know I don't complain to God?"

"I don't. I can only say what I think I saw. We were raised with good strong values, Sarah. Families suffered when women worked in wartime factories. It was necessary, not right or wrong. Prosperity came back when the war was over and families were reunited. Men came home from Europe, and women left the factories to again be at home. Your mother taught you the skills to create a loving home."

"If my mother were alive, she'd tell me I've failed. I can bake, cook, and clean, and I enjoy doing that—well, maybe not the cleaning so much. I tried, but I am not as strong as my mother. I should be able to give you more children."

"Sarah, dear Sarah, we've got Wanda. She's not of our flesh and blood, but she's in our hearts and will be forever. She's a joy, a beautiful young woman. She cannot replace Melissa, but no one can ever take her from our love, our hearts. You've already taught her skills, like sewing. Wanda made us a family."

"I know, dear," sighs Sarah.

They clutch each other tighter. The darkness is totally comforting, and nary a word pierces its cloak. The night slips away; the embracing couple forgets everyday cares. Fears are unspoken.

If Thomas is going to ponder his or his wife's words, it is not to be this night. Sarah's conscious state locks up her mind's secret for one more night.

Chapter Eight

Myron is at the south bin, an auger disgorging grain from its hopper into the bin. Unnoticed by Myron an unbuttoned left shirtsleeve dangles close to the unguarded auger pulley, his attention drawn up to the auger spout spitting out its ribbon of yellow shelled corn.

"Watch out Myron," a young voice yells.

"What the—" Myron cries out as he falls backward against the tubular cylinder of the auger. He grabs an auger transport wheel to steady and brace himself. "Where did that dog come from?" he blurts out to no one in particular.

"He's mine; I found him," shouts Oscar. The jacks-loving Anderson boy runs to where Myron is working.

The dog's reddish hair, streaked with brown, is thoroughly matted, a cocklebur or two along for the ride. With no clearly delineated ancestry, the dog most closely resembles an Irish setter, with a touch of collie in the face—its most distinctive feature. A prior life calamity is etched in a closed left eye covered with scar tissue.

"What's its name?" asks Myron.

"I don't know. I found him two days ago on the lawn in front of my house," replies Oscar. "He was just lying there, like he'd been hit by a car, but I didn't think so."

"What did you do?"

"Oh, I gave him a piece of chicken to eat. He's got only the one good eye." Oscar gazes at the shelled corn still flowing from the auger. "My dad looked at him and said he saw no blood and it probably lost the left eye when hit by a car a long time ago."

"You find a tag or collar with his name?"

"Nope. I call him Deadeye, and he don't care. My mom won't let him in the house. I give him food to eat, and he likes me. I want to keep him. I found him. Anyway, he'll like me more."

"What's he doing, running round?" asks Myron.

"He's always running. I'll go catch him." Oscar begins to turn.

"Aw, let him go. I'd like to ask you something," says Myron.

"What?" Oscar stops his turn. Puts his right hand into a pocket.

"Somebody told me you were in the old factory the other day or night and found the bones. Please, tell me what you found?"

"Can't."

Myron waits for more; Oscar puts his hand over his mouth.

"Why not?" asks Myron. "We're friends."

"Sheriff says I ain't to talk to nobody, not even my friends. Sheriff said it was important to tell the truth."

"I'm not asking you to lie, Oscar. I want to know how you got into the factory when I always lock the sliding door when I leave, and the exit on the other end of the building is nailed shut with boards crossing and you're too small to reach the windows."

"You don't need to open no door or window." Myron's eyes widen. Oscar continues, "Jimmy and me know a secret way to get into the factory. We promised not to tell. He's my blood brother. You can't tell. You must cross your heart and hope to die." Myron hears the corn stop flowing and looks away from Oscar to shut off the auger motor. "Myron, you must promise you'll not tell," an arm-waving Oscar repeats to a distracted Myron.

"I promise," says Myron. "Cross my heart and hope to die. You don't have to tell me if you show me how to get into the old factory. Maybe I might lose the door key. Then how'll I get in to my sailplane if I don't have a key to open the padlock?"

"I don't know," says a distracted Oscar. "Look, there's Deadeye over there. I'm going to get him."

"Why not show me?" pleads Myron. "That's not telling me. I could follow you and not say anything."

"The Sheriff will put me in jail, and my father said you only get bread and water behind bars. I have to go get Deadeye."

Oscar dashes off toward his new dog; it does not wait for Oscar. Myron loses sight of Oscar and Deadeye behind a building.

Myron thinks he'll have to find Oscar's secret way into the old factory. He must believe Oscar was not lying.

Chapter Nine

Sheriff O'Day picks up the phone. "O'Day speaking."

"Good morning, Jonathan. Glad to catch you in. Thomas Hamilton at the *Pioneer Ledger*."

"Well, I'd ask what I could do for you, but I can't tell you anything more about the factory skeleton."

"You know I'd like to learn all I can about the bones, but I can wait until next week, since the paper has already been published this week. Oswald over at the Elevator, though, has some cultivators or something locked up in the factory, and I'm asking you for a favor to let him get one of them out of there this morning. I don't think it would hurt anything. Have a deputy watch him. Make sure Gordie doesn't disturb anything." Thomas hopes for a positive response.

"You and I are friends, Thomas, but I can't. I promised the state criminal division honcho that nothing would be moved until his crime-scene technicians show up. One came down the day the bones … that is … skeleton was found to remove it to the funeral home here in Winterville. The only morgue we really have in the county. They're supposed to be coming back, looking for clues to solve this thing. If they ever found out I disobeyed, why they'd never trust me again. You're putting me in a box, Thomas. I'd like to help, but I can't."

"I still don't—"

"This time I'm forced to be hard, Thomas. Between you and me, this is an important find. It'll startle someone."

Thomas finishes a note he was writing. "Maybe, if you say so, or it could be just some visiting vagabond who lost a fight."

"You're smart, Thomas, and I won't answer that. My only answer is that the factory stays closed to everyone until I get an okay from the state boys, and that's final. I've put one of our special locks on the factory door. Sorry, Thomas."

"You're definitely being a hard man, Sheriff."

"I've got to do my job. Say, you asked about a cultivator. Who's the owner of that airplane?"

"Belongs to Myron Goostree, Jr., who works for Gordie Oswald at the Elevator."

"Interesting. Thanks, Thomas. We can talk more later."

"Sure hope so. I could've used your help today. You and me have been friends for a long time."

"Aye, best to you, Thomas."

Thomas and Jonathan are long-time friends. For years Jonathan would substitute for the vacationing Clinton barber and would come to help patrol at Clinton's summer and fall community parades as a volunteer member of the Lake County Sheriff's Department Auxiliary. After serving ten years in the sheriff's auxiliary, the county board hired him to fill a vacant deputy position under Sheriff Ed Hendricks. Jonathan was required to sell his Winterville barbershop to accept the law enforcement position. Jonathan's cousin, owner of his former Winterville barbershop, allows him to clip a head of hair now and then for free to keep his license current.

When Ed Hendricks did not run for re-election in 1962, Jonathan beat the odds to be elected Sheriff by defeating a fellow department deputy who had more experience and technical skill. County voters valued Jonathan's likeability more than any other factor and cast a majority of their votes for him. The voters, who knew the reality of the sheriff's position, did not deem it crucial that Jonathan lacked a significant crime solving background. For solving petty crimes, the sheriff's knowledge of specific family history and a discerning ear, rather than analyzing crime-scene evidence, would discover the perpetrator. Writing traffic offense citations was easily learned and required little technical skill. The state criminal division investigators on call to the sheriff handle rare major crime solving and evidence analysis, when necessary.

On this day, the rear window of the sheriff's patrol car reflects the blazing rays of the sun at its noon zenith.

A small group is assembled near the front bumper of the car—the Sheriff, his deputy, Oswald, Hamilton, and two men alien to local inhabitants. Sheriff O'Day pulls back the sliding door to the factory, barely wide enough to allow himself and the two strangers to slip into the structure. The others wait silently outside.

"Maybe now I'll get my cultivator," Oswald says to Thomas.

"Let's hope so, Gordie. Those two state crime guys should know what they're doing and be out of there in no time."

Thomas is prophetic. At twelve twenty-two p.m., the Sheriff leads the two state men back into the sunshine. Farewells are quick. The two empty-handed state criminal division technicians speed north in their unmarked panel van.

"Hey, Sheriff, can I get that cultivator, now that this damn business is over with?" Oswald calls out.

"Sure, but keep your hands off all that other stuff, and don't touch anything or walk behind the tape. And, make it quick. My deputy here will be going inside with you, just to make sure. I'm going to relock this factory door before I leave."

"Anything you can tell me, Jonathan?" asks Thomas.

"Not much you can print in that gossip sheet of yours, but buy me a cup of coffee and I'll bend your ear a bit."

"I'll sweeten that coffee with some fresh chocolate chip cookies if you have time to stop over at the newspaper."

"Deal."

Later, after placing the padlock back on the factory door, reposting the "Do Not Enter" sign, and sending the deputy off to answer a call, the Sheriff and the publisher sit at the latter's kitchen table.

"Help yourself to as many cookies as you like Sheriff," says Sarah, setting down a plateful. "I've been trying to get uptown all morning, so I'll not bother you. Thomas, I'll be at Goostree's." She keeps her hand on the front door as it closes so it doesn't slam shut.

"That's a great wife you have, Thomas. She's a great baker. You should be mighty happy." O'Day reaches for two cookies.

"I am. Sarah prides herself as a baker. Now, tell me about that skeleton. I still get these crazy telephone calls with all sorts of wild stories and speculations." Thomas refills his coffee cup.

"For your readers, you can tell them that the skeleton was very old, and I don't know if it was a man or a woman as of yet. The skeleton indicates a small to average-sized person. Our trouble is that the skeleton is not complete. That's all I can really say about the skeleton's condition." He dunks a cookie into his coffee.

"Where did you find the skeleton in the factory?" asks Thomas.

"You can't print this, or we will have every crackpot in the world coming into my office to confess. I've already had one. He claims the skeleton was of a Martian outcast he was forced to kill by alien invaders from another world. Some story, eh?"

"It'll make good reading, Sheriff. Sputnik and all."

"Yeah, and make me look like a fool for believing that poppycock. No, thank you," says the Sheriff swallowing a piece of his second cookie. "And I'll count on your promise not to let that story leave this table. Anyway, the state says the skeleton was human, not Martian."

"How do they know? Have they ever examined a Martian? How can they judge? Tell me that." Thomas has a wry smile on his face.

"Oh, just leave that story alone, will you? There's nothing to it, and you're beginning to talk like a first cousin to that fella who came to my office with the Martian story in the first place," replies O'Day.

"Then tell me some more about where they found the skeleton. You haven't mentioned that yet, and it's strange nobody ever discovered it before now, especially since you claim it's old. How old?" Thomas asks, sliding the plate of cookies closer to Jonathan.

"I can't answer that last question—at least, not now, anyway. The skeleton was … let me say it was found in the east corner of the first floor, found hidden in an old cistern nobody claims to know much about."

"An old cistern? Now that's a good story. Who would ever have guessed one existed, let alone contained a body. Surely, clothes should have given you a clue as to who the person is, or I guess more correct, was." Thomas stretches for a cookie.

"Yes, clothes would definitely help, if they existed, but they don't." O'Day's face is without expression.

"What?" Thomas rises from his chair, completely perplexed. "You're saying a nude body was sealed into an unknown cistern in our abandoned factory? Who would do such a heinous thing? Must have been a depraved person or persons."

"Looks that way, Thomas. The lack of human dignity has reminded me of those two bodies found during the summer two years ago in the swampy areas of Sand Lake—that's some eight to nine miles northwest of here."

"I remember that: two bodies, one man and one woman, caught on a ledge in what divers called a bottomless pit. If I remember right, both bodies had concrete blocks wired to their ankles with bullet holes in their skulls—one bullet in the woman, two in the man. Surely, that was gangland retaliation, as everyone suspected. One wonders if it will ever stop. We always feel so safe here in the country. Violence seems to only happen to those miles away, or in San Francisco or New York or Chicago. Murder is in the big city, not here in Clinton."

"You can talk about the big city if you like, but remember country life isn't all it's cracked up to be. You should see the crime scrapbook in the sheriff's office that was put together by Ed Hendricks. For example, near Clinton during World War II, there was an excavation, and lo and behold, up came pieces of bones that, when put together, equaled the remains of a man. Sheriff Hendricks dug up old court records and newspaper clippings, and, I was told, he had conversations with several old codgers who lived here back in the 1890s."

"Who'd Sheriff Hendricks think the man was?" asks Thomas.

"He traced him down to be a suspected outlaw who had shot and killed a former sheriff. Guy by the name of Mason."

"You mean Sheriff Mason?"

"No, no. Outlaw by the name of Charles Mason," explains Jonathan as he wipes his mouth with a paper napkin.

O'Day reaches for another cookie, takes a bite, washes it down with coffee, and then continues. "Story goes that Mason was wanted for a string of robberies and murders. He was holed up somewhere in the county. Sheriff found out, and he went out hunting for Mason with two deputies. The three of them caught Mason and his wife riding in a hay wagon. Mason whips out a rifle; while crouched behind his wife, he starts firing. Killed one of the deputies. As the deputy fell, his shotgun went off, and it killed the wife. Mason somehow escaped, only to be tracked down two days later when the sheriff got tipped off to Mason's hiding place. Four men ambushed Mason. He was killed with buckshot from close range, which matched a gunshot hole found in the skeleton's skull above the left eye socket. From what I've read, the town hung Mason's body in front of the court-house for two weeks reminiscent of what colonial authorities did to captured pirates, then put it in a hole in the potter's field marked only by wooden crosses and stones, which did not last the test of time."

"You got one good story there, but Jonathan it would hardly fit what you said earlier about the body being in a cistern. That cistern isn't a potter's field, and who would be ghoulish enough to dig up old bones from somewhere and put them in a cistern? I like your Martian story a whole lot better. Could be page one."

"Lay off the Martian story, or like I said, you'll be a candidate for one of my jail cells—although with your writing ability, you could add some intelligent graffiti to the walls, now that it looks like a battleship after the Better Government people painted it gray."

"Well, gray's not my favorite color, but tell me more about that fella with the Martian story." Thomas smiles.

"I've told you more than one time: stay away from that crazy. If you ever meet him, you'll find you've got better things to do."

"Okay, okay."

Chapter Ten

"Let's see if I heard you correctly: It's a fact, is it not, that once the body was found, you sealed off the factory."

"Yes, sir."

"Now, nobody was allowed into the factory, that is except you and other law enforcement officials until the body—or more correctly, the skeleton—was taken to and turned over to the mortician in Winterville. Is that correct?"

"Yes, sir."

"The official final report you got from the coroner stated specifically that the skeleton was not complete—that there were bones missing. Isn't that true?"

"Yes, sir." Perspiration beads appear on the witness' forehead.

"And that one of the missing bones was the pelvis?"

"Yes, sir." The jury watches the witness wipe a forehead.

"Now, isn't it true that the pelvis consists of three parts: the ilium, ischium, and pubic bones?"

"I'm not a doctor, but I would say that there are different parts to the human pelvis."

"Well, let's talk about the pubic bones of the pelvis."

"Okay." The witness' forehead perspiration reappears.

"Without getting too technical, you'd agree with me that there is a natural difference between men and women in the shape or structure of the human pelvis?"

"Yes, I guess so."

"Isn't it true a part of the pelvis called the pubic symphysis normally exists at a different angle for men, as compared to women, because women need—let's say, not to embarrass the ladies present here today—an opening to allow a baby to be born. Isn't that true?"

"Yes." The witness looks to find a dry, unused tissue.

"Now, you've already testified that no pelvis was found, so isn't it fair to say the skeleton was missing an important part critical to identify the rest of the bones as male or female?"

"Yes, but men don't wear gemstone rings."

"You positive about that in today's world? Withdraw."

A floorboard creaks. Half the jurors turn to sneak a peak, ignoring the present day Lake County Sheriff on the witness stand. A fan whirls on endlessly, unequal to the late summer heat, which at the moment seems to suffocate all those present in the Winterville court.

Handkerchiefs already soaked with sweat sop brows.

"Just one more question, Sheriff. ... No, that'll be all. No more questions. Thank you, Sheriff O'Day."

"You're very welcome, Mr. Windhurst."

Sheriff O'Day breathes easier now that this line of questioning is concluded. He hopes the jury, like him, finds the female hand bones, rings, and broken finger determinative, along with Old Man Peterson's lack of credibility, and not the failure to find a complete skeleton. The state crime chief had told him a skeleton's decay occurs faster in high-moisture areas, as moisture leaches out skeletal minerals, which corrodes the bones, and leads to bone disintegration. He also had been told that having the pelvis bone would have been of great assistance to determine the sex of the living person now a skeleton. However, the state crime report stated the bones of one hand found were most likely female and that a calcified finger bone had at some time prior to death been broken. It was proof enough for the sheriff that others had identified the gemstone ring and small wedding band found in the old factory cistern as belonging to Peterson's wife even if the law provided that Peterson himself could claim a constitutional privilege against self-incrimination and not have to testify as what he knew about the rings. Jonathan had his fingers crossed that Windhurst's attempt to have the jury doubt there was a female skeleton by a focus on a missing pelvis would be insufficient to acquit Old Man Peterson.

The judge looks at his gold pocket watch as the Sheriff raises himself from the witness chair. A court reporter changes paper. The bailiff yawns.

"Does the district attorney have another witness?"

"Yes, your honor, except that this might be a good place to recess for today, the hour being late."

"Any suggestions, Mr. Windhurst?"

"I'd agree with the DA, your honor."

"This court is in recess until tomorrow morning at nine-thirty a.m. to reconvene again in this courtroom. The jurors are again instructed not to discuss this case with anyone. Bailiff, please collect any exhibits or notebooks in the jury's possession. This court stands in recess."

Windhurst feels a hand grasp and tug his left arm.

A shout slices through the stuffy air: "It's Old Man Peterson!" The commotion is great. Windhurst shouts for the bailiff to get a doctor. The court reporter accidentally knocks over her dictating machine stand. Two woman jurors stand in the jury box with horrified looks on their faces. Curiosity to see what is happening rises and subsides as a hush descends. All eyes are on Arnold Peterson.

His pale almost ashen complexion, moistened noticeably on the forehead with beads of perspiration, exhibits not one sign of life as he slumps in an oversized wooden chair at the defendant's table. He manifests no telltale sign that he's breathing. His head hangs to one side. Attorney Windhurst again calls out for someone to please get a doctor.

The sheriff tries to get the spectators to stand back and succeeds only with the help of the judge, who has left the bench to stand between the jury box and counsel tables, asking people to make room, to move back. Most heed the black-robed judge.

The bailiff starts CPR after Windhurst, the Sheriff, and the bailiff place Mr. Peterson on top of the defendant's counsel table. There is little response from Arnold Peterson.

"I think it's too late," a woman spectator says softly to another.

Chapter Eleven

The onlookers stand in silence, dressed in their best mourning clothes. They, lining both sides of the church steps, number less than two-dozen. Six pallbearers walk solemnly in unison down twenty-one wide, fanned concrete steps after exiting through the large oaken entry doors of the First Lutheran Church of Clinton.

Each pallbearer grips a coffin handhold tightly with a white-gloved hand. A black hearse waits at the curb with its huge backdoor wide open and the funeral director standing at attention nearby.

A short funeral service asking God to look kindly upon the soul of the departed and grant eternal rest had ended only minutes before. There had been no eulogy, except for the Lutheran minister's few kind words.

Thomas, in attendance with other members of the Clinton Chamber of Commerce, rechecks the crowd to conclude that no family member of Arnold Peterson had been present.

No cemetery burial service or luncheon will be held.

Muffled background whispers go through the crowd as the casket bearing the body of Mr. Arnold Peterson is placed into the hearse, the door closed, and it is slowly driven away. The following Wednesday, the *Pioneer Ledger* carried this story:

Clinton Mourns Loss

Buries Arnold Peterson

Longtime Resident

Longtime Clinton resident Mr. Arnold Peterson, age 73, was honored last Friday by mourners in funeral services at the First Lutheran Church of Clinton. Interment was to be at a later private service in the church cemetery.

Mr. Peterson was born in Clinton to Robert and Abigail Peterson and for more than forty years worked diligently to have his great visions for Lake County become reality. As a community businessman he tried for many years to bring industry and prosperity to our town, which he loved.

In recent years he became the last family member to own the large factory building located at the edge of town.

It was a horrific shock to residents of this town when they heard of the sudden death of Mr. Peterson in Winterville a week ago Tuesday.

Mr. Peterson had no known surviving relatives at the time of his death except for one son, Gary. He was believed to be living and working in South America. One source said he was on his way to Clinton, although delayed.

Pastor Roman Johnson of First Lutheran Church conducted the funeral services.

Chapter Twelve

Myron kicks his right foot through the dying, decaying weeds alongside the old factory building perimeter. The unseasonably chilly early autumn air with its pulsating breeze stings his exposed skin. He keeps recalling his chats with Oscar. Several times, too many to count, Myron asked Oscar to divulge his secret way into the old factory. All of Myron's attempts were to no avail, as Oscar kept his mouth shut.

Myron also tried Oscar's playmate, Jimmy, with the same lack of luck. He is puzzled by their steadfast silence. Neither could be bribed with candy or ice cream, either. *The sheriff must have scared the living daylights out of both of them.*

Myron, frustrated, continues on, searching again and again for Oscar's secret entrance. Two weeks after Mr. Peterson's burial, Myron today returns to areas he had inspected time after time. The Sheriff made the Elevator erect a barricade at the first-floor's eastern corner cutting off interior access to the cistern, but Myron volunteered to do the work and knows nothing is hidden behind the wooden bulwark he constructed to prevent additional burials, unwanted spectators, and/or souvenir bone hunters. Once the barrier was constructed, the Sheriff removed his lock and Myron had factory access as he had before.

The first exterior spot Myron reexamines today is the boarded-up door on the first floor at the end of the building that's opposite the entrance. He checks every nail head but sees no sign of movement or paint chipped off in the last twenty years. He stands there, eyes fixed, focused on the last nail row.

"Got room in the dream for me?" The female voice is Wanda's, her sneakers sliding to a stop in the dirt.

"Maybe?" Myron grabs Wanda's outstretched hands and gives them a squeeze, then another.

"Whatcha up to today? Still hunting to find Oscar's nonexistent secret passage into this old factory?" She rubs dust from a sneaker.

"Yeah, I guess. I think I can trust Oscar and Jimmy to tell the truth. They wouldn't lie to me. I'm sure they wouldn't."

"Well, maybe not lie, but maybe they're letting their imagination run away with them. You know, how you told me that as a young boy you used to imagine Jolly Roger pirates attacking either your ship at sea or your seashore fort walls?"

Streaking rays of a setting sun radiate from the west. It is a crazy twilight as the sky is losing its last tint of azure and varied intensities of orange and red colors stripe the few grayish clouds before the creeping hidden blackness will take over.

"Let's sit over here," suggests Wanda softly. Without a word, Myron sits down first leaving her space to sit on an old well covering.

"Ouch! Damn nail!" shrieks Wanda jumping to her feet.

"What the—?" says a startled Myron.

"Oh, there I go again. Can't keep that word out of my mouth, but these old nails are going to ruin these new jeans. Did I tell you what happened to my other ones?" Wanda's fingers feel the snag.

"No. Not that I can remember," Myron lies.

"Well, last month I was trying to help Dad by carrying an old automobile battery. He told me to use some battery straps he had borrowed from the filling station uptown, but I said I didn't have to use them. I told him the battery wasn't heavy and I could carry it easy. Never thought much of it again until I saw my blue jeans when mother took them out of the wash at the end of the week. The whole front was nothing but big holes, almost shredded."

"Sure, you tipped the battery and some acid splashed out of a battery cell and onto your jeans," Myron guesses. He looks around.

"I didn't think so. I didn't notice any. Didn't feel anything either." Wanda kneels down to find the nail again.

Myron keeps a straight face. "Didn't have to. The acid merely took time to eat away at the cotton fibers of your jeans. Your skin was next." Wanda sticks out her tongue at Myron.

"I don't know why I tell you about all the dumb things I do."

"I'm your Father Confessor, that's why." Myron smiles.

"Oh, shut up and find something hard so I can get even with this stupid nail." Wanda's hand locates the troublesome nail.

"Let's have a look," says Myron. "You sat on the only nail in the board—and the board's been turned over."

"Must have come loose somehow," replies Wanda.

Myron lifts the board, expecting to find the never-ending blackness of an old abandoned well. That is not, however, what he discovers. The cylindrical brick walls of the well are about four feet in diameter but there is no great depth—someone seemingly has filled the well shaft with unknown material to a concrete cap. Myron can't tell if a hollow chamber exists beneath the poured slab.

"Here, Wanda, hold this board you sat on while I try to remove this one next to it." Wanda takes the board.

Myron wrenches free two additional well cover boards. It takes less effort then he estimates. As he studies the old well, he finds, counting rows of bricks, the brick wall is eighteen inches above ground level, with the concrete slab forty-two inches below ground level. Other well features are very indistinct in the failing light.

"Myron, want me to go get the flashlight from my car?"

"Yeah. That would be great." He leans over the well wall to see if he can feel anything of importance.

Wanda disappears around the factory corner and is back almost as fast grasping a flashlight in her right hand. She passes it to Myron's waiting hand.

Myron circles the flashlight beam around the inside perimeter of the bricks. There is a noticeable absence of cobwebs. The boards capping the well likely would keep out nesting rodents but not spiders. The flashlight beam shines upon nothing that strikes Myron as unusual.

"See anything interesting?" quizzes Wanda.

Myron shakes his head back and forth repeatedly indicating "no, no, no."

"Myron, if you want to look more, why don't you wait until tomorrow? Daylight should help. Besides, the mosquitoes are eating me alive right now." She slaps a mosquito feeding on her forearm.

"Hold on. Give me a hand with this one board, and I'll wait until tomorrow. Then maybe I can find out if the concrete is really solid. What do you think?" He reaches for the last board.

"I think I should go home. I must finish hemming the dress I'm going to wear tomorrow afternoon to Sharon's engagement shower."

Myron kisses her on the forehead. "Wait a minute," he says in a hushed tone. "There—that's all the boards back in place. Guess there's really no reason to nail them shut again. Let me walk with you back to the car. I need to stay awhile to finish some sanding on the wing front. Ain't no way I'm going to fly my plane this year. You still want to bet on 1984?"

Wanda doesn't answer.

An hour later, Wanda is tying off the last thread stitch when her mother appears at the open door to Wanda's bedroom.

"Hi, Mom. I'm almost finished. What do you think?"

"I think you always look good in blue."

"You always say that. I hope someone at Sharon's shower notices it. It's so depressing to spend so much time to look nice or sew a dress and then not have anyone notice or say anything other than 'Oh, how beautiful you look today.' It's all so phony." Wanda removes the spool of blue thread from her sewing machine.

"You mustn't think that way, Wanda. It's nice for you to stay in touch with other people in this town. You always seem to spend all your time down at that old factory."

"Do we have to talk about Myron again? It's not like we're already married or something," bristles Wanda.

"I know today's advice books say parents should foster their children's growing up by teaching them to be independent, but I can't disregard what my mother told me. I only wish she were here to tell you how living a full life requires selecting the right partner. Myron is a nice boy, but I think you should set your sights higher. All he thinks about is that airplane."

"Glider, Mother," corrects Wanda softly.

"Okay, glider, it's all about the same. I wish you and he didn't hang around the factory all the time. Although I haven't been there, several people have told me it's such a depressing building. While it may have been suitable years ago, it's not today, I'm told."

"Myron has to have a place to work on his glider. There isn't another spot in this town large enough. Anyway, I think Myron has discovered something important at the factory."

"What's important about an old factory that's ready to fall down?" Sarah waits while Wanda puts away her thread collection.

"Oh, Myron was told Oscar found a secret way into the factory. That's how Oscar found the skeleton. There could be more."

"That sounds impossible," replies Sarah. "All Oscar does is run after that new mutt of his, play jacks under foot on the bank steps, and who knows what else. His jeans always have a hole somewhere—reflects poorly on his mother. I rather doubt such a young boy tells the truth all of the time. He's probably seeking attention. Older people do that, too; they gather at the café when something sensational happens. Your father has been hearing all sorts of strange stories since they found … that body. We should now let everything rest peacefully in Mr. Peterson's grave."

"But Mother—" An exasperated Wanda stops before she bristles at her mother again. Sarah nervously runs her hand over her skirt.

"We should always let the past rest in peace. That's one piece of advice my mother said and I've come to learn it is the best way to live. It's best for one to put past events out of one's mind forever. We must live only for tomorrow, for the future. We can't change yesterday, now can we, Wanda?"

"Of course not, Mother, but shouldn't we try to make up for the sins of the past? There may be kinfolk somewhere in dreadful sorrow, waiting for a loved one to return, and if that someone was left for dead in the old factory, we can't let a whole family cry forever not knowing. I think it's better for them to know the truth so that they could live in peace, too. As for the dead person, prayers could be offered to heaven by his or her family." Wanda stretches her new dress out on her bed and returns to sit on the sewing machine bench.

"God knows and that's all that's important. We don't need the whole town gossiping," says Sarah.

"That's what the town is doing now," insists Wanda. "Why, in Goostree's the other day, two women were talking about the fact Mr. Peterson's family didn't show up at the funeral. I was even asked if I had heard about the guy over in Winterville talking about the Martians coming." Sarah inspects the hem Wanda had completed.

"Martians? It's now time this town quits fearing crazy improbable future happenings and gets back to reality. Gossip only creates needless turmoil and hurts innocent people. The only thing it's good for is selling coffee at the café."

"Well, tonight Myron lifted boards to find something interesting near the outside of the old factory building. He thinks it's why the Sheriff had scared the two boys into silence, after Oscar found the skeleton."

A blank expression creeps over Sarah's face.

"I sat on a nail I didn't see," Wanda explains. "The board was covering an old well near the factory." Sarah frowns.

"I suppose you put another hole in a pair of your jeans—your new pair? What will people think of you and me?" Sarah nonchalantly steps closer to Wanda, as if she is going to inspect the jeans, but, when Wanda slides to the opposite end of her sewing machine bench, Sarah steps back to where she was.

"Yeah, a little one," Wanda admits. "No big thing. I helped Myron take off some boards from the well covering and we saw there's really no well at all, just a hole with concrete at the bottom. There may have been a well there at one time, not now."

"I don't know what's so strange about a well being filled in if it runs dry," Sarah says logically. "Anybody would do that if they didn't want to worry about some child accidentally falling in."

"I might agree, but Myron said he's not sure the well is totally filled in. He wants to find out if there is really something under the concrete." Wanda stands to lift her new dress off the bed.

"I'm beginning to think Myron will become an older Oscar if he keeps on acting the way he does. First, there is the airplane—okay, glider—and now this old well. It all escapes me. He'd be better off trying to learn a craftsman's trade or work skill, something in demand, or completing the college program he started. My mother always told me it was the man's responsibility to obtain the best work he could to provide for his family. You should not be expected to continue working forever. I'm not a good example for you, working on the paper."

"Okay, Mother, I don't want another lecture. Would you help me test the back zipper if I slip this dress on?"

"Sure. First, let me see that nail hole in your jeans."

"No lecture, please."

Chapter Thirteen

arly morning dew dots the steel-reinforced toes of Myron's boots as he bypasses the factory entrance to walk to the old well. Quickly, he removes the previously loosened boards and stacks them off to the side. Taking one of the removed planks, he strikes it against what he thinks is the fake concrete floor. Only, his board splinters. Tying one end of a heavy rope he brought about his waist, he anchors the other end to a nearby tree. Gingerly, he steps backward, right foot first, then left, onto the concrete slab inside the well wall; for safety, he grips the top of the well wall with both hands.

Satisfied the concrete will support him, Myron stands up. He's still bewildered.

"What do I look for now?" he mutters. *There is nothing here except the concrete slab and old well walls.* His mind grapples with today's frustration. While he may not have received top academic marks in high school, he did his homework and listened to his parents' advice to work hard and never give up. His dad told him that success was ninety percent perspiration and ten percent being in the right place at the right time. He's done the ninety percent. His desire to find the secret entrance has meant time away from building his sailplane and not completing the sailplane has only added to his at home discomfort because his mother has begun to nag him every week that it's time he was married and started a family. She always mentioned grandchildren—and Wanda. "I bet her mother has taught her how to cook, sew, and do the things required to create a good home," his mother would tell him. "Young girls need to know those things. Women libbers will destroy America," she warned. He didn't know what his mother meant when she asked him one night at supper if he was getting Wanda in trouble at the old factory. He simply said "No, Mom."

He understood his mother's question when his dad took him aside after supper and asked him if he and Wanda used condoms. He said "No." He'll never be able to put into words the panic he saw on his father's face.

Myron doesn't know if his parents discussed their sex question to him with Mr. or Mrs. Hamilton. He hopes not. He and Wanda haven't even mentioned the word "sex" to each other—much less do anything. He would guess his parents still "do it."

He stares at the concrete slab. Surely, Oscar did not pour the concrete, but his boast of a secret passage into the old factory continues to haunt Myron. The latest trail, started when a nail tore Wanda's jeans, appears to have led him figuratively into an Old West box canyon.

The well floor is concrete, and Myron has no tool to break through it to unlock its secrets underneath. Without an answer, Myron begins to poke at the brick sides of the well. He tests one side and then the other. His stick causes loosened mortar, already cracked and flaking, to drift lazily downward to the concrete floor. A few whitish-gray mortar specks stick to Myron's shoes. Haphazardly, Myron continues to poke at the bricks. One moves.

Myron pokes harder. The brick falls—inward—away from Myron and the well's center. Caution aside, Myron is on his hands and knees inspecting the gap he made. He notices the ease with which several more adjacent bricks pop out or in. The mortar originally used to build the well wall is either missing or only adheres to a single brick; it does not hold two bricks together. Enough bricks are removed by Myron to provide an opening for a child's body to squeeze through into the waiting darkness.

A beam of light from Myron's flashlight crisscrosses the void behind the well wall. It's a tunnel, crafted out of brick, with a concrete patch here and there. A chocolate bar wrapper, surprisingly not faded, lays crushed on top of three bricks inside the opening, indicating a recent visitor—and odds favor a youth: Oscar, maybe?

Feverishly, Myron removes additional bricks until he can squeeze through. With a little grunting, he is into the tunnel. He is enveloped in darkness. Inch by inch, yard by yard, pushing his flashlight ahead of him, the distance between his entrance and the tunnel's mystery destination shrinks with every difficult effort forward he makes.

Suddenly, there it is: the factory cistern.

A realization slowly dawns on Myron: The small entrance, crumpled candy-bar wrapper, door nails un-tampered with, Jimmy's tall stories, and Oscar's promise. He has unveiled Oscar's secret factory entrance. The discovery now raises more questions for Myron than it answers. Surely, the Sheriff must have noticed the tunnel. *He had to have noticed it*—the phrase repeats itself in Myron's mind.

His hand undulates the beam of the flashlight onto the distant cistern wall. He sees nothing except old concrete and fresh scratch marks, presumably made by the examining probes of the state crime men. Time, he guesses, will eventually dull the probe marks, leaving only indentations for later generations to muse over. But now, he is more concerned he may lose his balance and fall into the cistern.

The return trip is no mean trick; reversing his body would have made his crawling easier and avoided the intermittent bumping of his butt against the abrasive brick face of the tunnel. He should have slid into the cistern and crawled out, but it's too late now. When he reaches the chocolate wrapper, Myron's left elbow rubs against the three bricks neatly stacked against the tunnel wall, the candy wrapper on top. Instinctively, he turns the flashlight beam onto them but sees only nondescript brick facing. His hands push his lower body backwards into the well and he twists his upper torso to be able to examine the three bricks.

On the backside of the third brick is scratched what Myron guesses to be three letters: G, O, and a backwards C. Checking his wristwatch, he realizes he's lost track of time and must hurry. While a Saturday, he's scheduled to report to work. He doesn't want to be late or have to explain why or where he's been.

Fully extricated from the tunnel, he stands upright and stretches. In his hand is the brick with the writing. In daylight, with the three letters plainly visible, he concludes the three letters definitely are a G, an O, and a backwards C.

The backwards C is the most interesting to Myron. "Why a non-letter for the third symbol?" ponders Myron. He thinks of possibilities, until his finger traces the last character into another O. "GOO" it would read—a baby's babbling. The paradox of symbols confuses him. If he's right, there's the written symbol of the sound of a baby, the beginning of life from a human body, next to human skeletal bones, which represent death and the absence of human life. Like alpha and omega. Then, too, he realizes, it could be the first three letters of his own last name.

As his high school English teacher had said: *Truth may indeed be stranger than fiction.* Hurriedly, he replaces the bricks to hide the tunnel entrance and lays the wood boards across the wellhead. He hides the brick with the three letters inside the factory and leaves the other two where he found them.

An important question looms: to whom can Myron disclose his discovery? What if he trusts the wrong person? What if—?

Chapter Fourteen

"Myron, when are you going to get this crate off the ground?" wisecracks Wanda. Her teasing question announces her arrival inside the old factory.

"Never, if I must take you over to Winterville every Friday to see a movie, as well as having to listen to your incessant yakking."

"Not lately, you've been holed up in this old barn all week, day and night, hiding," Wanda replies. "Are you practicing to become a religious monk? You got a good start."

Myron thinks of the condom question from his Dad. He's not going to open his mouth about that. Myron tosses a rag aside. "Oh, sure," Myron replies snidely. "I've got things on my mind, big things. Here, hold this in place. Damn bolt." Wanda frowns at him. "Why is it bolts never stay where you put them? This guide wire is supposed to be taut. I never get things right the first time."

"So? What else is new?" teases Wanda.

Myron ignores the sarcastic meaning that could be attributed to Wanda's question. "Plenty. I just don't know who to tell."

"You can tell me. We're not playing twenty questions you know. You can trust me to keep a secret."

"I just don't—"

"Animal or vegetable?" Wanda scoots behind Myron and puts her hands over his eyes.

"Please, stop it, this is important." Myron turns to face Wanda. "It's not like having a little nail hole in your britches and squirming to sit another way in order to hide it from the preacher on Sunday morning." Myron swivels his hips to illustrate a squirm.

"Come on, tell me. I'll stay here all night," threatens Wanda. "I don't work for my father, so you'll not be reading my exclusive in the *Pioneer Ledger*."

"Okay, if you promise not to tell anyone." Myron observes Wanda cross her heart. "Go find your chair." Myron waits. "It's about the old cistern. I found a way to get inside it through the old well. There's a tunnel. Shouldn't be there, but I guess it may have been built to prevent the shallow cistern from overflowing into the factory. Who knows? I don't. Maybe no one does, but it's there. I found some stacked bricks, three of them, and one is special."

"Is this some kind of a crazy weird story?" asks Wanda.

"No, it's true." Myron strides over to the corner of the factory where Wanda sees Myron reach for a gunnysack weighted with something. He returns to stand in front of her.

"See, this here." His outstretched hand holds one brick taken from the sack, the plain side facing Wanda.

"So it's a brick. What's the big deal?"

Myron turns the brick. "Look at this side. See the letters?"

"Wow! Why would these three letters be important? What if … what if the brick was only a brick later reused in the well?"

"Tunnel," corrects Myron.

"Well, cistern, tunnel, whatever. Those letters could have meant anything. Was there anything on other bricks?" asks Wanda.

"No, nothing that I could see. Yeah, they were blank." Myron hands the brick to Wanda.

"So, we have three letters that don't make sense. Could be lover's initials. Who it was, heaven only knows, but could be. You tell me." Wanda gives back the brick.

"I can't. I only found it week ago Saturday. I think they are important. You talk about lovers and initials, but what about my father?"

"How does your father fit in? That's weird, really weird." Wanda bites her lower lip.

"No. It's not. See, fill in this third letter to form an O, and you have the beginning of my family's last name. I reckon the person trapped in there, rest her soul, had begun to scratch out the killer's name before dying. Like in the movies or on TV."

"Sure, and Gary Cooper is going to ride in at high noon." Wanda mimics a rider on a horse. "That's a tall story, and the bit about your father's name is even weirder."

"Not so. Remember, my father was the last person to see Father Murphy before the priest disappeared. Maybe my father has information about this body. The name Goostree is in large letters across my father's storefront. Everyone knows him; even a tramp passing through could easily learn my last name." Myron pushes his hair back, off his forehead.

"You're incredible. Hanging your own father. I think your dream of reaching high altitudes in this here glider has marooned your mind at 20,000 feet. Right?" asks Wanda.

"I don't know, but who can I tell? They'll think I'm crazy, trying to pin it on my father, and, heaven knows, I don't want to do that. He's my Dad; I can't change that." Myron says forlornly.

"I know that, but what'll you do? You got to tell someone. Maybe my Dad can help?" Wanda stretches her arms.

"No, no. I don't think so. Your parents just don't understand me, and besides, I think they, or maybe it's only your mother who doesn't like me." Myron glances under the fuselage next to him.

"You're wrong, Myron," says Wanda. "They may want to protect me against life, but they don't hate or dislike you. You must understand." Myron walks three steps to where Wanda is sitting.

"Kiss me," Myron says as he leans over. "Enough of our babbling. I haven't talked this long since Aunt Helen promised me a sucker if I'd read a story and not make her cry." Wanda stands.

"Oh, Myron," says Wanda as she puts her arms around his neck.

Their bodies cling longingly in the tenderness of their embrace. The hot, searing first brush of the slightly parted lips is enough to smear, crumble, or crust the best of Wanda's fashionable lipsticks. Telltale signs of Wanda's lips brand Myron's face.

The brick, with its secret, sits on top of a gunnysack, ignored for the time being.

Chapter Fifteen

Wanda is livid. "You ain't gonna keep me buried forever in this little town. Honest, Mom, you're not!"

"Calm down, dear. All I want for you is the best, forever the best," Sarah tries to reassure.

"All you want is for me to live close and marry a preacher or maybe a doctor, if this town could ever attract one. And once married, I should stay home, have half a dozen kids, and bake apple pie for the county fair."

"That ain't, ah, there I'm saying words I tell you not to use, well, that isn't true. There's nothing wrong with being a stay-at-home wife and mother. My mother's generation worked in factories, but prosperity returned only when women came back to the home full-time and men returned to the jobs they left. There's nothing wrong with my wanting the best for my child, is there?"

"I'm not your child," snaps Wanda. She had been trying to sort through out-dated clothes in her bedroom closet when her mother had asked what she was doing. Her mother brought up Myron and that triggered the renewal of a previous heated discussion.

"Flesh of my flesh, bone of my bone, you may not be, nor did I carry you in my womb, but I've raised you these last ten years as if you've been my own flesh and blood. You can't deny that."

"Yeah, I can," is Wanda's quick retort. "You've treated me like a godsend, overprotected, and a person not to have a mind of their own."

"That isn't so, Wanda, and you know it," replies Sarah calmly. "You've never had it better, and this little snit of yours is only a stage in the process of growing up. You're changing, Wanda, and if you'd look in the mirror, you'd notice. Not so much the physical changes, since you bloomed early, but much deeper, maybe more subtle, like around your eyes—there are wrinkles, yes, the wrinkles every woman must face sooner or later. You've changed physically into a woman, but emotionally, you're still a girl—foolish, carefree, and afraid to face the reality that maturity brings. I know myself the pain of reality. I know the anguish that lives on in one's mind after one makes the wrong choice or follows a forbidden path. I only ask that you face life's reality with the mindset that women need to be strong, to avoid temptation." Sarah sighs.

"I've faced reality, Mother." Wanda thinks the word *reality* sounds strange and hard as she says it. "But I can't seem to express it to you. I've found a person, a man, to love, but feel like Juliet, where neither one of my parents respects the true feelings within me."

"Tell me that you and Myron are not ... how shall I put it?" Sarah looks away from Wanda; then turns her head back.

"No, Mother, we're not getting naked together, ... if that's what you're trying to ask."

Sarah's face turns beet red. Wanda is not sure she's blurted out the right thing. All her friends at Sharon's shower were talking about Helen Gurley Brown's book on sex, and, while Wanda did not understand half of what was written, she giggled at its sex references.

"My mother would never talk to me about creating babies," Sarah continues. "She said God would show me. These days, all these women are writing books and giving seminars about it. Women are working and talking about intimate things, and that's going to lead to our ruin. My parents' generation did not have all these divorces that we have today." Sarah's complexion returns to normal.

"Mother, you can't hide me from the world. I'm not some doll you can put behind glass in a cabinet. You talk about raising a family, staying home. You work just as much here as if you walked down the street to where I work," argues Wanda.

"You don't have to criticize that way," Sarah says as her mind reacts as if she had been stabbed with a knife. "You've been such a recluse these last few days, as if you're preparing to go to a distant mountain retreat to redefine the world or readying to run off."

"I don't want anything to do with redefining the world. Sure, I get and keep secret thoughts and inner feelings. If Myron and I talk about something that causes us concern, I will keep it a secret. And with good reason," says a defiant Wanda.

"There's no good reason for you to keep secrets from your parents, and you have to consider that Thomas and I are your parents. You're, at times, more a daughter to us than our own child."

"You've never had a child, so how can you preach to me about what women should do?" Wanda's defiant attitude flares up.

"You are wrong Wanda. Thomas and I had a beautiful child, a girl. You'll never meet her," sighs Sarah. "I don't have the words to tell you the guilt, yes, guilt; I felt at the time and still feel each and every day since our child's passing. I feel responsible, yet you'll never know this feeling unless you—heaven forbid—have a child and lose one. Oh, my God, it's terrible, devastating. More terrible if the generating circumstances are voluntary. Never mind the vengeance of an Act of God." Sarah feels exhausted by the vivid memories.

"I don't know exactly what you're saying or where you're going," says a perplexed Wanda. "Maybe my not knowing what it is you're saying is preventing me from telling you what's in my mind."

"Everyone knows what's in his or her mind. People may have trouble getting it out, but they do know."

"That's easy to say, but it's hard in reality to be able to express 100 percent of what is in one's mind."

"You can easily be 100 percent with me," coaxes Sarah. "I'm your mother. Mothers understand."

"I understand you don't like Myron, but he loves me and he is a best friend." Wanda would love to stretch out on her bed; however, she ignores the temptation with her mother in the room.

"Wanda, how many times do I have to tell you? That's not so—it never was. My feeling is that you could do better for yourself."

"Here you go again, trying to say nice things about someone you hate. It may be polite, but it's not honest. It's like hiding something dreadful behind a constant smile. Again, it's not honest."

"Well, what's honest about keeping secrets from your parents? There's no double standard, Wanda." Sarah rubs her hands.

Wanda hesitates. "I can't tell you anything about the brick. It's all so weird and silly. Besides, Myron is afraid I'd have it printed in the newspaper, and then there's no telling what would happen to his father or the grocery." Wanda's words raise a quizzical look on Sarah.

"You're now baffling me Wanda. Goostree Grocery is an institution in this town. It prospered because it was open Sunday after church to permit farmers to combine trips."

"You didn't see the brick."

"What brick? What brick?" asks Sarah.

"I can't say," says a solemn Wanda.

"Yes, you can. I have a feeling that it's becoming part of the wall between us, and I don't mean that literally." Sarah feels a smile at the corner of her mouth but, if she smiles, it would insult Wanda.

"Well, if I tell you, will you promise to keep it out of the paper? Even better yet, promise not to tell my father—I mean, Thomas. Promise?" asks Wanda.

"That's hard, Wanda. It goes against the vows we took years ago—to be honest and faithful. I can't now go against them. They are a sacred trust, rooted in the church's sacrament of matrimony and proclaimed by us in public to all," says Sarah with conviction.

"If you want something, you must give something. You talk about promises, vows, and sacred trust. I promised, too. My promises count," the defiance returning to Wanda's voice. "I don't know that I could live with myself if I were to be dishonest to myself and the promises I make."

"Wanda. I'll keep your secret. You must believe you can trust me, but I will try to talk you out of it. If I don't succeed, it'll be between only us. Promise."

"I'm grateful to you both for everything, but I have to grow to be my own person. I hope I can trust you. I need some answers, too. It's about Myron," says Wanda.

"Yeah," a concerned Sarah cuts short her reply.

"He found some old bricks at the factory."

"Gold?" Sarah smiles.

"Heavens, no. Just plain, ordinary bricks made of whatever, mud maybe, but who cares. The bricks came from the cistern, where the body was found, and there was a word written on one of them."

"A word?" Sarah focuses her entire attention on Wanda. "What word? Tell me, Wanda, quick, tell me."

"Just a word—only three letters really. There was a G, O, and a funny backwards C. Nothing really, but Myron was concerned. He thought it might be something to do with the skeleton and their last name. You know, Goostree." Wanda is pensive in trying to gauge the reaction of her mother to what she is saying.

"That's a tall story, Wanda. Some enterprising high school sweethearts could've put those letters on the brick. You never know where those things come from. It may have been part of a larger saying, maybe a slogan. You know how vandals paint and carve things. If that's the secret, I don't see the big suspense or concern."

"Myron does," answers Wanda. He thinks the brick connects his father with the missing priest."

"What? What the—?" A look of shock overcomes Sarah's calm exterior, like subtle cracks in the face of a china doll that has been dropped to the floor, but softly, not so hard as to shatter.

"It's true, and Myron doesn't want his father sent to jail."

"Myron Goostree won't go to jail for something he didn't do. He couldn't have." Wanda absorbs the conviction in her mother's voice.

"He was the last person to see Father Murphy. Why the look, Mother? The *Pioneer Ledger* said Father Murphy was last seen by him. Who can know different unless Myron's father tells us about what happened that day. And who knows if we'll get the truth—it's been so long?"

"Now I don't feel so bad about your not trusting me. You don't trust anybody, do you?" asks Sarah.

"Sure I do," says Wanda defensively.

"Not with what you're saying, or the way you've been acting, at least tonight. Mr. Goostree has been a fine, respected citizen of this town for years."

"Well, I don't know everything," Wanda admits. She pauses and then continues, almost in a whisper. "But I do know that Myron is scared, scared a lot."

"Don't you worry. Put the crazy idea about letters on bricks meaning anything out of your mind. Just forget it. It would be best if Father Murphy was forgotten, and we could live normal, peaceful lives. There's too much to worry about in trying to live one's life. Who has time for yesterday? If we all dwell on yesterday, who will have time to think about tomorrow? I try to think about tomorrow, the future, and you should, too. When you first came to live here, you'd always be about what will I be when I grow up. There'd be pictures in books of movie stars, even firemen, to interest you. You had dreams, big dreams, and I still feel you should keep them and that you can make yourself a better life. Don't get carried away with Myron. Maybe you should wait. Yes, definitely you should wait."

Wanda stares silently at her mother. Stillness engulfs the room. After what seems like minutes, the silence is broken by the shrill squeak of a door hinge at the front entrance of the newspaper office.

"Oh, my," whispers Sarah.

"It's me, dear," calls Thomas. He heads through the newspaper office to the family living quarters and sees the light from Wanda's room.

"Hi, Wanda. What's my favorite daughter up to?" He stops short, noticing that he apparently has broken into a conversation he wasn't invited to. He momentarily pauses and looks over his shoulder towards the kitchen.

"Come back in half an hour, Thomas," Sarah says quietly. "It's important."

Chapter Sixteen

I t is a rare day for Myron to be sitting at the kitchen table with Wanda's parents, but there he is.

"Would you like another piece of blueberry-pecan bread?" asks Sarah, trying to make him feel at ease.

"No, thank you, ma'am," murmurs Myron, wiping his chin with a paper napkin. Myron's eyes are riveted on Thomas as he closely examines the brick Myron found in the cistern tunnel.

"Maybe I should get my magnifying glass for a closer look," says Thomas, rising from his chair without waiting for a response, he returns quickly with his examination helper taken from a kitchen drawer. "Myron, anything special, other than the letters?"

"Nothing special to me. Same three-by-eight-inch brick you'd find in many of the houses here in Clinton. There are many in the tunnel wall."

"What tunnel?" asks Thomas.

Myron explains his checking the well, finding loose bricks in the wall, following the tunnel to the factory cistern, and his finding the three bricks under the candy wrapper. He leaves out his speculation on the three letters and his fear of a connection to his father.

"That third symbol doesn't make sense by itself," Thomas says. "There's got to be more—some further explanation."

"I don't think so," suggests Sarah. "That old brick is hardly anything to get into a hubbub about. Old bricks; it's best to let old things we know nothing about alone. Why kick up old dirt? Once it's settled. Leave it alone."

"No, Sarah, there's something here. We've got to answer the five Ws: who, what, when, where, why, and how. At most, we know a little bit about the where. You really start the mind working, Myron."

"Maybe I search for more than I should," replies Myron. "A little boy tells me he has a secret, and I go digging, literally. Maybe I should forget about everything connected with the old factory except for my sailplane. It's important to finish the glider. I've completed the fuselage sanding. I use up so much sandpaper, I should buy it in cartons for the wings."

"That's right, Myron, you should forget about the old factory," says Sarah. "Think seriously about what occupation you can learn for the future. Think about completing college."

Wanda glares at her mother; stays quiet. Myron nervously reaches for the last piece of homemade sweet bread.

Thomas looks at the group. "Seems I'm the only real Sherlock Holmes at this table. It would make a terrific story. Put the *Pioneer Ledger* on the map, ahead of all those big-city reporters."

"I would have thought you'd want to sell more or bigger ads to the town merchants or local church groups," says Sarah, trying to shift Thomas' mind away from his writing about the brick.

"A story on this brick will generate attention. Help convince advertisers that people do read the paper."

"You can't put it in the newspaper, Mr. Hamilton. That was a promise," says an animated Myron.

"Yes, Dad, you promised Myron."

"I know I promised Myron and for now I will keep my promise." Thomas moves his gaze from Wanda to Myron. "Myron, you have to consider letting Sheriff O'Day know what you found. The sheriff has kept the cistern sealed off from the public these past months, and while you didn't take down the barricade, you did get into the cistern by your tunnel crawling. You have to consider the Sheriff knows about the tunnel from Oscar. You might be in serious trouble for taking this brick away. Just think about it."

"I have, a lot. But I gotta keep it a secret."

Thomas hands the brick back to Myron.

Three days later, the *Pioneer Ledger* sparks a heightened buzz in Clinton with news on the factory skeleton. Gossip in the café sets a record for both creativity and volume. An overnight rainstorm brings two-dozen local farmers to town, and they join in the rampant speculation triggered by the following story on the front page of the *Pioneer Ledger*:

MYSTERY SOLVED

Skeleton Identified

EXCLUSIVE

The skeleton identification mystery was solved this week with the finding of old dental records. State crime officials told Sheriff Jonathan O'Day yesterday that the skeleton was Father Cornelius Murphy, who served as the parish priest here in Clinton at St. Mary's Catholic Church.

The Sheriff said the priest's dental records appeared during a second look at the records of a retired dentist. When Dr. E. K. Jones retired, he transferred his old patient records to other dentists treating his patients. Dr. L. Smithton of Oxford found the priest's dental x-rays within a file under the name of Corwin.

The skeleton had been found in the old factory on the edge of town. The factory owned at the time by the late Mr. Arnold Peterson. He was accused of killing his wife and hiding her body in his factory. A postcard he claimed to have received from his wife was proven at trial to be a forgery. He died in court during trial before a verdict was reached.

Sheriff O'Day said a new exhaustive analysis of the partial skeleton came up with the bones being more than ten years old. This coincides with the year and time the priest and Mrs. Peterson, a year before him, went missing. He further said he was told finding exact answers with decade old bones was extremely difficult.

Sheriff O'Day also stated that no exact cause of death was determined for Father Murphy. A bullet mark on his skull may or may not have been fatal and may have been inflicted after death, he said. The sheriff would not rule out fatal food poisoning or knife wounds. Who killed or why the priest was killed remains an unanswered question, the sheriff said. It is hoped that more information will be available next week.

Chapter Seventeen

Gordie Oswald stands reading the label on an instant coffee can in an aisle of the Goostree Grocery when owner Myron Goostree, Sr., startles him from behind.

"You're worse than a bear at a fishing camp," grumbles Oswald.

"No need to get all bothered," says the storekeeper sheepishly.

Goostree has been the main grocer in Clinton for almost twenty-five years. He has outlasted two competitors, including Sarah's father.

"Gordie, I was only wanting to say hello." Goostree is not as shy as he once was. He now ventures past his storefront door to participate in village events. Attending more community functions has meant he's added fifteen pounds to his six-foot, muscular frame since 1960. While he tried to diet in the last year, the pounds have stayed despite the daily manual labor of lifting and carrying required in his one-person enterprise.

"I was only looking," replies Oswald.

"I don't know why you're looking. You haven't switched from your Columbian roast coffee brand for as long as I've known you."

"They advertise coffee on the TV all the time, but I can't see that you have any of it."

"Not that new decaffeinated. Salesmen ask me to buy cases of decaffeinated, but people like you never switch. I have to buy by the case, maybe sell a can or two, and be stuck with coffee I can't drink—it's bad for my stomach."

"Guess you got a point. I'll take two cans of my regular grind. That's all I need for the Elevator pot at the moment. Say, did you hear any more about the priest?" asks Oswald.

"Just café gossip. It rains, and all the farmers drive to town to sit and chat. Nobody has answers, but one question keeps popping up: How'd that body lie in the cistern without someone smelling it?"

"Never thought of that," admits Oswald. "Peterson had been very secretive about that old warehouse for a decade."

"I thought Arnold only inherited the property three years back."

"No, no, not the Peterson that keeled over at the trial. It was his uncle or second cousin, damn, I don't remember."

"You mean the old suspected bootlegger?" asks Myron.

"Yeah, him. Very secretive he was and often traveling to exotic countries was that Peterson, especially South America."

"Still doesn't answer how come no one smelled anything. My thinking is now that we know it was Father Murphy and a decent proper burial was held, we should move on," suggests Myron. "No need to continue the gossip. Even those out-of-town newspapermen with their notebooks and stupid questions are gone. If I spent all my time worrying, I'd never open for business and would starve."

"Well, maybe so," says Oswald stiffly, looking down the aisle.

"Those reporters were real nasty. I kept telling them that I was only running an errand on the day that I saw Father Murphy. Nothing special. We may have said hello in passing but that was about it. I had known Father Murphy for the five years that he was in town. He'd come into the store from time to time. More frequent when he was looking for a money or food donation to help build the kids gym he was so keen on. But that day, he didn't even mention that."

Goostree hears his front door bell ring as a customer enters and seconds later a familiar figure walks down the beverage aisle.

"Hi, Godfrey. Can I help you?" asks Myron.

"I'm good. Need some sugar cubes and creamer is all."

"So how's business at the bank?" asks Oswald, looking across the aisle at Clinton's long-time banker, Godfrey Klempler.

Klempler worked his first two years at the bank as an assistant cashier. Townspeople grew to respect him; his stern facial features only infrequently exhibiting a smile.

Standing six feet and weighing 180 pounds, Klempler gave the appearance of an athlete beneath the dark business suits he always wore, but he was not. He and his wife, Rosie, are empty nesters after raising two sons. Both kids have moved away for employment and college. A very quiet person, Rosie has not for a decade participated in town activities, except church bake sales with her sought after German chocolate cake. She has one noticeable quirk: she always wears long sleeves buttoned tightly at the wrist, even on the hottest summer day.

Thinking that Klempler had not heard him, Oswald asks again, "How's business at the bank?"

"Looking up. It should be the best year since I became president fourteen years ago," boasts Klempler, a minority bank owner.

"We were just talking about the factory skeleton," Oswald continues. "Dreadful discovery. You knew Father Murphy, didn't you?"

"Sure I did. Knew him since he first came to town. Little long-winded in his Sunday sermon, but other than that he was pleasant.

Knew the other three priests who preceded and came after him, too. Been going to St. Mary's almost twenty years now. Rosie and I were married there." Klempler taps his foot.

"Did you happened to see Father Murphy that last day?" asks Oswald. "I heard he was uptown that last afternoon."

"Not that I recall. It's been so long." Klempler appears preoccupied. "If you'll excuse me, I have to get back across the street. I would have sent Sharon for this coffee stuff, but the employees are giving her a surprise party today at quitting time—she's getting married soon. See both of you later, maybe at the chamber meeting next week?"

"Oh, I forgot about the chamber meeting," says Myron, Sr.

"Bye," says Oswald.

With Klempler gone, Myron, Sr., continues. "By the way, how's my son doing these days at the Elevator? He's not goofing off on the job, is he?"

"Don't worry. He's doing a good job," assures Oswald.

"Got his mind fixated all the time on that sailplane he's building. I hope it's not causing any problems." Myron rings up the coffee.

"Customers like him. He's real helpful. You raised a good boy, if you ask me."

Chapter Eighteen

Charles Johnston hums, slightly off-key, an unmistakably bad rendition of a song of a cab driver driving once more around Mary's block made famous by his favorite group, the Mills Brothers. He saw them last year at Chicago's Aragon Ballroom, a historic big band venue with floor-length purple velvet draperies and a smooth, solid-wood dance floor.

The occasion was a weeklong school for crime investigation. The seminar classes were helpful in getting him started on his second career. A Navy veteran of WWII, he retired from the military to join the FBI, where for six years he was an expert in counterfeit stamps, money, and passports. He never traveled outside Washington, D.C. Questionable materials were shipped to him daily for analysis. His repetitious work was so boring it affected his after-work bachelor activities. He epitomized dull. Two years ago he was hired to be a State of Iowa criminal investigator, assigned to twenty rural counties including Lake County. Based on his last six months of case assignments, he today senses the director of state criminal investigations will be transferring him to full-time document examination.

His old, two-tone blue Chevy 210 still purrs from its last tune-up. The narrow tie he wears laps over his shoulder—a result of the wind whistling through the open driver window.

In thirty minutes, he'll be back in Clinton for the second time in a week. A box with three bricks, courtesy of Sheriff O'Day, sits on his car's backseat next to two unread detective novels received as Christmas gifts. He recalls crawling into the empty factory cistern to shoot crime scene pictures. He could discern no visible clues to the killer. He had noted the cistern rainwater input pipe value was rusted shut in the closed position.

Have to talk to that country editor, Johnston reminds himself. Yes, that's his first stop of the day.

The day is Tuesday, and Thomas puts the last slug of type into the chase, ready for lock-up, and then down to the basement, where seven other pages—only eight total this week—are sitting atop turtles ready for the short ride to the printing press. Thomas could only guess how the metal tables with wheels came to be called "turtles." His lack of a "turtles" answer is minor, compared to the pending questions he has about Father Murphy's death. Nothing more has surfaced. St. Mary parishioners want the incident laid to rest with the priest. When he visited the café last Sunday morning, he was surprised by the wild stories still circulating, none printable.

President Johnson may make an important policy announcement in Washington, but Thomas will never mention it in the *Pioneer Ledger*. If Mrs. Olson invites eight people to attend an afternoon tea party, however, everyone there will get a mention, especially if all are regular subscribers. When keepsake copies are purchased for scrapbooks, this generates income and a livelihood for Thomas.

Controversial people like Madalyn Murray O'Hair, the pugnacious founder of American Atheists, could disown her Baptist preacher son, appear regularly on the Phil Donahue television show, and fill a *Life* magazine column, but she would not merit one word in the *Pioneer Ledger*. Although there is no Baptist Church in Clinton, and townspeople consider themselves good tolerant Christians, any public atheist would find himself and his family shunned.

Two years ago Thomas received a check, along with an ad from a publisher for Helen Gurley Brown's book, *Sex and the Single Girl*. Thomas did not plan to run the ad, but he absentmindedly left the ad materials sitting near the linotype. Sarah saw them and went into a tirade against the book and him. She wanted to know how the U.S. Post Office could send such filth through the mail. He was wrong for having left it out where Wanda could be tempted to have improper scandalous ideas put into her head.

"I've worked hard my entire life to create a home with proper values," raved Sarah. "I learned how to cook, bake, and clean from my mother, and I take pride in what I do. No one can say I don't keep a good house. I work hard at it, even after I spend time helping you print a newspaper. I don't neglect my home or my family. I take the same pride in what I do as my mother did. Wanda will be proud of me, too. She'll make a good, loving, faithful wife and be fulfilled, as a woman should be. She'll learn sex from her husband, not some book teaching her to be a harlot."

Thomas said nothing when Sarah picked up the advertisement and check only to rip up both in front of him, and left to flush both down the toilet. He tried to apologize and explain he was not going to print the advertisement, but concluded time would be the best healer.

He would accept the journalistic Lovejoy award for courage and integrity, but he needed the cash register to ring more frequently. His *Pioneer Ledger*, with the exclusive on the death of the priest, made the state wire service as a three-line item. Thomas received calls, but they either sought information he did not have or he was asked if the priest's death was linked to a chain of area killings.

Thomas heard gossip that many Clinton residents and area farmers looked into their own cisterns for a skeleton.

Before he's completely lost in his own musings, Thomas hears the front door open. He lays down his wooden mallet and hangs up the stiff wire brush.

"Hi, there," a voice booms, echoing out of the throat of one Charles Johnston.

"Nice to see you. I guess. What's new?" asks Thomas.

"I thought you'd tell me," Johnston says in a coy reply.

"What about those bricks? Should be some telltale sign there, hidden from observation by us ordinary people but clear as a railroad crossing signal to you crafty investigators," responds Thomas. His railroad hat used for bicycle trips hangs on a visitor coat hook inside the office front door.

"We talking official, or are we just talking? You know what I mean?" replies Johnston.

"I don't go in for the hocus pocus big-city reporters use," says Thomas. "We speak openly in Clinton, and everyone realizes I do not print anything someone tells me not to print. I've got to keep all the subscribers I have. Absolutely, I do. Can't exist any other way."

"Okay, you've been straight so far. Can I look at your old newspapers, say, about ten, eleven years ago?" asks Johnston.

"Sure, some are yellowed, but they're all bound in books in the cellar. Off-the-floor racks keep them safe and dry."

"Thanks. Show me the way to the books. I can page through them myself, no trouble."

"What's in the books, anyway?" Thomas asks. "I thought all you guys did was check the body, the environs, or the crime scene, then analyze collected evidence to learn the identity of the culprit in what is left by the killer, and then tell us unknowing souls."

"Not that easy," explains Johnston. "On a big case, I'd not have to do this nitty-gritty, but the state director said I must do this old case by myself in my spare time. Where are the papers?"

"Follow me." Thomas steps around Johnston.

Thomas turns at the bottom of the steps into a basement room lined with books of bound, full-size newspapers. Dates scribbled on the front wooden shelf supports act as roadmaps to the year printed.

"Here—you can use this turtle to rest the book on. Should allow for easier reading," offers Thomas.

"Thanks," says Johnston as he takes down the book for 1951, a Korean conflict year, but no one would know it by reading the pages of the *Pioneer Ledger*—except for the story so-and-so enlisted or an occasional obituary written for a young citizen-soldier hero not old enough to have experienced a full life, become eligible to vote, or legally drink alcohol. Hamilton goes back upstairs.

Johnston pages through one volume and then another, covering the years from 1951 to 1955. He puts an entry into his notepad. *That's enough*, he decides after ninety minutes. He shouts for Thomas.

"Leave the books out; that's okay, I'll put them away," Thomas yells down the stairs.

Up the stairs, Johnston, ready to leave, pauses briefly to ask, "Did you know Father Murphy well, Thomas?"

"Not really," replies Thomas. "Sarah knew him better. She's Catholic and a member of St. Mary's. I go to First Lutheran, or, at least, that is where I'm registered. Why?"

"I have a question about St. Mary's and whoever controlled the church's operations there ten to twelve years ago. It may be important, or it may not. My curiosity was raised."

"About what?" asks Thomas.

"About activities at St. Mary's. I don't have concrete facts, but it seems that prior to the disappearance of Father Murphy, there was a lot of fund-raising events that stopped after he disappeared. Was there a new building, remodeling, or celebration in the works?"

"I don't recall any. I can ask Sarah when she returns from her errand." Thomas watches Johnston put his notepad into his pocket.

"Yes, please do. I'll give you a telephone call in a couple of days to be filled in on what Sarah remembers." Johnston departs.

Walking to his car, Johnston ponders his next move. He is staying in Winterville on a separately assigned counterfeiting case while he awaits St. Mary's financial information from the bishop's office. If it wasn't sex, it was money—one or the other always accompanied unexplained death. That was what crime school drilled into him.

Chapter Nineteen

Thomas had all but completed the printing of this week's edition of the *Pioneer Ledger* when he heard Sarah call to him she was home. She was preparing supper when he enters the family kitchen.

"Hi, doll, I'm ready for your help with addressing."

"That other fella still downstairs?" asks Sarah.

"You mean Investigator Johnston? No, he left shortly after you did. He did have a question after he looked at our old newspapers."

"What?" Sarah adds silverware to the kitchen table.

"He wanted to know about fund-raising at St. Mary's back in the early Fifties." Thomas finishes washing his hands at the sink.

"What?" asks an uptight Sarah. "I hoped we'd forget about the past. 1950? That's ridiculous, trying to remember back that far."

"That's why I was having trouble. Since you have been a member of St. Mary's, you'd have a clearer memory than me. You were active in the church then, although maybe not so much lately. I remember you were always baking for the church." Thomas sits at the table.

"Well, there was St. Ann's Circle, and some funerals where the church ladies served the luncheon for the family after the funeral mass. Father Murphy had a special project—a gym for the kids. It was his grand passionate dream. He approached the diocese, or at least he said he did, but they turned down his request for money. He changed his plan from building a gym to trying to get a hall. That had the potential of getting some money from the diocese, not one hundred percent. Father Murphy envisioned that a hall was just a gym without basketball hoops. If he built the hall, he thought it was just a matter of time until he added basketball hoops. I recall we once ran a special raffle at a holiday bingo. Other times, we gave him part of our bake sale money. Our help seemed like a good idea. The hall would provide additional space for church functions. The outdoor festivals could come inside if it rained. It could be rented out to the community, although some Legion member wives complained that it would unfairly compete with the Legion Hall." Sarah sits to join Thomas.

"Anything else you can remember? No hall or gym was ever built. What happened to the money?" asks Thomas, buttering a roll.

"I don't know," says Sarah. "Father Murphy said he created a special account at the bank so the money would earn interest."

"Was there a building committee?"

"Not that I recall." Sarah retrieves a pot from the stove. "Father Murphy heard about the Legion officers being upset, so he kept everything low key. I think Mr. Klempler at the bank was considered the special account treasurer. I know Father Murphy had a passbook to keep track of deposits. Where it is or would be, I have no idea."

"I'll tell Mr. Johnston when he calls back this week."

"I wish everything would just go away," she says with a sigh. "Most agree we keep upsetting ourselves by looking backwards all the time. Father Murphy is gone. St. Mary's went past a year before the diocese assigned a new full-time priest. Who knows anymore about bake sale money? There were no real records kept. We all donated cakes and cookies, sold them to our neighbors, and used the money for our projects." Sarah says table grace.

"I know." Thomas fills a glass with milk. "If Mr. Johnston wants more information, he can go to the church and leave us out of it. Any of that blueberry-pecan bread left?"

Chapter Twenty

A telephone rings.

Thomas jumps out of bed. In pajamas, he scurries to the kitchen from his bedroom.

"Hello. Thomas Hamilton," he mumbles. Rubs his eyes.

"Tom, George Windhurst here. Got great news."

"George, the rooster hasn't even crowed today."

"Sure it has, and the early bird gets the worm. That's you, Tom."

"What you talking about, George?" asks Thomas. His bare feet feel chilled on the linoleum without his slippers.

"Old Man Peterson's home, next door to you. Mr. Peterson left a will. I represent his estate and his son, who was in South America. He's coming back here this week. He wants to liquidate all of his father's property, including the house, and sell his personal effects."

"My offer is still $6,000.00. Should be less, considering that no one has been living in it for the past several months. Who knows what has happened to the house." Thomas shivers.

"You are without mercy, Tom. I need authority to draw up the sale papers for that amount. However, I do have authority to let you rent the house for one dollar per month until we can wrap up a sale. This way, you can make sure the utilities are working when winter comes, and when the sale is finalized, you will be in a good position."

"George ... sounds like a strange arrangement. What's the catch?" asks Thomas, rubbing his arm.

"Well ... well ... there is no guarantee how long it will take for Peterson's will to go through probate. The son's not sure whether or not his mother will show up and demand her share. He does not know whether or not she's even alive. He is guaranteed at a minimum the house next door to you and then there is the old factory. Who knows when it can be sold? At the least, if you rent the house, he's made a binding commitment to sell it to you when he can."

"Bring me the lease when you come to Clinton next Tuesday. I'll have a chance to discuss with Sarah by then. Consider it possible unless I call by Friday noon saying no deal."

"You've made a wise decision, Tom. I'll see you with the papers this Tuesday. Say hello to Sarah for me."

Sarah carries a pair of men's slippers as she joins Thomas in the kitchen. "Dear, who was that calling at this hour?"

"George Windhurst," replies Thomas, putting on the slippers.

"What did he want that couldn't wait?"

"He wanted to talk about the Peterson home next door. The son from South America is coming back to claim his inheritance."

"You mean he's going to be living next door?" asks a confused Sarah, retying her cotton robe.

"No."

"Then what is happening?" Thomas sees Sarah's befuddled look.

"Old Man Peterson was trying to sell his house and the factory before his death. My unaccepted offer, unenforceable because not in writing, was merely a conversation between George Windhurst and I.

"So, how much today?" asks Sarah, pulling out a chair.

"The same $6,000.00 I offered before; except now, there may or may not be a problem with how soon it can happen. Old Man Peterson's will gave his property to his son, but now it has to go through probate. And, there is still a question about Mrs. Peterson, who may or may not be alive. Since it wasn't Mrs. Peterson in the cistern, where is she now? What if she's not in the will? If she shows up, it could get nasty." Thomas opens a cabinet for a glass.

"Yes, it could get nasty dear. Why do you want to get involved?"

"I don't want to get involved in the legal things, but acquiring the Peterson home next door would be a plus for us." With a glass of milk, Thomas sits next to Sarah. "It would give us a proper home, not an apartment connected to the newspaper. We could have a spare bedroom for guests and grandchildren."

"Thomas!" Sarah gasps, grabbing his arm. "Do you know something I don't? Wanda told you something?"

"I'm sorry, no. I was just thinking ahead a little."

"Whew! You had me for a moment." Sarah releases her grip.

"Windhurst gave me a strange proposal," says Thomas, trying to carefully select his words. "He said I could rent the house for a dollar a month until the sale became final. I'd be responsible for utilities, but not property tax. He didn't exactly say this; I surmise he's trying to have someone in the house who would keep the heat on during the winter and avoid having the water pipes freeze."

"It's not like we would have to move in right away, is it?" asks Sarah. "We could take some time to figure out how we would want to fix up the house. We'd know if there were any major problems before we spent the money to buy it."

"Sarah, you talk like we're committed to renting."

"It would be nice to invite people over more than we do now. It would give us something to share, satisfy our future goal. I like that."

"Okay. All we have to do is wait until Tuesday, when Windhurst will bring the lease to rent the Peterson house. Please remind me to make it month to month, in case we find something wrong."

"I will. Now, please shave so you can get the *Pioneer Ledger* out of our basement and mailed to our many loyal, paying subscribers."

"Need a hug first. And, what's for breakfast?"

"Go, git," smiles Sarah. "Hug first."

Chapter Twenty-one

"Wanda, it's too cold today to expose your bare, naked bellybutton and midsection like that."

"Not if I desire to interest a certain non-attention-paying aircraft builder in my thermals."

"What's that supposed to mean?"

"Oh, Myron, you are so dense, or should I say 'up in the clouds,' oblivious to all that's around you."

"I'm not oblivious to you. What about your thermals?"

"I just wanted to talk in language you understand," says Wanda with a coquettish smile.

"Thermals are vertical air currents," replies Myron, missing Wanda's symbolism. "They are what I will be looking for to keep my glider aloft. Most people think that it's the wind that keeps a glider flying, but that's not so. The best days to fly are after a cold front passes, which clears moisture and dirt out of the air."

"So now you want me to be a cold front passing near you?" Wanda folds her arms to her midsection and shakes back and forth.

"Quit it, Wanda, you're just teasing and taking my words out of context. Finding vertical air currents or thermals is an important challenge for soaring. You find a thermal and go up in altitude and circle around in the thermal until you find the next thermal."

"You looking for another girl?" Wanda frowns.

"Didn't I say quit it, Wanda? I'm not looking for another girl. I've been studying for my private pilot's license so I can take this sailplane up for a test, solo." Myron waits; Wanda steps toward him.

"Kiss me," she says, closing her eyes and then opening them.

"Wanda?"

"Consider me a thermal you found. Kiss me."

Myron grabs Wanda, and their lips meet. If Myron was thinking thermals were the only things that rise, he was wrong. His tight blue jeans strain. His feet nervously shift his hips to keep his physical desire hidden from Wanda's clinging embrace.

They kiss once; then twice. Wanda undoes a button on his shirt.

"Wanda, this is not the place," Myron mildly protests.

"Why not?" teases Wanda, recalling her Mom's question about what the two of them do when they're alone. Myron searches for a reason to slow the moment.

"Wanda, someone was killed here in this old factory. Some bones may still be hidden under our feet, buried."

"You superstitious?" asks a pouting Wanda.

"Of course not, but there's not even a cot. We can't lie on top of a used, for sale cultivator. This place gives me weird dreams of an undiscovered body decomposing. I only come to finish my plane."

"But you did give the three bricks you found to the sheriff. That was a courageous move," praises Wanda.

"I guess."

"Your father is not in jail, is he?"

"No." Myron relaxes his hold of Wanda.

"So what's happened?" asks Wanda. "Nothing. The Sheriff said he turned the bricks over to the state crime guys, and you have not heard anything since. The Sheriff announced the bones Oscar found were those of Father Murphy, who disappeared a decade ago. His church buried him. The end."

"I don't know. My father asked an interesting question."

"What is that?" Wanda slides her finger across Myron's lips.

"If the body was in the cistern, he said, why didn't anyone notice the smell of rotting skin? I had no answer. Still don't."

"Maybe because the old factory was vacant for so long. That's possible. Right?" Wanda looks for confirmation. "How long was the factory vacant before the Elevator started to store stuff in here?"

"I don't know. That's the problem. I don't know the answers to a lot of things. The one brick with the letters, two completed and one unfinished still puzzles me. I know priests take a vow not to repeat what is said in the confessional. Why would a dying priest be compelled to keep his silence, if it was not a confession, but an act against him personally? Surely, a priest would not be bound to silence facing a loaded gun on a public street. Meeting a priest in an abandoned factory would not be, at least to me, the location for a confession."

"Myron, speaking about a dead body smelling is gross, but important—at least, I think it is." Wanda glances to the factory's corner.

"I don't know," sighs Myron. "It's a building abandoned for years, but that's not to say the place wasn't fumigated, which can leave an odor. Dead birds and bird droppings could fool a visitor."

"My father," says Wanda; "did not find anything peculiar about the brick when he looked at it through his magnifying glass."

"Your Dad was nice not to tell the Sheriff that he saw the brick before I turned it over to Sheriff O'Day." Myron smiles.

"He made you a promise, and he keeps his promises."

"I like that. And the Sheriff only said the brick came from a concerned citizen. I hope I didn't get Oscar in trouble."

"I'm sure you didn't," says Wanda. "Oscar obeyed the Sheriff's order and, as you learned, has not said anything to anybody."

"Oscar was in the tunnel before me, and I'm convinced his continued silence means he saw something in the tunnel or cistern I didn't," Myron confides in Wanda.

"There may have been something, but how can you be sure a boy his age would see it? You've crawled back in and said you saw nothing new or unusual. All you found were the loose bricks, one with writing, and the bricks are very common in this area. Probably all made by the brick factory in Smithton. We see them in houses, in barns, and in the garbage dump."

"I know the bricks are everywhere. It was the writing that was unusual. That is what puzzles me," says Myron.

"My Dad says the Sheriff looked at the brick with the writing and voiced no conclusion. I overheard my father say on the telephone there were no hair fibers, no blood, no nothing for analysis. A mystery person scratched the three letters at some unknown time. That is all we know."

"We should know more," wishes Myron aloud.

"Maybe, but my mother keeps telling me we should not live in the past; we need to focus on the future. I'm beginning to believe her. If there are things in the past that we cannot understand, we must forget them and live as if it were tomorrow."

"I can't totally disagree, but what about your father? He says we need to solve the questions in front of us. Be like Sherlock Holmes."

"Okay," Wanda tenses. "I don't feel comfortable pitting my mother against my father. I love them both, as I love you."

"I know you do," Myron whispers before clearing his throat. "I don't want to make you uncomfortable. I'm just trying to satisfy myself. Like the day I went kicking stones and weeds outside the old factory. Yet, it was only your snagging your new jeans on a nail that opened the door—or more accurately, found the loose board."

"You want me to sit on another nail?" Wanda grins.

"Of course not, Silly. I'm thinking there is a divine force somehow guiding us to the correct answers. Like the divine inspiration that brought you to me."

"We rode the same bus to high school."

"Yeah, but we didn't have to," says Myron with a smirk.

"You're now getting very deep into spirituality. That scares me."

"Kiss me again," requests Myron.

"Now, that does not scare me."

Their lips touch gently, passionately. Their bodies intertwine with each other, as grape vines cling to supporting wire. Silence. Serenity. Mutual bliss. Myron forgets to hide his rising manhood, even though it will go unfulfilled.

Light from car headlights bursts through the open sliding door of the old factory and quickly disappears unnoticed by those inside.

A flashlight beam through a window startles Myron and Wanda, who are clutched together next to his sailplane near the center of the first floor. They take a step back from each other.

Myron goes to the factory door and opens it wider.

It is Wanda's mother. "I wanted to see the old factory for myself. Everyone keeps talking about it," says Sarah.

"Hi, Mom," welcomes Wanda, feeling, not looking flushed.

"Hi, dear. Thought I might find you here. I saw your car."

"What's up?" asks Wanda as her mother stops to look around.

"Nothing specific. I thought I needed to see for myself what everyone in town is talking about," repeats Sarah.

"What's that?" asks Myron, reaching down for a sanding block.

"Oh, nothing special," says Sarah. "Just what the old factory looks like. I don't think I have ever been inside this building. Looks real dirty and dreary, if you ask me."

"I'm surprised that you would come here only to look around," says Myron, tossing used sandpaper into a box of trash.

"You shouldn't be. I've heard all this talk about the brick and the cistern at our kitchen table. My curiosity was raised." Sarah's eyes follow the perimeter toward the far corner of the old factory's first floor where the barricade to cordon off the cistern looms.

"This building represents the past, except for one future sailplane," Myron argues. "You always talk about being in the future. I don't see why you'd be here." Myron looks at Wanda.

"I still believe a person should live for future. And, Wanda is a big part of my future. I guess she is the real reason I'm here." Sarah's eyes move back and forth between Myron and Wanda.

"Mom, you're checking up on me, aren't you?" Wanda begins a quiz of her mother.

"No, I trust you. Wanda, I'm not spying on you; only this factory has been a place for ungodly evil happenings." She feels her wig.

"Wanda, I think we should get out of here," says Myron, wiping his hands with a rag.

"But, I thought you had work to do on the glider."

"I do, but not tonight. We should let your mother see what she came here to see." Myron watches Wanda walk to the door and turns to Sarah, "Mrs. Hamilton, I'll follow Wanda home now."

"Thanks, Myron. I may be a few minutes. Don't wait."

Sarah walks slowly around the sailplane's tail, along its side, and then past its nose. To her, it looks like it could fly.

"Mrs. Hamilton," calls Myron. "I forgot to tell you to padlock the sliding door you entered when you leave. The lock is sitting open on the chair over there. It's the only door to be locked."

"Thanks Myron. I'll do that."

"Good night." And with that Myron is outside and sees Wanda's car taillights down the dirt road, moving away from the factory. He jumps into his own car and is in quick pursuit of Wanda's Fairlane.

What a dreary place, thinks Sarah. She ducks as a sparrow startles her. She is alone with her thoughts.

Why would Father Murphy be found here? On the day he disappeared, I saw him after Myron Goostree, Sr. The *Pioneer Ledger* story was wrong. How did he get here? While I have misled others to believe I have achieved my mother's goals; my heart knows I've broken my vow to be faithful. I feel worthless. I have accepted God's punishment, but the nightmares continue. I can only make love to Thomas in the dark. My whole family, including my parents' memory, would be publicly ridiculed and scorned if the truth escaped.

As a little girl, my mother's first lesson, repeated until her death, was that I must always have an unquestioning trust in God, and all things would turn out for the best. She used herself as an example. She said she met a caring, wonderful Catholic man who married her, earned a good income, and was totally faithful. She bore three wonderful, healthy children, and provided a clean, healthy home with wholesome food on the table. She said I should do as she did.

My father was a caring man; growing up, he only told me to listen to mother. He always said my mother would help me learn the womanly things in life. He was a salesman and I saw him on weekends, and then, he'd spend most of his time with my brothers. They never spent time with mother, except when learning clean-up chores. They never cooked or baked. That was my destiny, alongside mother.

The big crisis came when I told mother I was going to marry Thomas. She cried for a week when I told her he was Lutheran. She demanded to know why I couldn't find a proper Catholic boy. The war was over, she said, nice Catholic boys were coming home, needing wives. When Thomas agreed to have our wedding in the Catholic Church, mother was only partially mollified. She kept saying my marriage would not last.

Two years after her 1951 death, her prediction began to torment me. I was happy with Thomas, following mother's teachings, and creating a wonderful home. My mother never faced the decision of American women who were joining the workforce. Excuse me, Lord, women were being told sex was no longer just for procreation. Conflict between Thomas and I began, not with sex, but his asking me to work on the newspaper. I knew mother would have me say "no." I told Thomas "no;" I would stay a housewife. I cried longer than mother did after my announcement to marry Thomas; I knew my decision was disobeying my husband, another thing mother said a good wife did not do.

My decision was the catalyst for other arguments, e.g., who did not answer the phone, or, who spent too much money on personal items. As long as I refused to leave the kitchen, the arguments were unresolved. Gradually, watching TV became the way to avoid conversation. Not going to bed at the same time, as we had always done, reduced—excuse me again, Lord—having sex.

The birth of Melissa intensified our marital tension. Thomas spent his time with Melissa, not me.

I cried myself to sleep; I lost twenty pounds; I avoided others. I could not dishonor my mother's memory. She had told me on her deathbed that she knew I would follow the Lord's fourth commandment to honor her and my deceased father.

After weeks of never-ending argument and tension, I felt the need to immerse myself in activities at St. Mary's. Bake sales were an enjoyable outlet and baking honored mother. The endless hours at church were untroubled. Thomas told me it was like working outside the home, but I refused to listen and said he was committing blasphemy. I gained lady friends, especially Hilda Swanson. They saw me as an admirable example; I felt like a girl experiencing adolescent emotions.

Father Murphy was very supportive. He was kind, inspiring and had a dream for the kids. We all wanted him to succeed and worked extremely hard for his dream. The money we raised was often several hundred dollars, which we give to Mr. Klempler for deposit at the bank. I was extremely proud of what we women were accomplishing.

I also enjoyed Father Murphy's presence. At first, he was there with all of us and then later I realized he would be there alone with me as others had departed to fulfill family obligations. I enjoyed talking to him; he listened to me. He praised daughters honoring mothers and said he prayed Thomas would understand it was God's law for a husband and wife to keep the home sacrosanct.

Then one night, I gave him an innocent hug, which lasted longer than it should have. Thereafter we stayed apart when others were present. Sunday afternoon was a special time; the rectory housekeeper left at noon leaving Father Murphy by himself. Thomas was often at the baseball park on Sunday afternoons to watch the amateur baseball team practice, youths play softball, or to observe people. He took Melissa after she was a year old.

Vulnerable, I found it easy to take a walk past the church, with the rectory next door. Cornelius Murphy's soothing words and confident demeanor put me at ease. I don't know why I drank the red wine he offered that March Sunday afternoon in the rectory. I sensed my head whirl; my soul was conflicted as I felt his right hand under my overblouse. He caressed my clothed breasts, then my naked breasts so tenderly. My mind said I could not let it go further. It was wrong—wrong for both of us. I had to put up the stop sign, but I didn't. On a divan, his weight separated my legs. My voice of protest was lost; I longed for tenderness. The soft kisses, tender strokes of his hand, and, finally, our climax high. His seed was inside me. Feeling completely ashamed, I rushed frantically to dress while promising myself it would never happen again. I was a married woman.

In one brief moment I had permanently stained mother's honor and my own. I was torn by following mother's wish to say "no" to Thomas' request to help with the paper and disobeying her by not saying "no" to Father Murphy.

While proponents of women's freedom argued for sexual liberation as the new healthy reality, I comprehended the forbidden lust with Father Murphy was not love. For the first time I had betrayed the sacredness of my marriage vows. Was God still watching me hustle home, eyes downcast to the sidewalk, for a cleansing shower, hoping feverishly I would not meet anyone?

I promised myself not to speak of my betrayal of Thomas' trust. Mother told me that good girls do not talk about sex. I wanted to go further and put everything in the past—to block it out of my mind and life forever. I vowed I would succeed with the future beginning with the restoration of my marriage with Thomas and I would make Melissa's life full of love and she would be a better homemaker.

I surprised Thomas two nights later when I agreed to help out with the newspaper as long as I did not have to abandon my desire to provide a clean, healthy, and proper household. I prayed my mother would understand I was not leaving my home for work.

I skipped a church circle meeting, then a bake sale. I lied saying I was busy or otherwise committed to avoid going to St. Mary's.

I was succeeding, … and then I missed a period. Horrified, I knew I was being punished. God had been watching. My mother's prediction was coming true: I was going to lose Thomas when he found out that I was carrying another man's child.

My life felt worthless, isolated. I couldn't tell Thomas. We had not been intimate for months before or after the day with Cornelius. Trying to convince myself it was a bad dream, I fantasized I would wake up and everything would be rosy, my bad dream was not reality. I deluded myself. A second missed period terrified me. Trapped, I had no one to turn to.

Living the shell of a life, I slept more and spent more time taking long walks with Melissa and giving others the appearance of a doting mother. Thomas was surprised when I twice offered to accompany him to Sunday services at First Lutheran.

Despite the diversions, I envisioned being captured in a downward spiral of events without end where this second pregnancy would make me the outcast of Clinton society, a person who heard others whisper behind her back, and the tour de force to destroy Thomas, both emotionally and financially.

With my mind grasping for answers, I prayed my trip to Winterville that Thursday afternoon would change my life. I told Thomas that Melissa needed a routine well-baby checkup. I did not disclose my appointment. Experiencing the same prenatal feelings I'd had with Melissa, I expected to be told I was pregnant and seriously pondered how I could terminate the fetus. My moment of lust had violated the tenets of the Holy Catholic Church; the sacred trust of my marriage vows, and had forced me into making a decision that would violate my entire upbringing, principles, and all the moral values given to me by my mother. My soul could no longer endure the painful irony of mother pressuring me to find a Catholic man, and then being ravished by a Catholic priest.

An overcrowded Winterville Clinic frustrated me, however, I was glad to be unrecognized. I cried in the exam room when told I was pregnant. The nurse thought they were happy tears; how wrong she was.

Still crying, I put Melissa back into the car for the return trip to Clinton. She does not see me cry, distracted by a lollipop the receptionist had given her.

On the highway to Clinton, I failed to observe another car swerve wide from an intersecting road into my path. I pulled the steering wheel hard to the right to avoid a collision. The sounds of breaking glass and metal on metal were the last sounds I remembered. Later, I learned the driver was drunk and his tire marks on the asphalt indicated he was driving excessively fast.

Thrown hard against the steering wheel by the impact, I was hurt badly. Melissa struck the windshield with her head. I saw blood everywhere. I called out for Melissa. I faintly remembered flashing lights, sirens, and voices telling me not to move. I feared my secret would become general knowledge; Thomas would learn it was not his baby growing within my womb. I fought hard to stay awake.

Men in uniforms told me to stay calm, breathe, tell them where it hurt, and explain if I was allergic to anything.

I don't remember much of what happened at the hospital. I was numb all over when I awoke—a deep, dull pain in my stomach, all the way to my thighs. I repeatedly asked to see Melissa. Thomas was there, day and night. His voice resonated strength, reassurance, and compassion, along with a repeated, "Sarah, I love you." Bandages across my head gave me a headache and my arm throbbed from multiple needle insertions. Out-of-focus images of unknown people came at all hours of the day and night.

I recall it was not until the morning of the third day that the doctor told me I was very lucky to be alive. He explained that part of my pain was from the hysterectomy—necessary to save my life. Initially relieved, I also understood my ability to have children was gone. I cursed my God for getting even.

The next day was worse when Thomas told me that Melissa didn't survive the crash. Told she was in my arms when the emergency ambulance arrived at the crash scene, I cried for hours.

A wheelchair carried me to the first pew when Melissa's delayed funeral was held at St. Mary's. A vacationing Father Murphy meant the funeral was officiated by a substitute priest. The face veil in my lap went unused. There were so many condolences; the entire town turned out. Shops posted "closed" signs for the Thursday morning funeral services. I could not bear to read her obituary printed the next week in the *Pioneer Ledger*.

These memories really exhaust me. Ten years later, I am as conflicted today as I was then, perhaps worse, now that his skeleton has been identified. I still have no one to confide in; the secret locked in my mind is as a prisoner in jail. I tried to speak with Father Murphy in the confessional, but couldn't force myself to be truly honest, and God took him, leaving only me to suffer. How can I tell Thomas that I saw Father Murphy in the evening the last day he was alive in Clinton? How can I be a source of strength for Wanda if there is no peace in my soul? I tell her to live in the future, not the past. Is a woman's future in the home or in working away from home? Society is giving conflicting guidance. The values that served my mother are being challenged. There is no reliable source for guidance.

A beam of light interrupts Sarah's thoughts. The light comes into the factory's lower-level interior through one of its windows near the ceiling. She's motionless. The light reappears, irregularly, twice more.

Sarah's muscles involuntarily tense for the unexpected, but she remains motionless. After three flashes, the light does not reappear. She dreads she cannot reach the unlocked factory door as she inches around Myron's sailplane. Where is the padlock? She has it. Is there a latch on the inside of the door? Is there a safer place to hide?

Step by step, she creeps slowly to the factory door. The hook for the inside latch is missing. Sarah feels her right hand go numb as she squeezes hard on her flashlight. It is the only weapon she has, facing the outside unknown. She turns off the lights in the factory.

She has to make a choice: sit tight or be brave and fully open the door. Two minutes pass. She is ready; it is now or never. Her left hand pulls at the factory door. It slides awkwardly. Sarah peers forward into the darkness. There is no shadow, no image, and no person visible.

She reaches for her car keys in the small purse slung over her shoulder. The ignition key pokes out from between her fingers in the middle of her left hand. No good, she thinks. She switches the flashlight and keys between her hands. If she has to swing her arm, keys would be better in her dominant right. She has the padlock, but she has to give it up to secure the factory entrance door, and then she has to traverse the ten to twelve steps to her parked car.

Her steps beat down on the dirt road as she runs as fast as she can toward her locked car. She stumbles to grab the exterior door handle. Behind the wheel, with the door lock pushed down, Sarah still does not feel safe. Her car lights show she is alone.

Only when her car turns off the dirt road from the factory to her *Pioneer Ledger* home does she feel out of immediate danger. Her pulse slows and her heart stops racing; her breathing returns to near normal.

It's not until she parks inside her garage that she sees the dusty smudge of a gloved hand on the exterior of her driver-side window.

Chapter Twenty-two

"**D**oll, you're home late."

"I was trying, dear, to discover and learn all I could about the old factory where Myron has his plane."

"Checking up on Wanda is perhaps more accurate."

"Not really; curious about what everyone is talking about, but yes, I did see Wanda there with Myron."

"And what did you see?" asks Thomas.

"Nothing, really. That old factory is really a dreary place, if you ask me. The cistern everyone talks about can't be seen behind the barricade. Just a few pieces of old farm equipment and that airplane that Myron is putting together." With no mention of the unexplained light, she goes on, "I didn't climb to the second floor to see what's up there. I think Wanda thought I was spying on her."

"And why would she think any different?" Thomas flips a page in the magazine he was reading before Sarah returned home.

"I guess she wouldn't. Still for her to be spending all the time she does in such a dreary place is beyond me."

"Perhaps, it's not the place, but who is there," says Thomas.

"I know you're right. Why there? That old factory is really scary, too. Someone should catch or trap the birds that live there, and it would better if there were an outside light that could be put on at night. Farmhouses around here have yard security lights."

"Myron's there because it's the only place big enough for his plane, and it helps that his employer uses the building for business. Perhaps Wanda is captivated by the same dream of soaring that courses in Myron's veins."

"What are you referring to?" asks Sarah.

"Just a condition of human nature. Young people want to share in the life dreams of each other." Thomas closes his magazine.

"We all have dreams. Sometimes they seem real, then a haunting illusion, and sometimes nightmares."

"Yes, and your dreams?" asks Thomas.

"I've had dreams, beautiful dreams when I was younger, but I've also come to appreciate that the future is the place where I should be. You, dear, are my future. I couldn't envision a happier future. No more looking at or living in the past, for that can only cause heartache and unnecessary hurt. This dreadful thing with Father

Murphy—I wish it would all go away. Death should be inevitable only after a long life. I don't want to think about Melissa or whatever else might have been. Her future and our future were taken away in a split second. You and I have tried to move forward in our lives together without Melissa. I visit her grave and here lately feel like someone I can't see is watching me. Wanda is our future, and I want her to have the best. A future my mother dreamed for me."

"Sarah, my happiness is here with you now. Wanda will find her own happiness. We should help, of course, but any further grief we encounter can only make us stronger, if we share and conquer it together. I only know part of your past grief. I might not be able to know a mother's sorrow on losing a child to death or from the child's disobedience. Still, knowing more is unimportant as long as we are together."

Chapter Twenty-three

"Charles Johnston, Thomas."

"Oh, hi Charles. Thanks for the call."

"I'm here in Sheriff O'Day's office. He's not here at the moment. Remember I had a question about St. Mary's back in the early Fifties?"

"Right. I talked to Sarah. She remembers that she took part in many bake sales and other fund-raising events. During those years there was a special raffle one time to support the priest's desire to build a gym for the kids. That's what Sarah remembers."

"Well, that confirms what I thought," says Johnston.

"What's so important about church bake sales?" asks Thomas.

"I noticed in looking at your newspaper files that there was a drop off in the mentioning of St. Mary's church activities after Father Murphy went missing. I wondered if perhaps the paper just stopped printing the information or if there was nothing to be reported. It may have been coincidental. I do know your paper did not mention that special raffle or the money raised. Did Sarah have anything to do with holding the money raised?" Johnston looks at his notepad.

"She said she didn't. She thought the money went to a special account set up by Klempler at the bank," replies Thomas.

"Ever recall hearing that St. Mary's had money problems?"

"No. Nothing unusual. Sarah said the priest urged tithes, visiting clergy from African missions, and similar appeals. Father Murphy's big push was trying to get a gym." Thomas checks the time.

"I appreciate your taking the time for my questions."

"Thanks. Say, what about the brick with the lettering?"

"Oh, that. Thomas, this is off the record. I have three bricks in the back of my Chevy. I was out to the old factory myself and found a pair of bricks in the cistern." Johnston is leery of saying more.

"I'll keep your confidence. I don't see how the bricks can be of much help, other than the one with the writing on it. Bricks would not, I assume, have fingerprints on them, as their roughness would not provide the necessary surface for transfer to it of the skin oils or sweat necessary to create fingerprints. Print ridges would not be unbroken to allow analysis."

"I must say you're correct about the fingerprints except for a possible rare exception. Thanks Thomas, I have to run." Johnston hangs up and waits to visit with Sheriff O'Day.

"What's up, Charles?" asks Jonathan.

"I have this feeling in my gut that I might be on to something in the Father Murphy case."

"Why? Those bones don't give us much to go on, and it's been a decade since he died. Any recollection would likely be hazy. The trail is cold, if you ask me." O'Day tosses his hat onto a chair.

"Cold, no. Frozen might be a better word."

"So what's your gut telling you?" asks Jonathan.

"Money somehow figures into the equation. But the amounts seem so small. The diocese may help, but they would not know about money collected and not reported to them. I've done my best to confirm that there were many extra fund-raising events, including a special raffle, at St. Mary's to help Father Murphy raise funds for a building project. And, all events stop when the good father disappeared. After the priest went missing there was a hodgepodge of people who had access to the church books. That went on for over a year, until the diocese assigned a new pastor. I may have a lead, if I can find the special building fund account. Determining what amount of money is missing may never be accomplished."

"Wish I could help here. Most of what you're talking about happened before I was elected sheriff two years ago. Heck, Ed Hendricks didn't even verify that Old Man Peterson's wife was actually where the postcard said she was. If his trial proved anything, it was that the postcard was forged." Jonathan shrugs.

"Jonathan, you have a copy of the crime lab report on the bricks from the old factory, don't you?" asks Johnston.

"Yeah, not much there. I could have told you that there would have been no identifiable fingerprints or fibers on bricks."

"We've got to operate under the assumption that Father Murphy's death was a homicide." Johnston opens his notepad.

"Okay, that's fine. That's pretty obvious," agrees Jonathan.

"I've tried to run several scenarios in my head. If we assume that the priest scratched the three letters on that one brick before he died, that would have been a decade ago when it was placed in the cistern. But there being no clothes in the cistern with the skeleton tells us the probability is that the priest was not in the cistern for the whole decade. Then again, the killer could have disrobed the priest before sealing him into the cistern, but why? It would not make much sense, unless the killer and priest fought, and the priest drew his killer's blood. Then the killer might want to get rid of the evidence of his blood by taking off the priest's clothes. If we assume the bricks were part of the cistern from the beginning, the two I found in the cistern that are not as weathered tells us that they were in the cistern first, and that the more weathered bricks, the three you got from young Goostree, were not in the cistern until later. If we assume the priest scratched the three letters on the one brick, it had to be at someplace other than the cistern."

"But that means the priest's body or bones were moved to the cistern after it had started decomposing."

"Right," says Johnston with an air of authority.

"That complicates the fact that we are missing some bones."

"Well, there is one other factor to be considered."

"What is that?" asks Jonathan.

"The odor coming from a decaying human body."

"Now where are you going? Your mind must have been working overtime on this case," says Jonathan, withholding praise.

"The café owner told me there was a great deal of conversation about a deceased person's smell. I heard someone ask the question that if the body had been in the cistern, why did no one smell anything? Then there was all that conjecture about Old Man Peterson. Most dismissed his involvement, as he had only been the outright owner of the old factory for three years prior to finding the priest. He could have been the killer and not disposed of the priest's body in the cistern to protect his relative from suspicion because he knew that the body could be discovered by its decaying odor. Only after he got ownership of the factory did he find the cistern as the best place to keep his secret. It would have been easy to put the bones in a box, put a piece of cardboard or fabric over them, and hold down the cover over the bones with the three bricks picked up near where the body was hidden," says Johnston, forgetting where his notes left off.

"What about the brick with the lettering?" asks Jonathan.

"Could have been easily overlooked. Or, given no mind. Obviously, whoever moved the bones would want to do it quickly to avoid detection. If it was night, who would have looked that close?"

"What motive would Old Man Peterson have had?"

"Best I can come up with is that somehow the priest was considered as having put ideas into Peterson's wife's head to leave him. When his wife told him she was going to leave him, Peterson concocted a way to get rid of his wife and forge the postcard to avoid suspicion. Peterson held the priest responsible for his wife's plan to leave him and waited until the time was right. The priest's wanting to build a hall to compete with the Legion could have angered Peterson, a past Legion commander and active in Post 167."

"I think you're stretching to make that last statement about competition between the church and the Legion," says Jonathan.

"Maybe he tossed his wife into Sand Lake and took advantage of its bottomless pit?" speculates Johnston, closing his notepad.

"Could be, but we'd never know if he did, unless the weight fails. So where do we go with the bricks we have?" asks Jonathan.

"We could stir the pot with some announcement."

"Let me think some about that. Okay, Charles?"

Chapter Twenty-four

"Sarah, I'm going uptown to the bank for a few minutes. I'm taking my bike and will be back as soon as I can."

"What for?" his wife asks.

"It's Tuesday, and George Windhurst should have those papers for renting the Peterson home," explains Thomas.

"Oh, yeah. Remember, month to month."

"What would I do without you?" A genuinely fond smile appears on Thomas's face as he gives Sarah a quick hug.

Up the three bank steps, he starts to follow the hallway access to Windhurst's law office when he sees Klempler in the bank lobby.

"Good morning, Thomas."

"Good morning," Thomas replies.

"Got a call from Mr. Charles Johnston late yesterday. Anything exciting going on?"

"He's helping O'Day on the Father Murphy case. He wanted to see 1950s newspaper back issues with a strange question about St. Mary's bake sales when Father Murphy was pastor. Sarah had to help me give him answers. She knew about raising money for the gym and was looking for old records."

"That was a strange inquiry. Laws prevent me from discussing people's accounts. See you later."

Thomas walks down the hallway and stops at George Windhurst's office door. He knocks.

"It's open; come in."

"Morning, George. It's Thomas Hamilton," says Thomas, pushing open the door to Windhurst's office.

"I have the lease contract in my briefcase."

"That's why I'm here. Just to double-check, we're talking a month-to-month lease until you can get this Peterson probate straightened out?" Thomas notices the office is still in disarray.

"Here's the agreement, simple, two pages, month-to-month rental with an option to buy for $6,000.00." Thomas reaches for the paper in Windhurst's hand as he continues. "Terms are one dollar a month; you're responsible for utilities. If you sign today, I've got the front door keys here somewhere in this desk. You'll need to call the power, telephone, and water companies to get the utilities changed over. Have last utility bill sent to my attention at my Winterville address." Windhurst waits as Thomas reads the lease.

"Looks fine to me," says Thomas. "Let me sign it here at the bottom and give you a five-dollar bill. Then you won't have to chase me down every month."

"That's great. I'll initial your copy, and we'll send you a copy with my client's signature as required by the probate court. Doesn't affect our agreement, and in good faith I'm releasing the house keys to you." Windhurst hands a key ring to Thomas.

"I'll keep that in mind. Would you be ..." Thomas clears his throat and hesitates momentarily. "Would you be interested in increasing the size of your business card directory ad in the *Pioneer Ledger*?"

"Let me think about that some. By the way, I heard you were out inspecting the old factory the other night," says Windhurst.

"Not me; Sarah was out there checking on Wanda, our daughter. Who said I was out there?" asks Thomas.

"Myron, Sr., said it. I was told second-hand. Information must have gotten mixed up. No prospective buyer has been near it."

"Sarah said the old factory is really a dreary place," says Thomas.

"Not really that bad, I wouldn't think. It's an industrial building. Got a rail spur. There's an opportunity there for a wise investment by some person or company."

"You can save the sales pitch."

"Have a good day," says Windhurst.

"Thanks, George."

Thomas clutches the Peterson home key in his left hand as he opens the newspaper office outside screen door with his right.

Sarah, in her front office, sees him return. "You're back quick," she says. Scraps of paper are spread out before her. A red pencil rolls off the desk and onto the floor. She ignores it.

"No problem. I signed the lease papers. Month-to-month lease. I have the key to the front door in my hand. I'll put it in the kitchen napkin drawer for now."

"You're not going over there now?" asks Sarah.

"No, it's more critical to work on this week's edition."

Sarah nods and looks around distractedly. "Now where is that red pencil of mine?"

"Check your right foot," suggests Thomas, before leaving.

Thomas slides out a drawer with its California job case, puts his pica pole in his back pocket, and looks around for his type stick. He has two or three classified ads left to assemble for this week—and these are prepaid.

Tuesday quickly passes into Wednesday. Thomas carries bundles of printed and addressed newspapers out the front door to his car for the trip to the post office.

"Sarah, you want to visit our new home next door when I get back from leaving these with Virgil?"

"Sure. I'll be ready to do that." Sarah resumes a silent prayer to St. Jude, asking the saint of hopeless causes to guide her heart from the darkness of fear into the peace of Jesus.

Thomas grabs the last bundle and is on his way.

At the post office, he greets Clinton's postmaster. "How's it going, Virgil? I got this week's hottest news in these bundles for you to get delivered."

As Virgil looks up, his reading glasses slide down his nose. He doesn't seem to notice that his blue shirt is only partly tucked into his khaki trousers. He just nods.

"Want these on the table?" asks Thomas.

"Good as anywhere," replies Virgil. "Say, Thomas, save me having to look. You got story in there about the dead priest?"

"Not his week, Virgil."

"Just wondering; it's been awful quiet this week. Oswald was saying over at the café yesterday morning that he saw some strange footprints in the soft earth around that old Peterson factory a couple of days ago."

"That's news to me," Thomas says with a faint smile. "Sarah was out there a few nights ago. Maybe they were hers."

"Oswald said they were large, like a man's size ten or eleven."

"That wouldn't be Sarah."

"Could have been Myron, I guess, but Oswald was convinced it was not Myron. Myron wears those steel-toed work boots with the patterned sole, and Oswald said he would have recognized those footprints."

"Myron could have changed shoes," offers Thomas. "He goes to the factory often to work on that glider of his. I'm sure he has more than just work boots."

"I guess you're right," agrees Virgil. "Oswald didn't know if the footprints were made at night or during the day. I think the town is really jumpy. It's weird why everyone seems so jittery; the priest went missing ten years ago. I also heard that an unknown guy visited your office last week. He was said to be a big guy in an old Chevy and carrying a notepad."

Thomas replies, "Oh, that was one of the state crime guys. He just wanted to look at some old newspapers."

"How would old newspapers help now?" asks Virgil.

"Looking for stories about St. Mary's Church."

"I guess that could be important, but I would doubt it. I'd think that brick the sheriff asked me about would be more important. If you ask me, I think the first two letters on that brick are the priest's way of telling us the killer's initials from the grave. Just so happens that the G and O could be Gordon Oswald, the Elevator manager."

"Gordie? The killer? You inhaling the stamp glue?"

"No. Just trying to think, like every other person in town."

"I bet Gordie would love to hear you're fingering him as the killer of Father Murphy," says Thomas, lifting the last bundle.

"Well, couple months ago, I asked him where he was the afternoon that the priest was last seen alive. And guess what. He said he didn't remember."

"Do you remember where you were?"

"Well, no. But my initials are not G.O."

"Did you forget there was a third letter on that brick—or part of one?" asks Thomas, waiting for Virgil to stop canceling envelopes.

"No, the way I see it, that third letter was just a clumsy C to begin the word: Co-op. There wouldn't have been time or space to scratch out a full name or 'Farmers' Elevator.' The priest was probably in a great deal of pain, dying and all, and losing his memory. We all sometimes refer to the Farmers' Cooperative Elevator Company as the Co-op. Everyone in town knows that, and Father Murphy would have been here long to know that, too."

"Virgil, have you given your theory to the sheriff?"

"I hadn't thought of it then. I told him I didn't know."

"You should call him. He might be interested."

"I don't want to get involved. I got to live here, too. It is one thing to talk like this, but—" Virgil stops stacking envelopes and turns a little pale. "You're not going to print this in the paper, are you?"

"No, of course not."

"Good. Klempler at the bank thought it had merit."

"I don't see how Oswald could have killed the priest and put him in that cistern and have it go undiscovered all these years. Myron, Sr., says someone should have realized something was wrong when there was a smell," says Thomas.

"Oswald would have been the only person who went inside. A dead pigeon or two could have disguised the smell from the outside or have been a ready reason for people to accept."

"That's still far-fetched," Thomas argues.

"Okay, okay. I got another idea. Oswald could have taken Father Murphy out to his fishing shack near Sand Lake, killed him, and later, to avoid suspicion, tossed the skeleton into the cistern because he got scared that someone might find the skeleton on his property."

"I guess that would take care of the smell part, but Oswald does not go alone to his fishing cabin. He has three or four others out there several times during the summer. The cabin has no basement. It's only one room. The largest hiding place is the one closet, and Oswald—I know myself from being out there—locks his hunting rifle in the closet, in case a guest gets drunk and loses control."

"Thomas, you seem to have a way of knocking down all my ideas. You have an answer to who killed the priest?"

"No. Can't even rule out an accident," asserts Thomas.

"Accident? Never heard anyone claim there was an accident. No, I think it was murder. And, when someone figures out how that brick with the letters fits in, we'll know who the killer is."

"Let's hope so. I still think you should give Sheriff O'Day a call. You may have a good piece of the puzzle. The sheriff knows more than any of us, I'm sure. Thanks, Virgil. See you later, next Wednesday at the latest, same time. Stay well."

"Bye, Thomas. You remember, now. I don't want to see my name in next week's paper."

Thomas closes the post office door behind him. It's a short drive back to the *Pioneer Ledger*.

"So, how did it go at the post office?" Sarah asks. "You were longer than usual."

Thomas signals an "okay" with his fingers. "Want to go next door? I'll get the key."

Thomas locks the front door of the *Pioneer Ledger* and adjusts the hands of the clock on a "We'll return at _" sign, showing they'll be back in an hour.

"This could be exciting," blurts out Sarah.

"Probably just dirty," answers Thomas matter-of-factly.

The porch boards creak at the pressure of Thomas' feet. So does the lock when he inserts the key. Leaves have piled up and are decaying in the front porch corner. Arnold Peterson's porch rocking chair is tipped on its side. Sarah sets it upright. A hornet's nest clings to the far upper porch corner. The dirty windows also advertise that the house is uncared for. The faded green exterior paint is peeling in too many places on the Masonite siding to allow a touchup.

"What a mess," exclaims Thomas on his first look inside. He stares into the one-story rambler interior. The front door opens into a living room, with the kitchen off to the right. Directly across from the front door is an archway into a short perpendicular hallway. Straight ahead is a full bathroom. To the left a door leads into a small bedroom. To the right a door leads into the bigger of the two main floor bedrooms.

Slowly, Thomas edges himself inside. He steps to the right into the eat-in kitchen. An L-shaped work area with sink and counter are to his right. A window above the sink showcases the front yard. Opposite the two-bowl sink is the refrigerator. Straight ahead is the range with its vent hood. To the left of the stove is a doorway, and through the doorway is a half-door in front of the basement stairs; a pair of closed mahogany folding doors for a coat closet; and a door that leads to the single-car garage.

"Sure could use a woman's touch," says Sarah, two steps behind Thomas. "Oh, this door leads to the garage from the inside the house. Just like at the rectory." Sarah bites her lip, hoping Thomas has missed the reference to St. Mary's.

"Why do you say that?" he asks.

"Oh, no reason," says Sarah. "Pretty common I guess for houses with attached garages to have an inside access, especially to the kitchen. I was saying this house could use a woman's decorating touch."

"Not until we get this place cleaned from top to bottom. The cobwebs are everywhere. We need to get some air circulating. The carpets should be shampooed. The kitchen linoleum looks in good shape."

"Could be because Old Man Peterson never cooked."

"Now, Sarah—" Thomas lets the two words hang there.

Sarah is glad he makes no further mention of her church. "Are we going down to the basement?" asks Sarah.

"Yes, brought a flashlight in case we needed one?"

The stairs leading down to the basement are carpeted in worn bright-red shag, and the stairwell walls are paneled in a dark natural mahogany color. However, the light at the bottom of the stairs is a bare bulb. Thomas tries the wall light switch and remembers the electricity has not yet been turned on.

"We'll have to explore," says Thomas, leading the way.

"Smells musty, if you ask me," replies Sarah.

"I hope it's because the house has been empty and closed up for so long. I'd hate to find a crack in the foundation."

"Can you move a little faster?" she asks.

"Sure, I was feeling this wall here. The panel seems to have some give to it. Finishing nails are of a different color."

"Maybe it came loose or wasn't nailed properly. This might be a do-it-yourself fix," suggests Sarah.

"Could be. Look around here. The carpet covers this entire half of the basement. And there are some pub chairs and a bar at the far end. The carpet is run up the front of the bar. Could be nice with new carpet," says Thomas.

"Let me look behind the bar with the flashlight," Sarah suggests as she edges past him. "There's nothing here but some shelves under the bar and a cabinet unit on the outside wall."

"I think we should get rid of these chairs and sofa."

"I don't think there is one piece of furniture to stay."

"Okay, I'll talk to Windhurst. I'm ready to lock the door again. How about you, Sarah?"

"We didn't look in the garage, but let's save that for another day. We first need to know what we can toss."

"Should we get Wanda to help clean?" asks Thomas.

"Sure, and I'd be willing to hire both her and Myron, especially if we are going to get rid of some of this furniture. There's a lot of lifting that needs to be done."

"Let's have another look upstairs," says Thomas.

"What's on the other side of this basement room?"

"I peeked in while you were behind the bar, Sarah. There's a sink and toilet enclosed in a small room next to what looks like a makeshift bedroom, and the other part is an unfinished utility room with the furnace."

Sarah walks through a door separating the basement areas. "Oh, I see a faucet and concrete washbasin. There's an electrical outlet."

"Okay, then, let's go back upstairs."

Thomas is halfway up the basement stairs by the time Sarah starts up. He pauses in the kitchen, tempted to check out the garage, but Sarah has caught up to him, and she turns sideways and scoots past him toward the front door.

"Sarah, wait. Let's take a quick look at the bedrooms."

"Okay. But I'll take you at your word: quick. Until we have enough time to clean and get utilities, it's too dirty to stay here."

The small bedroom is cramped with a twin bed, small dresser, and a nightstand. The larger bedroom has a double bed, a dresser with mirror, a nightstand, and a small desk in the corner with a telephone. The double closet is full of clothes, which are mostly men's but which also include a few women's clothes pushed back into the hardest-to-reach section of the far end, almost hidden by a large plastic garment bag.

"Sarah, look, nobody's sorted through these clothes."

Thomas is most intrigued by the desk in the corner. He guesses it can't be more than thirty inches wide, barely space enough for one row of small drawers along the right side. A two-foot hutch atop the desk allows for two small drawers and several pigeonhole slots. There is no chair.

He pulls open the top drawer. It is crammed full of folders, some open and some with flaps closed with rubber bands. A rubber band crumbles in his hand when he picks up one folder.

"What have you got there?" asks Sarah.

"I don't know," replies Thomas. He pulls back the flap on the folder and peers inside. He grins. "Guess what?"

"Thomas, I have no idea."

"It's a Harmon Killebrew rookie baseball card."

"Wasn't he with the Twins?"

"Sure, but this card is the old Washington Senators. It's got to be worth something. Why else would Peterson put it away in his bedroom?" asks Thomas.

"Maybe he was saving it for his son and forgot about it."

"Could be. Let's see what's in this one." He takes out another folder. "Oh, my. It's a land survey; sure looks faded and earmarked."

"What land? Peterson or his family owned several pieces of property. Could it be this house?" Sarah stretches to see more.

"No. See the top? Looks like it's near some stream. That wouldn't be this house or the old factory."

"Thomas, why don't you just take all the folders, and we can go back to the newspaper. We've been gone longer than we said we would be. I'd also like a drink of water, and I'm not turning on any faucet in this house, not now."

"Okay, doll. Is there a box or something we can use for these folders and papers?"

"I don't see one," replies Sarah."

"Okay, there's not too much here anyway. I'll just carry it home. I'll leave the Killebrew baseball card by itself in the top drawer."

"Thomas, give me the front door key from your pocket before you gather up all those folders."

In less than two minutes, Sarah locks the front door, and they are back in their newspaper office kitchen.

Thomas dials the kitchen phone, waits for an answer, and then says, "George Windhurst, please. ... Okay. Would you leave a message for him that Thomas Hamilton called? It's a question about some papers found in the Arnold Peterson house next door. No rush. He can wait until the next time he comes to Clinton. Thanks." Thomas puts back the receiver.

"Windhurst was not in and probably won't be until tomorrow at the earliest. After you finish your glass of water, Sarah, want to look at these papers with me?"

"Sure."

"I'll put this land survey to the side for the moment," says Thomas, looking directly across the table at Sarah.

Thomas begins sifting through the open folders and finds mostly old receipts, a three-by-five card giving the serial number of a Pentax SLR with date of September 1962, a list of baseball cards, a list of what looks like bank account numbers or saving certificates, a copy of army discharge papers, and several newspaper clippings, all completely yellowed by time. Nothing seems unusual to Thomas, except he thinks keeping baseball cards was quirky for a man of Peterson's age. There are still two more closed folders.

He hands one of the closed folders to Sarah, saying, "Here, you open this one. I'll get this last one."

"I must say this is somewhat eerie, going through someone else's things when he's no longer living."

"I guess so. We can't live in that house with this stuff in there, though, but we can't really throw it out. Who knows when that son would do it? He hasn't even come to Clinton. It would have been nice of him to have purchased at least a small card of thanks for publishing in the *Pioneer Ledger*."

"Not everyone pays to have a card of thanks printed."

"Yeah, I know. What's in your large envelope?" asks Thomas.

"Looks like old documents relating to the house. There's a receipt for a window pane replacement; copy of a letter written to the village a few years ago, complaining that the water bill had been wrong for months; bill of sale for a cabinet; warranty on the refrigerator and stove; and a receipt for some concrete work three years ago. I can't read the full date. The corner of the receipt is missing."

"We need to check closer to see if there was work done on the house foundation or the basement floor," says Thomas, looking up from his own folder.

"With that musty smell in the basement there might be mold," replies Sarah, turning the receipt round and round. She thinks of Wanda and the well near the old factory. Three years ago was when Old Man Peterson inherited the factory, and the bones of Father Murphy were missing. She'd seen strange lights when she was there. Now the town was talking about unexplained footprints there. Perhaps the person was not following her or trying to scare her, but checking the old wellhead to see if it had been disturbed.

"I thought I was buying a house, not a swimming hole with a roof," says Thomas with a twinkle in his eye.

"Next time, we should examine downstairs more carefully."

"I'm not ready for a next time yet. This here envelope I have seems to be stuff related to the old factory. Copy of the will page, or so it seems, that says the factory was bequeathed to one Arnold Peterson. No ownership papers. Those must be some someplace. Maybe locked up in a safe deposit box? Or maybe Windhurst already has them—Old Man Peterson could have given them to Windhurst before his death, as he was trying to unload his property as far back as three years ago."

"What about the land survey?"

"It's here. Give me the folders you have, Sarah, and let's put the contents back into each folder like we received it."

They finish the task and then stack the folders. Thomas spreads out the land survey to get a better look.

"What are we looking for, Thomas?"

"Beats me. First, I'd like to find out where this land is."

Sarah's eyes open wide and her jaw drops as she waves her hand to get Thomas' attention. "Thomas, look, there are those … those initials in this margin."

"What initials?" Thomas is standing.

"It's a G and an O." Thomas switches to a chair nearer Sarah; leans over to be closer to the survey.

"Let me see." Thomas slides the survey around to get a better look. "You're right. Do you see any other writing?"

"No," says Sarah. "There is a hand stamp at the bottom corner. 'Certified by H. L. Hofmeister, State of Wisconsin, Land Surveyor.'"

"That could indicate the land is out of state, in Wisconsin. Maybe the surveyor was hired so the survey could be completed without local people knowing about it. Do you see any stamp indicating this survey was officially filed with a recorder of land records?"

"I don't," says Sarah, still anxious about finding the G and O.

"Neither do I. And the back of the one sheet is blank. I don't see a cover or overlay that might have been used to protect the actual survey drawing itself."

"Let's see the survey again. Put it facing north, like this, Thomas. There are three sides—east, south, and west—that have straight lines. This top north line is somewhat curved inward at the center. It looks like about twenty acres total, if it is completely rectangular. I don't see any building markings or symbols anywhere on it."

"How do you know?"

"Oh, I don't really, but proofreading the legal notices we print of sheriff sales of repossessed land has given me some familiarity with how surveyors draw diagrams."

"You're a genius, Sarah."

"Now what do you mean?"

"Do you have a ready file of those legal notices, or do I have to dig out past copies of the *Pioneer Ledger*?"

"I got a file of invoices and attached to each invoice would be a copy of what is actually printed. It's filed under 'Sheriff—Legal Notices.' I'll go get some recent ones." Sarah is out of her chair and walking to her front office and the file cabinet to the side of her desk.

Before Thomas can open the refrigerator door and decide what to munch on, Sarah is back with a handful of invoices.

"Let me see here," says Sarah, starting to page through the stack of invoices she has brought back to the kitchen table. "Here are two in our county, one from two months ago, and one six months ago.

The latest survey gives a description, but then says 'Village of Clinton' so that can't help. This other one talks about north of County Road One about five miles, eight miles east of the county line, then a bunch of numbers with degree marks that I don't understand."

"That really helps, Sarah. On this land survey, down in the bottom corner opposite the hand stamp, there's a reference to being north of County Road One about seven miles, and eight miles east of the county line, then a bunch of numbers with funny symbols. Sarah, we're looking at a land survey for a piece of property that's probably near to Sand Lake."

"What makes you say that?" asks Sarah.

"The references from your sheriff invoice and this land survey are definitely similar. The land must be physically close."

"But the invoice land survey states there are straight lines joining at four different points. The survey we have from Arnold Peterson's house only has three straight lines."

"True, and that is why I think it's a piece of land on Sand Lake. Sand Lake is not square; it has a point somewhere, but it mostly would be a curved line if one owned only a piece of land or a lot on the lake."

"Why would Old Man Peterson have a land survey for a place on Sand Lake? Was there a fishing boat in his garage or a fishing pole?"

"We didn't go into the garage, remember?" shrugs Thomas.

"What are we going to do next? Ask Windhurst?"

"No. I'm going to ask Gordie over at the Farmers' Co-op."

"Why him? He's no surveyor, to my knowledge."

"He might recognize the land that this survey details. If it is Sand Lake, Gordie would know it—he's fished there for years. He has his own place there as well. It might be worthwhile to talk to him. Windhurst let it slip to him that I called the sheriff when Gordie was trying to get that piece of machinery out of the old factory after the bones were found there. Anyway, we're members of the chamber."

"Are you going now or after supper?" asks Sarah.

"I think I'll ride my bike over to the Elevator now. Nice day out. Who knows who I might run across?" Thomas winks; Sarah frowns.

"You want brussel sprouts tonight?"

"You betcha," replies Thomas, rising from the table.

Tucking the land survey back into its original folder, Thomas grabs a new rubber band from Sarah's office desk, dons his railroad signalman's hat, and, when Sarah hears the screen door slam, she knows Thomas is on his way to see Gordon Oswald at the Farmers' Elevator.

Sarah realizes that by now Oswald has told the entire town of the mysterious shoe prints. She's not told anyone, not even Thomas, of the strange light shining into the old factory during her visit or the smudge she wiped off her car's window. *No need to worry him*, she decides. *It's enough that I worry.*

Chapter Twenty-five

"I thought we paid our bill this month."

"You did. I'm not here to collect money."

"Then, Thomas, what's the reason for this unexpected visit? You need to get some miles on that favorite bike of yours?" asks Gordon Oswald, his face covered in a fine, powdery dust, as is the rest of him. Only his beloved fishing cap has been spared.

"I have a mystery question and thought your experience and vast expertise would give me the answer."

"A mystery? Huh. Let's step across these grates and out of the grain unloading area and go into my office. I need to brush off first; you can wait for me in the office. Pour yourself a cup of coffee. I got a new can of regular the other day at Goostree's."

"No coffee, thanks. I'll be in the office." He turns to leave and sees his daughter's boyfriend. "Hi, Myron," he says cordially.

"Good afternoon, Mr. Hamilton."

"Myron," says Thomas, with a hand over his mouth, "I might have an extra job for you in the next couple of weeks. I'll tell you more when you're not working."

"Okay, Mr. Hamilton."

Inside the manager's office, Thomas finds a chair and sits down to await Oswald. The office looks the same as it did the last time he was here. The same old trophy walleye hangs on the wall, collecting a layer of dust. Two fishing-buddy pictures hang on the neighboring wall, each boasting of one fine day of fishing. File cabinets at the back of the room blend in with the beige paint on the walls.

"So, what's this mystery we got?" asks Oswald, stepping into his office now that he's wearing less dust.

"I'm trying to locate a piece of land," begins Thomas.

"Well, how big? Do I need to find my county map?"

"Might not help; let me start by showing you this land survey." Thomas slips the rubber band off the flap folder and onto his left wrist. He spreads the survey over Oswald's desk, moving it around to have the map's north indicator point toward his stomach.

"Looks interesting," says Oswald. "Isn't there a notation somewhere that tells you the name of the county or state?"

"No."

"Did you call the surveyor?" asks Gordie.

"No. Name is followed only by State of Wisconsin. For operator directory assistance, I would need to know the name of the city in Wisconsin and that would take a long time—I'd just be guessing. I'm hoping you might be in a better position to help."

"Say, what are these initials? G and O? Those are mine. But I've never seen this survey before in my whole life."

"I thought you might have recognized the survey. The two letters could stand for a lot of things. I'm thinking that the property is at Sand Lake. I know you have Sand Lake property; that's why you might be able to help me," explains Thomas.

"I've never had my property surveyed. Didn't see a need to spend the money. I only wanted access to the lake. When I bought it around 1952, the real estate agent told me the land circling the lake was being subdivided by the farmer who owned it and that my property was marked by yellow stakes driven into the ground. I guess there should be official surveyor markers buried in the ground, but I don't know where. After a year or two, I built two brick pillars to replace the yellow stakes. The one pillar with a mailbox at the top identifies the eastern edge of the property. The western edge has a matching pillar without a mailbox. Helps me know where my cabin road is in the wintertime if I want to do some ice fishing. The gravel township road runs along the property's southern edge."

"How many acres you got?"

Oswald looks to the ceiling. "About twenty, give or take what the lake fills in or erosion takes away from the northern property edge."

"Looks about the size here, one-half of a section," says Thomas.

"No, it's smaller. A section would be 640 acres. Putting my property together with that survey would be about one-sixteenth of a section or forty acres total."

"Well, twenty acres is still a decent plot of ground."

"Let me look closer at this survey." Oswald turns the survey. "The way the northern edge is drawn is interesting. Sand Lake near me used to be scalloped. That is, the shoreline indented a little, came out, and then went back in. I've had it explained to me that a boat dredging the lake bottom anchored itself away from shore and used a bucket scoop to dredge the bottom. It was easier for them to swing the bucket out on a boom, do an arc, and then move the boat to start over. That's what gave the scalloped appearance from overhead. Really is not that way now. Since 1950, when the dredging was done, the lake has washed away the little arc points, at least on the surface.

I'd say there's good chance that this property is at Sand Lake. Who gave you the survey?"

Thomas gets a moment to think as Oswald's phone rings. After answering a customer's question, Gordie looks toward him.

"I really don't want to say today." Thomas hesitates. "My main purpose is to get this land survey back to its rightful owner."

"A mystery—and you're being more mysterious."

"Just bear with me a couple of days, please."

"Let's see this other corner. Seven miles north of County Road One, eight miles east of county line. Dang," exclaims Oswald.

"Dang! … What is it Gordie?"

"That's almost the exact mileage to my Sand Lake cabin."

"How close?" asks Thomas.

"Within a tenth of a mile. I'm just under seven miles from County Road One here in town."

"What you're telling me matches my guess that the property was on Sand Lake. I didn't think it was so close to you as to be next door. That would be amazing." Thomas' face is animated.

"That it could be. Those initials might have been put there to indicate that is my property abutting," speculates Oswald.

"How would the land surveyor know, if he was the one putting the two letters there?

"Could have asked someone. I'm known there."

"Doesn't seem to fit. If you recollect right, the survey would have to have been done after the dredging but before you bought your piece in 1952. It's unlikely that the surveyor made the notation to reference you before you bought the place. Who's your Sand Lake neighbor to the west?" Thomas asks eagerly.

"Don't know. Don't care if it stays unused either."

"What do you mean, you don't know?" Thomas exhales, shrugs.

"Never met the person. There is no cabin, no road. Just trees, shrubs, brush, some native prairie grass, and a whole nature's collection of weeds—dandelion, thistle, cocklebur, creeping myrtle."

"You go there enough. You must have seen someone."

"No. Seen the embers from a fire on the shoreline once or twice. But that could have been anybody. Kids on the lake coming ashore late at night to build a fire. That part of the shoreline has some reeds growing in the lake that make a good spot to locate crappie in cool weather. In summer, no; the shallow water would be too warm."

"I thought you were a walleye man," asks Thomas.

"Just for trophies and sport challenge. For eating, I enjoy crappie or the lake's bullhead for variety."

"Thanks, Gordie. You've been a big help."

"Do me a favor?"

"What?" A puzzled Thomas asks.

"Tell me first who my neighbor is. I could invite him or her—boy, wouldn't that be extra special, if some body-shop-calendar model bought the place as a secret retreat? That'd add a fine diversion from unshaven, belching fishermen in underwear, telling stories of the one that got away, while still in the stupor brought on by emptying a six-pack."

"Sure, but I'd not be dreaming of any calendar girl. If one owns the land next door, I'm sure she'd be erecting a six-foot fence, not coming over with a six-pack to share."

"Now, how am I going to get anything done?" smiles Oswald.

"You'll make it. I almost forgot. Heard you found strange footprints outside the old factory the other day."

"Yeah, they seemed out of place. I've chalked it up as nothing to be worried about. Asked Myron, but he doesn't remember anything out of the ordinary that night. Says he left early, though."

"Just wondering if what I heard was true," says Thomas.

"Remember, you tell me first who my lake neighbor is."

"Yes. You'll be the first to know."

Thomas finds his bike where he left it. He mounts the seat and begins pedaling with the land survey in his right hand. He turns opposite to the way he had come to ride past the bank. Oscar, with his jacks, is not on the bank steps.

He'd have to ask Sarah if Windhurst called. Klempler comes walking up from behind his bank.

"Hi, Godfrey," says Thomas, slowing, but not stopping.

"Oh, hi, Thomas. Nice day, isn't it? See you later."

While Thomas was at the Farmers' Elevator, Sarah is busy trying to catch up with the laundry. Most women in Clinton did the laundry on Monday, but Monday for Sarah was out of the question, because of her work on the *Pioneer Ledger*. She hears the screen door open.

"Hi, anybody home?" calls a male voice.

Sarah shouts, "Just a minute!" She quickly runs her hand over and adjusts her wig and tugs at her skirt as she emerges from the bedroom on the way to the newspaper office.

"Hello, Mr. Johnston," she says, opening the front door to let him inside. "Thomas isn't here. He went over to the Elevator."

"That's fine. I wanted to ask you a question about St. Mary's at the time that Father Murphy was the priest."

Sarah's stomach tightens and her entire body reacts to tense up all at once. Her mind is racing; thoughts crash into each other. She wipes her mouth with a hand towel she holds in her left hand. "I thought Thomas told you."

"He did," explains Johnston, as he glances over his shoulder to see if anybody is there. "I don't know if I got everything right. Got a moment?" Johnston is standing, shifting weight between his feet. His notepad is in his right hand, a finger sticking between two pages. *No,* he thinks, *better leave the notepad closed.*

"Well," Sarah begins slowly, "there's not much I can remember. It's so far back."

"I know. How well did you know Father Murphy?"

Sarah tugs at her skirt again and clears her throat. "Like everyone else, I guess. Everyone in the parish had good words to say about him. He always had a kind word. You could call him at all hours of the day. He really only kept to himself on Sunday afternoons ... er ... no ... I'm sorry, I meant to say, Wednesday afternoons."

"What about his desire to build a gym?" asks Johnston.

"Oh, he really wanted to do that. He talked about it all the time. The church ladies tried to help with bake sales. Ah, I guess you already know that from the articles that were printed in the *Pioneer Ledger* back then."

"How much money was raised?"

"I really don't know. I wasn't involved with the money. Oh, I guess there was one time when our circle treasurer, Hilda, had to miss one of the sales, and I took the money home."

"Didn't the church have a lockbox?"

"I guess so, but it would have been locked. I ... I ... didn't have the combination." Sarah glances at the notepad in Johnston's hand.

"You needed a combination?"

"I think so. Really, I can't remember," replies Sarah.

"So what happened with the money you took home?"

"I had it in an envelope. The next morning, I walked over to the rectory and gave it to the housekeeper."

"Know how much you had?" asks Johnston.

"Well, not really. One of the other ladies had put the money in the envelope. I didn't see the need to look."

"Can you guess?"

"I don't really remember. Bake sale—maybe $400.00."

"Were there any other times that you handled the money?"

"Not that I remember. Can you excuse me?" asks Sarah. Johnston nods. "I think I heard the washer cycle change; I should add bleach. I'll be right back." Sarah turns and goes to take care of the laundry. Out of his sight, she wipes her moist forehead with the hand towel. Johnston still stands inside the front door when Sarah returns. She sees him close his notepad, as if he had been writing.

"Everything okay?" asks Johnston.

"Yes, fine."

"Did Father Murphy ever attend fund-raising events?"

"Sure. He'd stop by, normally toward the end. He was interested in how it was going and always would thank the ladies who were helping out. He might even have been there when I locked the door after an event. It was not unusual for me to be the last one to leave. Some ladies had to drive back to the farm; others had small kids to tuck in. I was in town. It was no big deal. Just worked out that way."

"Anybody complain about having to raise the money or say that Father Murphy's idea was bad?" Johnston waits for Sarah to answer.

"No, not really. I think Amos' wife said that the money could be better used for something else. She said the Legion had a nice hall and there was no need for another to take money away from the Legion, its veterans, and their families who had served their country."

"Who was this?"

"Jane Johnson, wife of Amos Johnson. They farm north of town. He was post commander of the Legion."

"What happened?" asks Johnston.

"I told Father Murphy about the comments. He suggested that there would always be someone not entirely happy, but that everything would turn out in the end."

"When was this conversation with Father Murphy?"

"Ah …" Sarah hesitates and glances toward the ceiling. "I … I don't really remember. It's just so long … so long ago. I really don't want to … I really don't remember when."

"Did you have anything to do with the other money collections at St. Mary's?" Johnston tries not to become impatient.

"I don't know why you keep asking," replies Sarah. "No. I think Father Murphy handled that with the secretary of the church."

"Who would handle that money?" Sarah flattens her dress sleeve.

"The ushers, the secretary, Father Murphy, someone at the bank, I would guess. I really don't know."

"I appreciate your talking with me. Say hello to Thomas for me. Terrible thing, this thing with Father Murphy." Johnston pauses to look around. "Did I ask before if Father Murphy was particularly close to anyone at St. Mary's?" Johnston shifts his weight so that he's standing completely erect.

"I think I answered that before," Sarah swallows hard. "Everyone really liked Father Murphy."

"So to your knowledge, Mr. Goostree at the grocery store was the last one to see Father Murphy alive?"

"That's what he said. I think we should not disagree."

"Thanks again." With that, Johnston pushes open the screen door and walks down the street. Sarah looks at her hand holding the towel. It is clenched tightly, knuckles white. She sighs; glad Johnston was gone. All these questions had caused her mind to gallop, holding her mind in the past. She wants to forget the past. When would it be over? A tear slides down her cheek, then another. Father Murphy had been the third death in the same year. Why was the church focused on the number three? The Father, Son, and Holy Ghost. Three crosses on Calvary—two thieves and Jesus. Twelve apostles. A number divided evenly by three—and the digits 1 and 2 equal three.

"I've endured enough pain in my life," she says aloud, as if speaking the words will make them less painful. "I've gone through enough heartache. My transgression was only once with Father Murphy. Let it stay in the past. Oh, how I have prayed for forgiveness. I've not sought my own gain or glory but have worked with humility to bring joy and happiness to others, especially Thomas and Wanda. I've now agreed to help with the newspaper. I try to help Wanda, although not always with the best result."

Sarah closes her eyes; she speaks the mind's troubling thoughts: "How often have I felt worthless? Too many times to count over the years, mostly because I could not live up to the ideal set by mother. I've been doing more to live up to mother's ideals, but the pain has not lessened. I have not joined women who agitate for equality or for society's approval of sex outside marriage. I have not burned my bra."

The hand towel drops to the floor. "Stop thinking of the pain!" she instructs herself. "I can salvage Thomas and Wanda if this preoccupation with Father Murphy would end. He is dead, God bless his soul; let him rest in peace. Let me have my peace in the future."

She grabs a pot, fills it with water, rinses off several vegetables, and turns on the stove. She wipes her face.

The screen door of the *Pioneer Ledger* slams shut.

"Is that you, Thomas?"

"Hi, doll. We get any telephone calls on missed papers this afternoon? Windhurst?"

"One of the Isenbergs said no paper was in their mailbox today. Little Ralph came over, and I gave him one of our extras and a sucker. He was happy. I need to check if one of the addressing machine templates skipped or dropped out. What about the survey?"

Thomas explains what Oswald said about his property at Sand Lake and how the land survey could be the property west of him. Leaving out the fantasy calendar girl, he tells Sarah about the similarities in mileage, the shoreline shape, and the fact Oswald has never seen his neighbor at all in these many years.

"That's really strange," says Sarah. "Someone buys a piece of property at the lake and then doesn't use it for years and years. There had to be some purpose. Why go to all the trouble to get a survey done to let the weeds grow?"

"Maybe it was Old Man Peterson who bought the property and then somehow forgot about it," offers Thomas.

"I thought he owned a ton of property, or at least his family did. Weird we found only one land survey. There were no other papers, like a deed dealing with specific property."

"We looked only in the bedroom desk; other papers may exist. I still need to talk to George Windhurst. Did he call?" asks Thomas.

"No. Not today," replies Sarah.

"I smell brussel sprouts."

"Supper will be ready shortly. Wanda said Myron is taking her out for a hamburger. Did you see that Mr. Johnston today?"

"No, why do you ask?"

"Oh, no reason." Sarah glances away.

"I'll be back in minute. I've got to see if I have the right paper stock cut for the Kluge job press run tomorrow."

Chapter Twenty-six

Thursday morning, and Charles Johnston taps his fingers on the steering wheel as he drives and listens to Mary Wells' "My Guy" hit song. The backseat of his Chevy is getting full—a journal ledger book is stacked on top of the box of bricks.

He hears the ledger book slide off the box of bricks as he abruptly brakes to a stop in Sheriff O'Day's Winterville parking lot. He retrieves the journal for his visit and report to the Sheriff.

"Good morning. Rebecca. Sheriff in?"

"Yes, he's alone in his office."

"So how are you today? Keeping the outer office peaceful?"

"No problems today. I'll be better prepared tomorrow, after my karate class tonight."

"If I leave quietly, do I need to put my hands up?" Johnston smiles and takes a step sideways toward the sheriff's office.

"No," giggles Rebecca, covering her mouth with her hands. Her eyes tell the world she is smiling.

"Sheriff, good morning," says Johnston, leaning against the doorjamb, the journal clasped against his right side.

"What's so good about it?" replies O'Day in an uneven cadence. He doesn't look up as he runs a pen across a newspaper page.

"Whoa, there. Rebecca smiled at me. You must have gotten out of the bed on the wrong side this morning."

"Nothing of the sort," snorts the Sheriff.

"Well, anyway, you should be interested in what I've learned about that dead priest found in Clinton." Johnston glances briefly at the book in his hand. "We got some help from the Catholic Diocese after I did a little cajoling, and a judge helped out with a limited subpoena for financial records. I got a look at the reports for Clinton's St. Mary's Catholic Church, and I was permitted to take some notes."

"Refresh my memory. Why church financial records?"

"Well, the victim was a priest. I decided my best way to go was to follow the money." Johnston opens the journal.

"What money is missing? I don't know of any," says the Sheriff.

"That's just it. I don't have a solid grasp of what money is missing, but my gut tells me there is connection between the priest's murder and money." Johnston peers over the Sheriff's desk. O'Day slides a tablet over his newspaper. Johnston continues: "Father Murphy needed money to fulfill his preoccupation with building a gym for kids—that was the firefly in the darkness. The local newspaper showed the increase in money-raising activities prior to the priest's disappearance. Then a great drop in fund-raising afterward and, curiously, no publicity relating to money being spent. We know no building was put up; no Father Murphy memorial fund created."

"Do we know how much money we're talking about?"

"No. Not really. That's why I thought the diocese would have more specifics. But they did, and they didn't. St. Mary's reported a gradually increasing revenue stream matching post-WWII prosperity. Then, in 1952, the revenue decreases. First, it fluctuated a couple of hundred dollars weekly; it then was a thousand dollars a week less, on average. I checked the records on registered church members and the numbers remained constant, if not an increase. And, it was not the baby boom adding more children of attending members increasing church membership without adding more weekly offering envelopes. The number of church weddings, funerals, and other functions during this time was normal. Only lower reported revenues stood out."

"So what you're saying is that over the two years at $1,000.00 per week, you're looking at a missing $100,000.00," summarizes O'Day.

"No, not that much. I'd say about $40,000.00 to $50,000.00 total, including maybe up to $5,000.00 from bake sales and other fundraisers over the two-year period. Remember, not all money raised would be diverted, only a portion."

"That's still a fistful of dollars to have stashed someplace. Who at St. Mary's had the opportunity to know about the money?"

"Well, a lot of people would have a general notion that part of the fund-raising money was earmarked for the new building. Since that was the smallest portion of the money, it should not have raised any parishioner concern. Only a small number of people would have had any knowledge about the diversion of the weekly offerings. And, it may have been only Father Murphy."

"Why do you say that?" asks Sheriff O'Day.

"Why? Because it looks like—in order to keep the money hidden from parishioners and the diocese—large foreign mission donations were claimed. A time or two, the parish bulletin would have a purported donation thank you."

"You're saying the money never went to the overseas recipient, for example, the World Overseas Mission?"

"That's what I'm saying, Jonathan. It was a way to hide the money diversion. There would be little chance that parishioners could verify what they were told. Perhaps the diocese could have done so, if it'd had an inkling of what was happening, but there was no alarm going off. The diocese was getting its parish tithe from St. Mary's. It really had no desire to tell the parish how to spend its other money. Sure, it could appeal to the parish for support, but as it had denied St. Mary's request for a building fund grant, it could readily understand if St. Mary's was going to respond in kind. Not very charitable, but we're dealing with humans and human emotions."

"Who would have known about the missing money? Father Murphy? Any money committee?" asks Sheriff O'Day.

"There was no official money or finance committee. The priest was supposed to be in charge and be hands-on when it came to financial affairs. The head usher and one or two of the other ushers would have access to the collection envelopes, but would not have opened them. There was a fireproof safe located behind the altar in the room where the priest stored vestments and prepared for mass. That's where the collected envelopes were taken after each mass. Cash offerings were sealed into a manila envelope with the date marked on the outside and placed in the safe. On Monday, the church secretary would take money out of the envelopes, writing the inside amount on the outside of the envelope. She'd stamp each check 'for deposit only,' count the cash, and fill out a bank deposit slip. She'd give the money and paperwork to Father Murphy to take to the bank. If Father Murphy were not available, she would call the head usher. The combination to the safe was known only by Father Murphy, the secretary, the head usher, and one alternate head usher."

O'Day finishes scribbling the information Johnston has given him. He then looks up, expectantly. "Now who were these others?"

"During the time period—that's 1952 to 1954—there were two secretaries. One was Esther Peterson, until 1953, and the other was Anita Halberg."

"Wait a minute. Is this Esther related to Arnold Peterson?"

"Yes, she was his wife. She donated her time to the church. I didn't find Mr. Peterson was active in the church. One person told me that Peterson converted to Catholicism when he married Esther. There was one son, Gary, who went to church with his mother, but seldom did the family go together. No one could tell me where the son is today; most said they heard South America. He's thirty-eight, thirty-nine. Obviously, it's murky what happened to Esther."

"What about Anita Halberg?"

"Deceased. Two years ago. She was sixty-eight. Death certificate states it was natural causes. I couldn't otherwise confirm."

"Who was head usher?" asks O'Day, making a list.

"Amos Johnson, still there, became head usher when he returned from WWII military service as a decorated veteran. He has an impeccable reputation. Served as commander of the local American Legion Post No. 167 for three years after 1952. Took over running his parents' farm when they passed away in the mid-1950s. Purchased the 120-acre farm that adjoins his parents' homestead in the late Fifties, so he has been very successful. To anticipate your next question, the substitute head usher was Elmer Anderson. I talked to Elmer the other day, and he had a very fuzzy recollection. He was a friend of Amos, but said he only substituted for Amos maybe a couple times, and that was when Amos took a week of vacation in Texas. He thought that at both times, the secretary went Monday to open the safe. In late 1952, he recalled the combination to the safe was changed, and Amos told him he'd get it, but Elmer couldn't remember ever getting it."

"Did you talk to Amos? I know Amos."

"Yes, drove up to his farm on day I talked to Elmer Anderson. He is an impressive person, isn't he? Straightforward, seems to have a strong recollection of events and strong community ties. And he is well connected, going to church every Sunday, going fishing sometimes with Oswald at Farmers' Elevator, shopping every week after church at Goostree Grocery. I didn't learn anything new from him."

"Anybody else who should be on the list?"

"I'm hesitant, but when I talked with the publisher's wife yesterday about Father Murphy, I noted an unusual hesitation in her speech and a measured response—it made me think she was being very careful in choosing her words, not a lack of memory."

"You mean Sarah Hamilton?"

"Yes," says Johnston, now looking at his notepad.

"How does she fit in? Any past church office or position?"

"No church position, but she was involved a great deal in the fund-raisers to support Father Murphy's gym for the kids. She has an influential position in the community, as she talks to people frequently, and the entire town knows her. She can help groups or individuals with her ability to print items about bazaars and open houses, and she can help people *not* have embarrassing news printed. People trust her. She has compassion and an empathy for others."

"Yet, you sense something?"

"Yes, by her own words, she would often be the last person to leave, other than Father Murphy. She held money overnight on one occasion, but there is no evidence of irregularity. One has to weigh that these fund-raising monies were the nickels and dimes, not the dollars involved. She knew Father Murphy as well as anyone in the whole church and was in the group of most active parishioners when he was there."

"Any other persons come to mind?" asks O'Day.

"Only one more: Godfrey Klempler at the bank."

"Why him? Did he have an official money role?"

"No. Someone told me he was like a finance chairman. I couldn't confirm that. There is no doubt that Mr. Klempler's bank, as the only bank in town, would be a repository for funds, such as those from St. Mary's. The church had multiple accounts at the bank—a checking account, a savings account, and a special account for activities like the annual church dinner."

"Have you talked with Klempler?"

"Only briefly by telephone. He was out of town recently. He was courteous, but unwilling to go into any specifics, told me he was prohibited by law from talking about people if they had accounts or divulging the specifics of those accounts. He's been the banker in Clinton for almost twenty years." Johnston closes the journal.

"What about those bricks you keep in your Chevy?"

"If we could decipher the code that would help. I assume Father Murphy made the letters. The color difference on two of the bricks when compared to the other three troubles me. The human remains had to have been moved at least once. What bones were missing? I recall the pelvic bone and one forearm or hand bone."

"Correct. I hate to remember that—not having the pelvic bone caused us such a headache, and we weren't sure about the gender— we assumed the bones were of a female. The small wedding ring and a red-colored jewel said female. The rings had no known connection to the priest. The lab, in its best guess, said the hand bones were fe-male, but time had seriously degraded them. And, we had the forged postcard that Arnold Peterson claimed he'd received from his miss-ing wife after she left—that damaged his credibility. His wife had been missing since 1953, and then there was his wife's finger injury. The condition of the bones matched the time she'd been missing, the crime lab said. I regret it now, but who would have known we would come up with misplaced dental records? I was told initially that none were found. We had none for Esther Peterson, and she lived in the same community for decades."

There was a light knock on the closed door. O'Day shoots a glance at Johnston and motions for him to be quiet.

"Yes, come in."

"Mr. Hamilton of the *Pioneer Ledger* is on the telephone for you. Do you want to take it, or shall I take a message?" inquires Rebecca.

Johnston is shaking his head "yes."

"Rebecca, transfer the call in here," directs the sheriff. He and Johnston wait for his desk phone to ring.

"Hello, Thomas. No, you're not interrupting. Always glad to hear from you." O'Day sees Johnston open his notepad.

"Tell me again what you found at the home of Arnold Peterson. A land survey for what looks to be a property on Sand Lake. Had margin notation with the letters G and O. No, you keep it. Investigator Charles Johnston is in town today. I'll have him check the county land records. Property, about twenty acres, west of property owned by Gordon Oswald on Sand Lake; got it. I'll request Charles come to Clinton and personally look at what you've found. Don't worry; I'm sure he'll be able to find you. Thanks for calling."

Charles is writing as the Sheriff ends the call. Charles looks up.

"Charles, did you get that? Old Man Peterson had a land survey for property on Sand Lake. Those letters from the brick are showing up again. It was those letters that caused Hamilton to call."

"I don't know about the value of the land survey Hamilton found. However, I'll get a chance to casually talk to his wife again. That should be more important," offers Johnston.

"What about Gordon Oswald? His initials are G.O., the same as on the brick you have. The skeleton was found in a cistern on the property rented by the Elevator."

"Oswald is a Lutheran. There's no connection I found with St. Mary's. He never dated or had a relationship with any woman who was a parishioner. I'm sure he knew the priest, but by that criterion, we'd have 800 suspects. No, we still need to consider that there was a third letter, a backward C. If the letter were filled in, like an O, the letters would be G-O-O, not Gordon Oswald initials. I'm inclined to believe that the writer was not finished scratching when he stopped. The three letters lead more to a name like Goostree than any other, especially when it is so prominent in town."

"Maybe so. What is Oswald's middle initial?"

"Sheriff, honestly, I don't know. I'll put that question in my notepad for further checking," says an embarrassed Johnston.

"Good. Could the last letter be part of a P?"

"Could be. It's one of the possibilities. Nothing seems to be going in that direction, however. I need to be off now."

Johnston stretches his legs out, reaches for the journal he brought, and slowly stands up. He watches the sheriff slide back the tablet he had been writing on to expose the newspaper beneath, but Johnston isn't able to read anything. Walking backward, Johnston steps out of the sheriff's office.

Should've asked about the newspaper, Johnston thinks.

At his desk, the Sheriff renews his search to find his grandson's name in the newspaper, which he was told was in a box score today.

Chapter Twenty-seven

Wanda inches herself across the cloth front bench-seat of her Fairlane, getting ever closer to the car's steering wheel, a seat already occupied.

"You need more cola?" asks Myron, sitting behind the steering wheel of Wanda's car. A tray from Debbie's Drive Inn is hooked over the window and balanced against the driver-side door.

"No. They don't have the new diet cola."

Myron's sees a carhop on roller skates whirling past the car's hood ornament. Her short red-and-white candy-stripe skirt flashes a shapely pair of legs that entice from the tops of her bobby socks all the way up to her trim waist.

"I could do that," says Wanda, noticing Myron's eye movement.

"I'm sure you could, but it would cost a lot of money to drive up here to work every day, now that gasoline is over thirty cents a gallon." Embarrassed that Wanda caught him staring at the carhop, Myron quickly changes the subject. "Did you know that your father found a mysterious land survey?"

"No. What land survey?"

"I don't know exactly. Mr. Oswald said your father came over to the Elevator with a land survey that shows land that could be next to my boss's cabin at Sand Lake."

"Is my father buying a lake cabin?" asks Wanda.

"No, I don't think so."

"You know where the survey came from?"

"I don't know that either," says Myron.

"So what do you know?" Wanda's straw gurgles.

"Only that my boss said the land in the survey was next door to his Sand Lake property. That, and the land was nothing but weeds and trees. No one has been seen even visiting. We should go tomorrow after work and check it out. Then I could be one up on my boss."

"But that would be trespassing," Wanda says with concern.

"It wouldn't hurt anything. Besides, I'm exhausted from working on the sailplane. That's why I proposed we drive to Winterville to have supper. Another day won't matter. What do you say?"

"Okay, I guess," agrees Wanda, her voice tentative.

"We could be treasure hunters," suggests Myron.

"No way. Let Oscar and Jimmy do that. On the other hand, there'd be no skimpy-skirted distractions roller skating by."

"We could invite a couple of carhops to go with," teases Myron.

Wanda playfully punches him in the shoulder. "Let's turn on the radio. Maybe Mary Wells will be singing, or maybe a Beatles song."

Work did not go fast enough for Myron this Thursday. He does not tell Mr. Oswald he is planning to visit Sand Lake that evening.

At four-thirty p.m., he plans to meet Wanda at the old factory. The sun is still up, but the days are getting shorter. Myron doesn't fathom why he is doing this. When he searched for Oscar's secret entrance into the factory, he at least had some idea of what he was hunting for. The old well was again boarded up. As far as he knows, the concrete in the well was undisturbed.

"Hey, Myron!" calls Wanda. "Sorry I'm late. I had to change clothes. My mother said she was proud of me for finally putting on old clothes to come here, as she's often suggested."

"I got a flashlight, pocketknife, some matches, and a large bag of marshmallows."

"You're a regular explorer, a Columbus on dry land, or Lewis and Clark, if you ask me." Wanda locks her car.

"Yeah." There was no thrill in Myron's voice.

"So where are we going?"

"We'll go County Road One and turn north toward Sand Lake on the township road. I think I can find Mr. Oswald's place. He keeps telling others to look for the two brick pillars on the township road that runs south around the lake. I don't think we'll have any trouble identifying the place once we get close."

And they don't. Myron's route allows them to be approaching Sand Lake in minutes.

"I see the pillars to the right," says Wanda. "The one has a mailbox; I don't see a name."

"I don't think there is a name sign. But I'm sure we're in the right spot. Look at those bricks. Same type as I found in the tunnel."

"Myron, those brick types are everywhere." Wanda ties the strings at the top of her blouse, thinking: *Why did I wear this old thing?*

"Let's park in the driveway to Mr. Oswald's cabin. I'm sure no one is here. As far as I know, it's only used weekends, if at all."

125

"Myron, this land to the left of the driveway is nothing but this-
tles, weeds, and briar. Looks like it's been neglected for years."

"If we stay on Mr. Oswald's driveway, we can find the lakeshore.
Then, we can follow the shore to see if there's less bramble."

"Good idea. Lead the way, Captain." Wanda salutes.

The pair begins walking along the driveway toward the cabin and
Sand Lake. Only the squawks of disturbed birds are heard. A cooper
hawk circles. Myron keeps glancing from left to right. The sun casts
shadows across their path and from their bodies.

"There's nothing here," says Wanda.

"Keep looking. We're not to the lake yet."

"There it is Myron; the lake is beyond the sugar maple tree losing
its yellow leaves. This was a quick few minutes."

The shore beach is narrow, more like a strip of sand, not wide
enough for two persons to walk side-by-side.

"Turn left, Wanda." The distance sound of a motorboat is heard.

"Maybe we have visitors, Myron."

"I don't think so. Sounds like someone started a motor and
turned it off. Probably drifted from a fishing spot before changing
his mind. I'm not surprised that we've not seen any fishing boats.
Those reeds to our right would keep most motorboats away from
the shore. Crappie should come back to shallow water this time of
year."

"How come you know stuff about fish and fishing?"

"Wanda!" Myron shakes his head in disbelief. "Who is my boss?
Ever been in his office? See the fish trophy? Duh."

"Okay, I wasn't thinking. Look, a fire pit. It's old, but someone
came prepared. There's fresh charcoal around the edges."

"Good, we can build a fire later and roast marshmallows. Now,
let's search for a path or someplace where the overgrowth is not so
high. I should have brought a hatchet. This pocketknife of mine will
be worthless."

"How were you to know what we would find? We can go home
now, or build a fire to toast the marshmallows," says Wanda.

"We have an hour of daylight left. Let's see what we can find. We
can light a fire later. I'll leave the marshmallows over a branch in this
tree until we return."

"I'll follow you," says Wanda.

Myron inspects the dense bushes and weeds. Slowly, he walks up
the shoreline several paces. He spots what he thinks is an old trail,

but he is not quite sure. Branches, four feet above the ground, have been bent back. *Surely, not by an animal*, he thinks.

"We got any bears in these woods?" quizzes Wanda.

"Nah, probably rabbits, woodchucks, pheasants, wild turkey, mice, maybe a skunk or two," replies Myron.

"A skunk? No way; I'm out of here now."

"Hold on, Wanda, I am merely guessing. Besides, you can hide behind me if we run across any."

"Thanks loads," she scoffs.

"Come on; this way," directs Myron.

Myron scrutinizes what appear to be old footprints under the bent branches. The ground looks more compact between two trees, indicating a former path leading from the shoreline.

Wanda grabs the loop in Myron's jeans with her two fingers. She is going to stay close as Myron turns south.

Deliberately, Myron parts the branches; careful to hold them long enough to let Wanda pass. It is slow going. He has to watch every step. Cockleburs stick to his shirt and jeans. One cocklebur hitches a ride by sticking to a shoelace.

He keeps the sun to his right and the lake to his back. His path is definitely not straight. He nearly trips over an exposed tree root.

"You still with me, Wanda?"

"Yes," says Wanda, a little frightened.

Myron is more serious than normal, Wanda thinks. He has always been driven by a need to get things done. Any other person would have given up when the bank refused the sailplane purchase loan. Not Myron; the bank could not deny his dream. He sought a way to achieve his goal and, if it involved hard work, no problem. Yet, it was out of character for Myron to stop working on his sailplane for a wild goose chase. Maybe he has set up a prank. She dismisses the thought; he wouldn't do that to her, and besides, there's no sign of other people.

"Hey, Wanda, you still there?"

"I'm holding on as tight as I can. You are *not* going to lose me."

A twig snaps ahead. Wanda jumps back. Myron almost topples backward on top of her. Fortunately, Wanda releases her fingers from his belt loop.

"What was that?" asks Wanda, her growing fright heightened.

"Just a twig," replies Myron. "Just a twig breaking."

"Would that be a skunk?"

"No, shush," he whispers. "Might be our neighborhood bear."

"Wha-a-at?" Wanda's eyes become as big as golf balls.

"Just kidding," says Myron softly. Wanda exhales, loud and long, but Myron cautions her: "Be quiet a moment." Wanda freezes, not daring this time to release her reacquired finger grip of Myron's belt loops. "Let's go," says Myron, finally. "It probably was just an animal wandering through. If it had been a bear, we'd have heard more noise, as it would have had to move branches from its path, like us."

"What about a skunk?"

"I don't know. Nothing worse than a stinky shower. We can hope that he's as afraid of us as we are of him. If we leave him alone, he'll do the same to us."

"I hope so." Wanda's breathing is regular again.

Myron starts forward again; Wanda follows. They advance pushing branches aside, watching their step, and swatting mosquitoes.

I should have thought of wearing one of those safari hats with the nets protecting the face, thinks Myron.

After a half-hour, he is tired of the drudgery of trying to walk. The pair's progress is painstakingly slow. He doubts they'll reach the township road by dark. They are already losing the sun's helping rays.

About twenty feet ahead, Myron beholds an opening in the trees. He strains to see past the weeds. "Wanda, I'm going to go faster for a half dozen steps." She keeps pace, but a low branch whips back at her foot, and she feels a fresh scratch on her ankle.

Myron and Wanda are in a small clearing. A dozen trees have been cleared away to form an oasis. The weeds are still there. Several purple flowers highlight a late-blooming thistle patch. Wanda sighs, thankfully for relief from the bushes they had clawed through.

"Can we stay here?" asks Wanda, pleadingly. She releases her finger hold on Myron's jeans.

"Yes, until I figure out what's next."

"How far are we from the road or the shore?"

"From the shore, maybe 200 yards."

"Is that all?" asks Wanda.

"We didn't walk very fast or straight. It may be faster going back, since I broke off branches. We'll definitely need our flashlights."

"Let me rest a moment," says Wanda, dropping to one knee in the weeds, careful to protect her face.

"You and me both, but we better not stay too long. The sun is below the horizon. We're going to be walking back in the dark. Stay here. I want to quickly walk to the other side of this clearing. I'll be right back. Keep a grip on your flashlight." Myron bulls his way through the knee-high weeds, high stepping and swinging both arms.

Wanda stands, watching Myron's shadowy figure and the faint singular beam of light that precedes it.

Gnats swarm her face; she takes six steps diagonally backward from where she had been standing. She still watches Myron, hoping he will soon turn around and they can get out of there. It was scary to begin with, and now it is even more so. It was fine for Myron to go crawling through dark, cramped brick tunnels, but she would never do it. Not even on a dare.

On her sixth step backward, she almost falls as the crack of a board breaking rises to her ears. "Myron! Myron!" she shrieks.

"Wanda, hold on!" yells Myron; he pivots on his left foot, trampling weeds as he runs toward her. "Wanda, you all right?" he gasps, struggling to breathe.

"Yeah, I think so. My heel seems to have fallen into some kind of hole. I heard a board crack."

"Let me have a look." Myron starts to part weeds, moving the flashlight beam in a circle. "Looks like an animal was digging here, exposing a piece of wood. It's hard to tell in the dark. I can move some of the dirt. It's about three inches deep before more wood."

"Do you think something is buried?" asks Wanda.

"I don't know. Let me move this way a couple of feet." Pulling at a clump of weeds, Myron easily tears their roots from the ground. Reaching down, he digs with his hand. He touches rough wood again. He hits the wood with the end of his flashlight. The sound is hollow. The spongy wood gives slightly as Myron strikes it again.

"Wanda, we have to get out of here tonight. Whatever is buried there can wait until we have daylight."

"Do you think it's like a utility connection box?"

"I doubt it. Those boxes are usually metal, and this is definitely wood. If I remember, the electricity coming into my boss' cabin is on a pole. We walked past two utility poles on the side of his driveway. I don't think there's a sewer line way out here. Everyone uses septic tanks or outhouses."

"That's it, Myron. It's just an old outhouse pit someone covered up. Phew! Phew!"

"Could be. This clearing could have been a campsite. I don't see any signs of a campfire site, but then again, it could have been a long time ago, and with these weeds, we're really lucky to see much of anything. The other side of the clearing is just as dense as what we came through, so I'm saying we should go back the way we came, as best we can, and think about what to do next."

"You lead the way."

"Put your flashlight over my shoulder, pointed straight ahead. I'll try to keep mine pointed lower."

"Yes, sir," Wanda says, giving him a mock salute. The return trip is demanding as Myron stumbles into branches that snap back, hitting Wanda's raised arms. The only enjoyment comes from watching a few fireflies light up the darkness. The croak of a bullfrog, crickets, and several eerie bird sounds fill the still air. Nothing breaks the silence between Myron and Wanda as they trudge forward, trying to retrace their steps. The only twigs snapping are beneath their feet.

At last, they see the outline of a nearly full moon behind streaky clouds. They hear water lapping gently. With one last step, they are out of the bramble and onto the shore. Both stand still, holding hands, watching a mallard in the moon's reflection on the water.

"I'm going to grab the bag of marshmallows, and we can head back down the shoreline to Mr. Oswald's place, walk out along his road, and find my car."

"I'm with you. I'll enjoy a few marshmallows riding in the car."

The reflection of the chrome around the car headlights is a welcoming sight to them both. The trip, short in time, was physically and emotionally draining.

"Thank you, Wanda," says Myron, giving her a long hug.

"What are you thanking me for? I sat on an old board, a nail puts a hole in my jeans, and you find a secret passage into the old factory. Now, I go with you into the middle of the jungle and step into a hole of some kind that hides who knows what."

"I was hoping to find something Mr. Oswald didn't know or learn why this land was important to your father. It's very different from other lake property for some reason. That buried wood was suspicious; if a board, it should not sound hollow. I'd like to discover what was buried, but not get in trouble for digging. We have to decide who we should talk to."

"First, I think we should talk to my father. He won't believe this. Last time you were worried about your father getting into trouble. Well, this time I'm worried that my father will order me to my bedroom, lock the door from the outside, and I'll have to open my window to get food smuggled in."

"Wanda, your imagination is one of a kind."

"If it is, you should get awarded an explorer badge and retire. Maybe we should bring Oscar and Jimmy out here to do the exploring. They're shorter so they can walk under the branches without ducking, and we could sit on the shoreline, eat marshmallows, and talk to them with walkie-talkies."

"They'd probably love it. Oscar wouldn't come without Deadeye and I nominate you to pick all the cockleburs from the dog's fur. By the way, check your hair. Nobody will believe walking through the woods at Sand Lake put all that vegetation in your blonde hair."

"I've got a brush in my car. My hair should be okay. There's enough gossip in town. I'll not be starting more."

"Do you think anybody is watching us now?" asks Myron.

"No, why?"

Myron kisses Wanda and hugs her again. He picks one cocklebur from her hair. A bullfrog croaks in the distance. "Let's get back to town. It's a weeknight, after all. Work will come all too quickly."

Myron backs his car out of Oswald's cabin driveway. While Myron is turning the front wheels, a red pickup truck zooms by from the west leaving a cloud of dust. Wanda reaches over to turn the radio dial but finds only commercials.

In the fifteen minutes it takes to reach Wanda's car at the old factory, they agree to tell her father about the buried wood. Myron says he will come to the *Pioneer Ledger* the next evening after supper.

Chapter Twenty-eight

"*Pioneer Ledger.* This is Thomas." Picking up the receiver in Sarah's front office.

"Thomas, George Windhurst returning your call."

"George, at the Peterson house here the other day—"

"I hope everything there is okay," Windhurst interrupts. He has a premonition that something is wrong.

"Appears to be, except, you know, the dust, cobwebs, and a musty-basement smell. I was only over there once and didn't look at everything. The place is still full of furniture and Arnold Peterson's personal belongings. I would have thought the family would have removed the personal items, at least."

"I hired an heir locater firm; Mr. Peterson's closest relative is his son, Gary. He stands to inherit everything, however, his only interest is getting a check. Now that his father died, the previous monetary gifts have stopped."

"I didn't think my neighbor had any income other than his pension and social security. I know he had property, but there has to be upkeep, and I would not have believed the Farmers' Elevator paid enough rent to make him rich," says Thomas.

"You're right, Old Man Peterson was slowly depleting his bank account with wire transfers to Gary. Now, I didn't tell you," Windhurst warns.

"I understand. Back to the house belongings, I found a land survey along with a Killebrew rookie baseball card."

"A Killebrew rookie card! Now that's a find. Killebrew would have been playing in Washington when that was issued. Who would have guessed that Clark Griffith would have moved the Senators to Bloomington? What else did you say was found? A land survey?"

"Right, a land survey. I talked to Oswald over at the Elevator, and we came to the conclusion that it's a survey for a piece of land next door to him at Sand Lake."

"What lake was that?" asks Windhurst.

"Sand. S-A-N-D. Just northwest of Clinton."

"Got it. I know of that lake. Now, your question was?"

"The question was: what should I do about the personal items?"

"Let's do it this way: I know Gary doesn't want the furniture, appliances, or any knick-knacks in the house. On his behalf, I'd ask that you not destroy any personal pictures or family albums. Save all baseball cards. I thought I had all the land deeds and other real estate records, but save the land survey. I would consider it a personal favor if you saved for me any record by Yogi Jorgensen. I need an extra copy of his song, 'I Jus' Go Nuts at Christmas.' Tomorrow, I'll ask the heir locater company to run a search for property."

"I understand," says Thomas.

"Thanks, Thomas. I know you'll be fair and honest. About that land survey ... what can you tell me about it?"

"Not much. Looks to be a twenty-acre parcel of land about seven miles north of County Road One and eight miles west of the county line. Like I said, it may be next to a similar parcel owned by Gordon Oswald. In fact, the survey document had the initials G and O in the margin."

"The survey margin had Oswald's initials?" repeats Windhurst.

"Yes. Oswald and I determined the land survey was done some-time between 1950 and 1952, although no date appears on the document itself." Thomas sips orange juice.

"This is all news to me. Mr. Peterson never told me he had bought land for a cabin on Sand Lake. He didn't fish."

"Oswald said he never saw any neighbor who may have been the owner of the land west of him. He found that odd."

"Well, yes and no. Could have been investment property initially, and Arnold just forgot about it," speculates Windhurst.

"Wouldn't Mr. Peterson, if he were the owner, have received a yearly real estate tax bill?"

"There would have been taxes due. Mr. Peterson relied on his accountant to receive notices like tax bills, pay when due and add the amount paid to his charges to Mr. Peterson. Considering that Mr. Peterson owned or had an interest in several pieces of real estate, the individual tax paid would not have stood out. If the property was not improved—that is, no building was built on the property—I'm sure the taxes were in the agricultural category, and twenty acres would not be a large yearly sum."

"You make good points, George. Sarah and I will probably be in the house again over the weekend. But I now know how to proceed, so thank you, George."

"You're welcome, Thomas. Say hello to Sarah for me. You call me collect if you find the Hope diamond."

"Bye." Thomas hangs up the telephone. Sarah enters the office.

"What did Mr. Windhurst say about the items?" Sarah asks.

"We can exercise common sense," replies Thomas."

"It's still going to be a big task. Would have been better if the family could have taken the responsibility," sighs Sarah. "By the way, Myron and Wanda want to talk to us both after supper tonight."

"They're not announcing their engagement, are they?" asks Thomas, hiding his face.

"Oh, heavens. I hadn't thought of that." Sarah's face turns red; her body quivers. "You're scaring me."

"I was thinking out loud." Thomas winks.

"Wanda did seem evasive when I asked her why she and Myron wanted to know if you were going to be home tonight."

"We'll just have to wait and wonder all day, won't we?" says Thomas with a twinkle in his eye. He gives Sarah a quick kiss on the forehead. "I've got to get back downstairs to finish a commercial print job for the Legion Post. Say doll, have you checked our wedding announcement order books for Wanda's fingerprints?"

"Shush, Tom, dear. Get back to work while I think up something to make you nervous with." She begins looking for a pen.

Hamilton is halfway down the basement steps when the telephone rings. He hears Sarah answer, and within seconds yell, "Thomas! Telephone for you!"

He returns to Sarah's office and takes the receiver from Sarah as she leaves, pen in hand. "Hello, this is Thomas."

"Charles Johnston calling. Sheriff O'Day was talking with me, and he told me you called him about a land survey for property next to Gordon Oswald at Sand Lake."

"Yes, I did." Thomas sits in Sarah's desk chair.

"I went to the county land records office. Jonathan said I should share my findings with you. I found Oswald's property at Sand Lake on the official courthouse map. Mr. Oswald's land was part of a large subdivision created in 1950 by two farmers who owned all the land on the south side of Sand Lake. They saw a profit opportunity when the county got a federal environmental grant to dredge Sand Lake. All the lots were sold in the early Fifties. The parcel next to Oswald's was sold in late 1951 to one Arnold Peterson in joint tenancy with one Esther Peterson. Ever since the purchase, the taxes have been regularly mailed to the same Winterville accountant. Taxes are up-to-date and I could find no building permits of record. It is still listed agricultural; neighboring lots have been changed to recreational.

There was one strange record in the file—a document, signed by Esther Peterson in April 1953, gave her property ownership interest to St. Mary's Catholic Church in Clinton. There was no notation the recorder received the original document; there's just the one copy. Without an original signed by Mr. Arnold Peterson, the recorder said she had no legal basis to change the parcel ownership. This was all public record information, except the recorder's statement to me."

"So, if I hear you right, the land was bought by Arnold and Esther Peterson, jointly, and is still owned by them," says Thomas.

"That's correct. Since Arnold is no longer alive, Esther is now the sole owner of the property. Or, if Esther predeceased Arnold, then Arnold would have become the sole owner, with his heirs inheriting the property now that he's dead."

"What about St. Mary's?" ask Thomas, ready to make a note.

"They have no right at all to the property. There is no valid record transfer. I talked to George Windhurst about this, as he is handling the Peterson estate, and he says the church has no valid claim to the property," says Johnston.

"What do you want me to do with this land survey?"

"Hang on to it for safekeeping? I'll bet your wife is excited about the prospect of a new home."

"I think she will be excited once everything settles down. She wants all this business about Father Murphy to be over with. There's so much gossip—and people like you coming to town, asking questions. I know it must be done, but many folks find it unsettling."

"I appreciate your help, Thomas. I was planning to visit and talk with you face to face, but I got sidetracked. Next week, maybe."

"I'd appreciate it if you did it later in the week. Monday and Tuesday are my busiest days."

"Fine. Then we'd have time for a cup of coffee, too."

"Thanks, Charles." Thomas hangs up the telephone and returns to his upstairs work area. After a few minutes he hears footsteps and knows its Sarah because the front door has not squeaked.

"So tell me," Sarah says. "Who owns that land on the survey?" Sarah's hair is wet from the shower. "Come back into the kitchen, Thomas, so we can talk. I'd hate to have someone walk in and see me like this."

In the kitchen, Thomas begins relaying the information given by Charles Johnston, including that the land ownership passed to Esther Peterson upon Arnold's death.

"But is Esther dead?" asks Sarah, wrapping a dry towel around her head.

"Who knows? While Arnold was accused of killing Esther, it was never proven in a court of law. Could she show up and claim the property, along with her other inheritance? Sure, it's possible, but I don't think probable," says Thomas.

"What about the house next door?" Sarah readjusts the towel.

"Same situation, I think," replies Thomas.

"I was talking to Rosie Klempler last weekend in Goostree's, and I asked her if she remembered Esther Peterson. I got this unusual frown from her, which prompted me to ask if she disliked Esther. I knew Esther, years older than Rosie, as always courteous to fellow parishioners. Rosie said it was because her husband had been spending a lot of time at church functions, and Esther always seemed to be present. While Godfrey is probably ten years older than Rosie, he's considerably younger than Esther. He was draft-deferred and matched with Rosie by an organization helping ladies displaced by the war, especially from Germany. I reminded Rosie that Esther had been the church secretary, however, Rosie didn't see it that simply. She told me that at one point, when she saw Arnold Peterson uptown, she asked him if he was happy with his wife spending all her time at church. She said she told him that her husband was spending too much time at St. Mary's, too, and she didn't like it. She didn't say what Mr. Peterson's response was." Thomas scratches an ear.

"Seems like petty jealousy to me," Thomas suggests. "I know many times I felt lonely when you were at St. Mary's,"

"Thank you, dear. It was lonely without you, too," replies Sarah.

"Anyway, you sidetracked me. The owners of the land survey property are Arnold and Esther Peterson, jointly."

"Where do we go now?" asks Sarah.

"Nowhere. Sooner or later the probate court will make a decision. I'm not concerned about the lake property. Even if Esther shows up, Gary, the Petersons' son, should inherit one-half of the estate, and Windhurst tells me Gary's share will be the house next door—he's committed to carrying through the rental and sale agreement we have. I'll stay on George's good side and play along with his silly old phonograph record requests."

"Let me finish dressing. I must look a fright in this housecoat and not wearing a wig."

"You'd look divine, with or without the housecoat."

"Oh, now I've figured it out! You want us to live next door by ourselves, leaving Wanda to live here in this apartment. Then you'd have me all to yourself."

"I always said you were smart. Pretty, too."

"You need to get back to work," says Sarah. "And wipe that silly grin off your face. By the way, I'll be gone from one to three this afternoon for a St. Ann's meeting."

All afternoon the clink and clank of metal was heard as Thomas worked in the basement. The small job-press piston labored mightily—impression, release, impression, and release.

Sarah sat in St. Mary's church hall at a table with six other women planning activities to support an overseas mission appeal. Following a diocesan outline, the project was completed smoothly.

Hilda Swanson and Sarah are the last two present. The two, Hilda graduating high school a year after Sarah, have been friends for years and Hilda's daughter, Sharon, is Wanda's best friend.

"Sarah, do you mind if I smoke?" Hilda asks. "I've tried to quit repeatedly, but I can never last long."

Sarah is envious of Hilda's five-foot ten-inch height and her constant 120-pound weight. Only their brunette hair color is the same, but Hilda's is natural. Sarah likes Hilda's vivacious, although occasionally reticent, personality and does not repeat gossip that Hilda is an overly prim and proper clotheshorse.

"No problem. Tell me, are you excited about Sharon's wedding to Roger?" asks Sarah clearing away revised worksheets from the church hall table where they sit.

"It's a lot of work, but it's coming together. I'd be surprised if there was no last-minute snafu. I'm glad I don't have to worry about Sharon looking good at the wedding."

Sarah has first hand observations that Hilda has kept her cosmetology skills earned in a two-year course completed after high school graduation. Sarah had patronized the Clinton beauty shop Hilda started at, but Hilda only worked there six months before she married and became a full time homemaker.

"What's Sharon going to do after she's married? Will she still work at the bank?" asks Sarah.

Hilda moves her ashtray away from Sarah. "No, Roger is going to expand his auto repair business in conjunction with the service station. They're going to live over on Fourth Street. If she works at all, it will only be until the first of the year. Then she'll be a full time homemaker."

"That's fantastic, Hilda; her to be a homemaker. You brought her up right."

"I'm proud of her. There are so many distractions today. I know America has to change. While we've more modern appliances to help at home that shouldn't change our values. You must be careful with what's on TV or what books are sold in stores or even in the public library." Hilda notices Sarah nod, and continues, "The Winterville High School, where my husband teaches, last week had a controversy over a book assigned to be an English reading. My son, luckily, has a more responsible teacher."

"You're absolutely right, Hilda." Sarah refills a stapler.

"I recently had to scold Sharon. After her engagement shower, when all the girls had left, I found that single-girl sex book by Helen Brown in the living room."

Sarah suddenly looks horrified. Wanda was at Sharon's engagement shower.

"Sharon said I was old-fashioned," Hilda stops to verify Sarah and her are still alone. "Sharon said the Pill being invented has changed everything. After we talked a while, I think she finally understood how dangerous that book was."

"You're absolutely right. I don't think the birth control pill benefits anyone. The only good thing is that since it came into being three years ago, it's been available only to married women. I'm glad Sharon will follow your example to build a strong family home. I see on TV where all these women want to give up the home to work full time. Who's going to rear our children and teach them the values of right and wrong and prepare them for life?" asks Sarah.

"Aren't you part of this new wave? You work."

"It's different, very different, Hilda. I haven't left the home. I still work full time as a homemaker. Monday and Tuesday I help to make Thomas' life easier. I don't get paid or clamor in front of TV cameras. It's a sacrifice I willingly make. When other people say thanks or are pleased with the recognition the paper gives to their good works, that gives me a happy feeling."

"I see what you mean. You're a strong woman, Sarah. You can be humble, too. I've seen it," says Hilda, crushing her cigarette.

"Between us, to this day it causes me pain that I've never done everything my mother said I should do," admits Sarah.

"I hope Sharon does everything I've taught her, but I won't be surprised if she fails to. I never did everything my mother told me."

"What did you do, if I may ask?" Sarah slides her chair slightly to fully face Hilda. "It must have caused you so much sadness."

"It did at first. I remember one time I talked to Father Murphy about how I had felt."

"You did!" exclaims Sarah.

"I'm embarrassed, but I know you won't gossip. As a teenage girl, on a dare, I took off all my clothes at the beach when boys were there. I exposed everything from head to toe including private parts in between. No boy touched me, but my mother found out from one of the boys' mothers, who overheard her son and his two friends wondering if all naked girls show hair below the waist. I couldn't lie and I was restricted and fed only bread and water for a week. My father, with his hand, tanned my rear, hard."

"But you talked to Father Murphy? Why?" asks Sarah.

"He was talking to another circle about the need for a safe place for kids to keep their growing minds focused on following the Commandments and away from the world's evil temptations. He made reference to a movie in the theater that was condemned as C-rated by the Catholic Legion of Decency because of sexual language and full female frontal nudity. He said nudity, except between husband and wife, was a sin. And any child who disobeyed his or her parents to go to the movie was sinning against the fourth commandment to honor one's father and mother. I felt so ashamed of failing my mother—the beach dare. I found him alone in the hall kitchen and asked him if there was hope of salvation for one who sins, like he had said, or was the person forever condemned?"

"What did he say?" asks Sarah, eagerness in her voice.

"He said we must believe that God is compassionate. He sees all, but if one prays, forgiveness can be had. It might not be instantaneous. The goal is to keep trying, not to despair if one is not always perfect. He said the Bible says Jesus proclaims that if you follow him, the promised happiness will be with him in heaven, if not in this world."

"How can you not feel worthless when you fail to meet what is expected, what you're taught?" Sarah tries hard not to stare.

"You can't. You could if you were perfect, but no one is. I've convinced myself that one should not look to the past or the future; you live only in the present. You live for today, period. That's all— nothing more, nothing less."

Hilda takes the last puff of her second cigarette. "Sarah, I must go. I have to keep a florist appointment."

"I look forward to the wedding. It should be beautiful."

Later, in her kitchen, Sarah had wiped the last soapy dinner dish before Wanda and Myron arrive. Wanda appears apprehensive.

Sarah smiles. "Hi, Myron. Want to sit in the kitchen or parlor?"

"Kitchen works." He scans the floor behind to be sure his boots are not leaving any dirt trail.

"Thomas, Myron and Wanda are here," calls Sarah. She turns to the two young people. "I think he's catching up on the late news broadcast."

An upbeat Thomas enters the kitchen. "Hi, Myron. Hi, Wanda." Perceiving an anxious Wanda, he asks, "How's everyone?"

"Fine, Daddy."

"I'm good, Mr. Hamilton."

"So, what is it the two of you want to talk about?" asks Thomas as they take seats around the table. Myron sits next to Wanda.

"Well," Wanda begins, "Myron and I were out to Sand Lake last evening—"

"What?" interrupts Thomas, irritation spewing forth. Wanda waits. Myron does not move his hands from his lap.

Breaking the silence, Wanda softly continues, "Myron learned about the land survey you found. We were curious and went out to Sand Lake to see what we could see. We knew where Mr. Oswald's cabin was and had no problem finding the property next door. What a jungle we saw."

"Was there anything special about the place?" Thomas asks, less agitated. Sarah sighs.

"There was. You tell them, Myron."

Myron's caught off guard. He clears his throat. "Well, let's see. It was hard to walk through the bramble, but we did, starting from the shoreline. Then we came into a small open space. That's where Wanda stepped backward into a hole, and she heard wood crack. I looked at the ground, and it was about three inches of dirt over wood." Wanda is shaking her head up and down. Sarah sits there speechless, rubbing her hands.

"I checked two other spots, one close by and one farther away," explains Myron. "The dirt was about two to three inches deep with wood underneath in those places, too. I tapped my flashlight against the wood, and there was this hollow sound. It was dark by then, so we decided we needed to get out of there."

"What do you think, Thomas?" Sarah is inwardly comforted that she did not hear any engagement news.

Thomas shakes his head in disbelief. "Tell me more about the wood sound, Myron," he asks.

"It was really weird," replies Myron. "There was something strange. I did not expect buried wood. If an old pallet, there would have been gaps between boards. Any storage box I'm familiar with at the Elevator would be smaller. Wanda was right when she called it a jungle. No one is going to be walking through there. Other than an old fire pit on the shoreline, Mr. Hamilton, there was no sign that anybody has been there recently." Myron peeks at Wanda.

"That confirms what Gordie Oswald told me," offers Thomas. "He said he has never seen a neighbor there. Myron, you've added another unknown to the letters, G and O, on the land survey, and ownership by Old Man Peterson. You need to show the sheriff what you've found—and do it quickly." Myron and Wanda exchange puzzled looks on hearing these two bits of information.

"You mean, I should call the sheriff?" asks Myron nervously.

"Well, I could call for you tomorrow morning. You need to tell your boss about your visit. He'll appreciate knowing that the sheriff might be prowling near his lake cabin."

"Are you sure, Thomas?" asks Sarah, hoping to seem matter-of-fact. "That Mr. Johnston—do you think he will be here again?"

Thomas nods. "Yeah, I'm sure he will be."

Sarah tenses, and then distracts her mind by offering everyone something to eat. "Myron, would you like a slice of banana bread?"

"That would be awesome, Mrs. Hamilton."

Chapter Twenty-nine

"Sheriff, I know you're busy, but this is important." Thomas struggles for the right persuasive words without begging.

"Thomas, what do you say I get Charles over there today to have a look. I know it's Saturday, but he's still around. From what you're telling me, it could be anything. I'll get back to you in a few minutes."

Thomas hangs up the phone and turns to see Sarah pacing the kitchen floor for no apparent reason.

"Thomas, what did the sheriff say?"

"He said he was extremely busy. He's going to get Mr. Johnston to investigate. I'm supposed to wait for a call."

"What about the deputy?" asks Sarah, pacing.

"Didn't think to ask. If Johnston can't come, I'll ask Jonathan about the availability of his deputy."

"You'll get soaked if you wait too long. Sky appears threatening."

"Is Wanda up yet?" Thomas asks.

"Think so. I heard her close the bathroom door a few minutes ago. What about Myron?"

"We're going to pick him up at the old factory; he wanted to work on his glider while he waited. I wish there was a telephone there. That would save time."

Wanda enters the kitchen and draws stares from her parents.

"Where's the party, Wanda?" asks Thomas with a smile. "I haven't seen you wearing so much makeup since you went to Sharon's engagement shower." Sarah shoots Thomas a penetrating glare. He guesses he has crossed some unwritten boundary. Quickly, Thomas says, "I'm waiting for the sheriff to get back to me right now to check out that hole you stepped in at Sand Lake."

"At least my jeans didn't get a second hole in them, like near the old factory," quips Wanda, failing to be funny. The ring of the telephone saves her from having to comment on her makeup.

"*Pioneer Ledger*. This is Thomas. Yes, Charles. Okay, forty-five minutes at the driveway to the Oswald place at Sand Lake. Got it. See you shortly."

"Was that Mr. Johnston?" asks Sarah.

"Yes. He's going to substitute for the sheriff. It's almost ten. If we leave here in twenty minutes we can stop to pick up Myron and still have plenty of time to hook up with Mr. Johnston at Sand Lake."

"Wanda, you want some toast? A banana?" asks Sarah.

"Maybe a banana. I don't feel like eating much."

"Thomas, you want a refill on your coffee?"

"Sure. Are you coming?"

"No, you go with Wanda and Myron. I'm going to stay here—I have things to do. I'll be ready with a late lunch when you get back."

"You sure, dear?" probes Thomas.

"Yes. I won't mind missing my chance to walk through bramble. Please take an umbrella or two."

"My raincoat is in the closet. How about you, Wanda?"

"I have a jacket with a hood," replies Wanda.

"Then let's go." Thomas kisses Sarah on her cheek.

"Good luck," says Sarah, watching from the backdoor as Thomas and Wanda leave, rain gear in hand.

In a matter of minutes, Thomas stops at the old factory. Wanda jumps from the front passenger seat and dashes past the sliding door.

"Ready to go?" she asks.

"In a sec," says Myron. "You look pretty for going into the woods. No, that came out wrong. You're always pretty, but today you look extra-special pretty."

"Kiss me, quick."

"Why?"

"Before my Dad gets in here."

Myron needs no second request. He gives Wanda a quick kiss before turning away from her. He spies Thomas standing at the entrance to the factory. "Hi, Mr. Hamilton. I'm ready. I need to wipe my face to get the dust off."

Wanda smiles, somewhat coyly.

"So that's your glider. Looks pretty impressive."

"Thank you, Mr. Hamilton."

"When will it be ready to fly?" Thomas walks past the nose.

"I don't think before the winter snow, but definitely by spring."

"How many can fly in it at one time?" asks Thomas.

"Just the pilot. There's no room for passengers."

"Interesting." Thomas gazes at Wanda. "I think we should be leaving now. We can talk in the car on the way."

On the seven mile trip to Oswald's place at Sand Lake, Thomas tells Myron of his call to the Sheriff and that the Sheriff sent Mr. Johnston in his place. Myron says he told his boss, Mr. Oswald, about his and Wanda's foray into the neighbor's jungle and about finding a mysterious hole.

"He said he's catching up on Elevator paperwork and chores at his house," says Myron. "He told me where to find a cabin key he said he hides at the lake, in case we need to use a phone."

"Here we are," says Thomas, announcing their arrival at the Oswald mailbox. "We could drive in, but let's wait on the shoulder for Mr. Johnston. Myron, didn't you say the best way to get to this hole is to come from the shoreline?"

"I don't know if it's the best, but that's the way we went."

"I see dust kicking up down the road. That must be Mr. Johnston. Stay in the car; I'll tell Mr. Johnston to follow us to the cabin." With that, Thomas is out of the car to stand by the brick pillar near the drive. He waves. The approaching Chevy 210 slows to a stop. Charles rolls down his driver-side window.

"Good morning, Charles."

"Same to you, Thomas. Tell me, what kind of adventure are we on today?"

"The kids found some mysterious hole with wood in this overgrown lot owned by Arnold Peterson. It's the property you checked up on in the county recorder's office. Follow me up the driveway to Oswald's cabin. That'll get us closer to the shoreline, where the kids went into the woods."

"Lead the way," replies Johnston, shifting car gears.

At the cabin, everyone gathers and Thomas makes introductions. "Mr. Johnston, this here is my daughter Wanda, and her friend, Myron Goostree."

"Good morning," says Charles. "Myron Goostree—that name rings a bell. Are you related to the grocery store owner in Clinton?"

"That's my father. He's senior. I'm junior."

"Weren't you the young man who found the brick with the letters at the old factory—and the bones?"

"I found the brick; little Oscar Anderson found the skeleton."

"This property to the west looks like it would be hard to walk through. I've a hatchet and shovel in the trunk," says Johnston.

"Yes, I have a small spade in my trunk," says Thomas. They each retrieve their tools; Myron leads the way, walking toward the shoreline. It quickly becomes single file, with Johnston second, Thomas third, and Wanda. At the shoreline, Myron makes a left turn.

"We should go in near the fire pit," suggests Myron.

"Did you use the pit when you were here?" asks Johnston.

"No. We had a bag of marshmallows and were going to, but darkness came too fast." Johnston nudges a briquette with his shoe.

"Did you see anybody? Anybody see you?"

"No. We heard a distant motor, but never saw the boat."

"The shoreline is rock hard. Did you happen to see any object that you would not have expected or that looked out of place?"

"Not I. Wanda, did you see anything the other night?"

"No, Myron. Not here on the shoreline," says Wanda softly.

Charles had intently watched Thomas, as the latter walked gingerly along the shore. Charles makes a mental note that Thomas had not said one word since departing from the cars.

"Here's where we went in," Myron interrupts Charles' thoughts. "See those broken branches between the two trees?" he says, stopping and pointing his hand to his left.

"Let me step in front of you, Myron. I need a closer look," says Johnston, taking charge. He kneels down, checking the opening: back and forth, left and right, up and down. His notepad remains in his pocket. "Myron, I will go ahead," he directs, speaking over his shoulder. "You stay close behind me and keep me retracing how you went in. I'll keep the hatchet; you take this shovel."

Again, single file, Johnston first, they push back the two broken branches between the trees to enter the thicket and bramble.

Wanda thinks about, but doesn't put her fingers into her father's belt loop. She hears the wind rustling through the trees before it dies down. A twig snaps. Wanda's entire body tenses. She relaxes, and worried about running into a skunk or a bear, takes a tentative step forward. *Why did I have to come?* She wonders. *Why did I have to come?*

"So how far ahead is this clearing?" asks Johnston.

"We're almost there," says Myron, but he is guessing.

"I see it," exclaims Johnston. In minutes, the four are standing in the clearing.

"I see uprooted weeds to my left. Is that the spot?"

"Yes," replies Myron.

"You all stay right where you are. I'm going to check this area out myself."

The three stand silent. The wind picks up again. A gust, Thomas estimates to be twenty miles per hour, blows his signalman's hat off his head. *The predicted storm must be coming*, Thomas thinks.

"Myron, I'm going to need you with that shovel," Johnston calls out.

Myron almost tiptoes to where Johnston is standing; next to one clump of weeds Myron pulled out the night Wanda stepped into a hole. In the daylight, he has a better look. The hole is only about five inches in diameter, two inches deep. The rotted board Wanda stepped on is at the bottom of the hole.

Johnston takes a camera from his jacket pocket. He snaps pictures from three different angles before putting the camera back into his pocket. "Myron, take your shovel and scrap off the dirt, starting from where the hole is over toward where this clump of weeds has been pulled out. Be careful when you do it."

Myron follows directions. Slowly, he slides the shovel into the ground to scoop up a mixture of dirt and weeds.

"Put the dirt behind you," directs Johnston. "Off to the side; that's good. Now, do the same thing all over again."

Myron continues his task. Thomas and Wanda watch intently, never moving their feet. Thomas hails Johnston. "Want my shovel?"

"No. Not right now. I need to know much more without disturbing everything too much."

Inch by inch, Myron unearths what looks like the top of a wooden box. It is at least eighteen inches in one direction and getting close to five feet in another. Johnston's interest deepens as he watches the pile of dirt and weeds grows ever higher.

"Myron, stop there for a minute. Take away some of the dirt on this end. The box, or whatever it is, looks wider than what you've scrapped off so far, but stop for now."

Myron leans on his shovel. Johnston takes the blade end of his hatchet and slides it under the still-fastened end of a piece of wood. Slowly, with a creak, it splinters as Johnston fails to pry loose the four-inch wide board in one piece. Finally, the end is free, and he pulls it upward. The board is broken where Wanda had stepped on it. Johnston reaches into his pants pocket for a penlight. He casts its beam into the darkness.

"Oh, my god," he mutters.

Myron is close enough to hear. Thomas and Wanda are unaware.

"Wanda, we found something!" shouts Myron.

"What? What?"

"Myron, hold on there. Let's be calm," says Johnston.

"Mr. Johnston, what exactly is it? What's there?" asks Myron, leaning over, trying to get a better look.

"Looks like ... bones." Johnston enunciates slowly, "Bones big enough to be human bones."

"Oh, no!"

"Let's join the other two," Johnston suggests. "Be careful where you step. Try to follow the same footprints you've already made. I'll be right behind you."

"What is going on?" Thomas calls out. "What is there?"

Johnston ignores the question, "We need to get ready for rain. Looks like the predicted thunderstorms aren't far away."

"Charles, what did you find? Tell me, or I'll go see for myself," Thomas says insistently.

"Thomas, there were bones. Human bones. What I saw looks like a foot bone, and there was another bone, a shorter, smaller one."

"Could they be animal?" asks Thomas. Wanda covers her mouth.

"I'd bet you a week's pay it was not an animal bone I saw. We need to cover it up again to protect it. And we're going to need more than a rain jacket, judging by the look of that sky."

"We can go back to Oswald's place. I remember seeing a tarp over an old rowboat along the side of the cabin. I'm sure he won't mind if we borrow it."

"Great idea, Thomas. I'll stay here. You three go back and get that tarp. Don't forget any rope. If there is anything to weigh it down, bring that, too. While you're gone, I'll cut down a branch to make makeshift stakes we can tie the tarp to. Now hurry."

Myron takes the lead; they struggle to backtrack to Oswald's cabin. Thomas stumbles once, but he quickly recovers. When they reach the cabin, they quickly remove the tarp and refold it. It's heavy, but Myron offers to carry it on his shoulder.

"Mr. Hamilton, can you take the section of rope and the twine?"

"Yes, Myron."

"Myron, there are scattered bricks over here, if you need something to add weight," interjects Wanda.

"I'll grab four," says Thomas. "Myron, let's get back to Mr. Johnston before we get drenched." Lightning flashes in the distance. "Wanda, you stay here at the cabin. The small awning over the door should keep you dry. Take my car keys."

"Okay."

Again, Myron leads. He keeps peering over his shoulder to make sure Mr. Hamilton is not too far behind.

"You guys are back quick," shouts Johnston, as the two re-emerge from the bramble. He is squatting on the ground, trying to shave a point to a branch he had hacked off a nearby tree.

They all go to the digging site where Thomas gets his first look at the broken board. He tries to see through a crack to what is underneath, but it is too small, and the darkness hides what is beneath the replaced board.

"This tarp works just fine," says Johnston. "Thomas, toss me a piece of rope. Thanks. These stakes should hold down the corners."

"I have these four bricks," says Thomas, "to weight it down."

"Good idea," snorts Johnston, reaching out a hand. "Boy, these bricks look familiar."

"Nothing special," replies Thomas. "Oswald probably had them left over after building those pillars that stand near the township road. Everyone has bricks. More bricks per square mile than people."

"Guess you're right. Are we going to beat the rain?"

"If we're fast."

"We've done the best we can. Let's get to the cars."

With that, the male trio strikes out for the Sand Lake shoreline and the two-parked cars—and in the nick of time as the rain starts, lightning flashes, and thunder claps. Thomas is momentarily concerned when he doesn't see Wanda under the cabin awning. He's relieved to find her already in his car, stretched out on the backseat.

Johnston jumps into the front passenger seat of Thomas' car. Myron gets in the back, next to Wanda; his hand pushes her foot off the seat.

"Thomas," says Johnston, "we need to contact the sheriff as quickly as possible to let him know what we found. This rain is not going to help, seeing that we opened up the ground somewhat."

"Let's go back to my place," Thomas suggests. "We could try to call the Sheriff from Oswald's cabin, but he won't want to traipse under wet trees and through bramble and we probably should leave that tarp where it is until the rain stops."

"Sounds like a good plan to me." Johnston dashes back to his car, and as he pulls his driver-side door closed, he thinks it is also a good thing that he'll be able to observe Sarah Hamilton. He wants to see her reaction to this news of more human bones.

Chapter Thirty

Sarah wipes down the kitchen counter, and then pushes aside hangers to locate her bright yellow, full-length raincoat in the closet. With the raincoat draped over her arm, she tucks the grocery list into her purse, ready for her trip to Goostree's.

"Hi, Sarah," Myron, Sr., behind his store's front counter, greets her as she enters. "Looking for anything special today?" he smiles.

"Just a few staples. I have to walk home."

The bell above the front door chimes twice. Myron and Sarah both look toward the door.

"Hi, Rosie," say Sarah and Myron, almost in unison.

Myron turns back to Sarah. "Check out the squash. Just arrived, locally grown." He hesitates momentarily, and then says, "Say, I've heard certain townspeople mention while shopping you're solving the mystery of who killed Father Murphy."

"Who told you that?" asks Sarah, abruptly turning to Myron, Sr.

Rosie interrupts, "I didn't like Father Murphy. He thought he could do anything he wanted, even if the diocese told him no. If someone needed to talk to a priest, he would be nice in the beginning, but then he'd turn his attention away. Anyway, that's what I was told."

"I never heard that Rosie," blurts out a surprised Myron.

"If you ask me, we should stop talking about Father Murphy," says Sarah, her throat tightening. "He may have had secrets—any priest would—but he was required to keep confidences."

"Odds are being given at the café that the 'priest killer' is going to kill again," Myron says. "But this time, it might not be a priest. Since Vatican II's new church rules two years ago, priests dress in street clothes—without the collar. A priest could easily be mistaken for an ordinary citizen and be a robber's target, like anybody else."

Rosie shrugs and turns to go down an aisle. Sarah shakes her head and soon follows. Myron trails after them, still wanting to chat.

"What happened to your eye, Rosie?" asks Sarah as Rosie stops to inspect an item on a shelf.

Medical tape had been stretched across a white gauze patch over Rosie's right eye. Discolored skin peeks out from under the edge of the patch. "Got a sty. Puss caused my eyelid to stick shut. To quit rubbing it, I put this patch on."

"Hope it heals fast."

"Same here," joins in Myron, Sr.

"Thanks to you both."

Myron turns to Rosie again. "I was praising Sarah the last time she was in here for her efforts to solve the mystery of Father Murphy's death. The killer had to leave an identifying clue. I don't have much faith in Sheriff O'Day, although I like him, to discover it. He mistook the factory bones for Esther Peterson's." Neither woman responds. Myron, undeterred, decides to try a different tack, "I think all you ladies liked Father Murphy because of his good looks. If he hadn't been a priest, I bet he would have been considered quite the catch as a husband."

"He was handsome," Rosie agrees. "And it's terrible that he died. I wouldn't be surprised if some woman didn't killed him."

Sarah fidgets, feeling uncomfortable with the remarks about marriage and Father Murphy. She distracts herself by rummaging in her purse before saying, "I don't think Father Murphy purposely made an enemy with his desire to build the gym. I find it hard to believe trying to remember where bake sale money went and finding old bulletins, as I've been asked to do, might help the Sheriff find the killer."

"You might get this town back to normal," says Myron. "It has been too gruesome around here lately. All the black humor."

Sarah wants to extricate herself from this conversation. "Rosie, excuse me, I need to get a few things and get home. Hope your eye heals real fast." She quickly moves down the aisle and finds the sugar, muffin mix, bread, and luncheon meat on her shopping list.

"No squash?" Myron calls out to her.

"Maybe next time." Sarah glances above the sale signs out the front windows before pulling paper money from her purse. "I'd better hurry home or I'll have these groceries ruined by the rain."

"Say hello to Thomas and Wanda for me, please," says Myron.

Sarah nods. The bell above the door chimes as she exits.

The clouds are definitely ominous. Lucky for Sarah, her route is short, and today, the street is deserted.

It had been a short walk the night when she last saw Father Murphy. The memories are still vivid. She replays in her mind the brief events of that day. …

She had left the *Pioneer Ledger* a little after sunset. All she wanted to do was take a brief walk. The day had been beautiful—

clear skies and warm—in strong contrast to the past month of cold and ice.

She'd been longing to get outside, to breathe the fresh evening air. It had been earlier in the day that she'd learned a friend needed major surgery.

She hadn't expected to see anyone; she walked rather aimlessly, without purpose. As she came around the corner of the block where St. Mary's Catholic Church stood, she saw the church lights were out.

She kept walking. The door to the rectory garage was open, but she didn't see anyone. Then she heard a voice. Father Murphy was standing in the shadows.

"Sarah, please come in," he'd whispered. She slowed her steps, feeling a rising sluggishness in her legs. *I have a husband to think of,* she'd told herself. *I have gone through enough. I do not want to be alone with Father Murphy, ever.* The anguish seared her soul, and the scarring of her emotions left sleepless nights. Her psyche was not whole—she did not want to relive the past.

"Please, Sarah," he whispered. "I need to talk to you."

She felt pulled forward as if by some overwhelming force—*a spirit I could not see or touch seemed to push me forward.*

For a third time, she heard him, "Sarah, please come in."

She stepped inside the garage and immediately heard the overhead garage door come down. Father Murphy stood in the dim light by the door leading into the rectory.

"Step closer," he encouraged her. "Soon the light will be out."

"I'll stay here," she had said, her hand on his car for support.

"Please, come in. I offer no harm."

"I don't want to be here," she remembered insisting. "You don't know what you did to me when I closed my eyes to obeying God's Commandments. I took pleasure in the flesh; God-given free will let my body enjoy a moment of forbidden lust. I do not compare myself with Eve, only that when Eve tasted the forbidden fruit, she was cast out of Eden, together with Adam, as both were stained with original sin. I have new life from God. Life you created. Adam suffered along with Eve. Now, only I feel the torment, the shame, and the anguish of having to hide my failure to abide by the vows of sacred marriage. From that Sunday afternoon I have suffered, and it is unrelenting." She took a step backward and glanced around for a way to get out. "God took his revenge on three of us: me, the unborn life that had been growing within my womb, and my precious daughter, Melissa, a total innocent. He gave the doctors reason to cut out my ability to conceive again. One moment. Two vehicles. Two paths. One collision. God knows I have confessed my sins. I continue to pray for forgiveness. I only hope I can continue to hide the past and keep living with the burden of my sins."

I saw Father Murphy extend his hand. "Sarah, you can't shoulder this burden all by yourself. If only I could change myself—exorcise the demons from my soul. I pray every day that I will be given the strength to return to the vows I made when becoming a priest. We humans are not perfect. God has given us free will. He has given us the grace necessary to lead a moral life and has called upon his angels to help us. Jesus died on the cross for you and me."

She stood silently, head bent forward, eyes cast to the floor. An observer might have thought she was praying, but she wasn't. Her fear of being this close to him was conflicting.

"Sarah, I cannot change our past together. I only stand here asking that you believe me when I tell you to be careful, to watch out for your life."

She couldn't believe her ears. "Watch out for my life?" She felt her knees would buckle, as her mind started swirling.

"Sarah? Sarah, are you all right? I don't want to cause any further harm, but you must listen to me. Heed my word. I have misplaced money I hid from the diocese so St. Mary's could build our gymnasium for the kids. When Esther Peterson went missing last year, I thought she'd taken the money. She and I had had many private discussions about church finances, and I trusted her completely. But she has been gone for almost a year." Father Murphy shook his head. "Now, more money is missing. I'm not sure who's taking it, but it seems to me someone opposes my goal to build a gym. It may not be simple thievery but a plan to discredit me, to make me out a crook."

"Why you telling me this?" she asked, her voice barely audible.

"Sarah, you must believe me. You need to protect yourself. Guard your life." He took a small step away from the door to the rectory. "You can walk through the rectory kitchen and out the backdoor. You will have a better chance to get safely home if someone followed you."

But Sarah had refused. She didn't want to be alone in the rectory with Father Murphy, nor walk past him. She asked him to press the garage door opener so she could go back out the way she came in.

A day or two later, she learned Father Murphy was missing. She had remembered his words of warning for her safety.

A clap of thunder jars Sarah back to the present. She realizes it is not the high humidity that has caused her blouse to show perspiration.

Chapter Thirty-one

Sarah, we're home."

Lying on her bed atop the covers in the clothes she wore grocery shopping, she had heard the backdoor open before the greeting and dashes into the bathroom, flushes the toilet, and grabs a towel to wipe her face.

"I'm coming," Sarah replies, walking into the kitchen. A pot of soup, straight from the can, simmers on the stove's back burner.

"Sarah, I've invited Mr. Johnston, here, to share lunch with us. We're all a little damp from the thunderstorm outside."

"I hope it's no burden," says Johnston, standing behind Thomas.

She shakes her head. "Please take a seat at the table. There's chicken noodle soup ready on the stove and I can make sandwiches. What would you like to drink, Mr. Johnston?"

"Coffee or water, whatever's convenient." He removes his jacket.

"Fruit drink for me," says Thomas.

Wanda and Myron enter the kitchen. "Hi, Mom, guess what—we found more bones at the lake," Wanda says excitedly.

Sarah becomes deathly still. Her lips part, but she does not speak a word. Johnston watches her without trying to stare.

"Good afternoon, Mrs. Hamilton," says Myron.

Sarah requires a second or two before her words finally come out. "Both of you need to hang up your wet jackets on the wall hooks inside the backdoor. They need to dry out fully and not drip all over the kitchen." Johnston rises to follow them with his jacket.

"Yes, Mom," replies Wanda. "Did you hear me? We found more bones at Sand Lake."

"I did hear you, Wanda. First, hang up your jacket."

Sarah ladles chicken noodle soup into bowls and begins making sandwiches. Johnston continues to observe her as she bustles about the kitchen. He senses nothing out of the ordinary, except her initial reluctance to hear about the bones.

"Sarah, we've got another front page story for next week's *Pioneer Ledger*," begins Thomas. "Myron led us back to the hole on the land survey lot at Sand Lake where Wanda stumbled. That was where, after some digging, we found more bones. Human bones."

Sarah's feeling slightly faint. She takes a sip of water and asks, "What are you going to do now? Are you sure what you found were human bones?"

"Oh yes, they were human bones," speaks up Johnston. "Everyone here has to promise not to talk about this until we get the Sheriff updated." Heads nod "yes." Johnston continues, "The box we found was too big to have been a casket for some pet. I would venture a guess that the box was formerly some sort of equipment crate. One of the top boards had a faded shipping stamp imprint. We might be able to determine where the box came from by that imprint. Somebody went to a great deal of trouble to hide that box from being found." He wipes a napkin across his lips and pushes back his chair. "Sarah, lunch was delicious. Thomas, can I use your office telephone? I need to call Sheriff O'Day."

"Straight through this door," Thomas points to a door. "Down the hall, last door on your right. Telephone is on the desk."

"Thanks. I won't be long." Johnston exits the kitchen.

"Thomas, this is getting more serious all the time," says Sarah. "More bones. The first discovery has been giving me bad dreams."

"Mom, how do you think I feel?" whines Wanda. "People in this town will think I'm a jinx—all these discoveries of bones taking place near where I have been." Myron finishes his second sandwich.

"Wanda, you're overreacting," her father scoffs.

"I'm not overreacting. I think this town has some evil force."

"Thomas," says Sarah, ignoring her daughter, "do you think the box could be some prank by students burying a laboratory skeleton? You know, a way to scare unsuspecting classmates?"

"Sarah, I'd say no. There were no signs kids had visited the area—no bottles, pop cans, or candy or gum wrappers. Nothing one associates with kids. And, the land appeared abandoned."

"Well, maybe it was years ago," suggests Sarah. "Kids from past generations played pranks on each other, too."

Thomas shakes his head. "No, dear, I doubt it was a prank."

Johnston returns to the kitchen and waits until he has everyone's attention. "Sheriff O'Day has given this his highest priority. We are not to speak about this until he says so. He's dispatched his deputy to Sand Lake to guard against intruders and curiosity-seekers. In addition, a state crime lab crew will be there tomorrow to begin an investigation. I suspect a full examination of the property."

"Does the sheriff want to talk to any of us?" asks Thomas.

"I'm sure he does, but his first action was to protect the evidence. Just between us, I think Sheriff O'Day is concerned about panic. He fears someone went to a great deal of trouble to bury a body on that property. And that someone may react with the bones being unearthed." Johnston slowly turns toward the backdoor. "Anyway, you now know what's going to happen. I'll be leaving. Mrs. Hamilton, thank you for lunch."

"Mr. Johnston, here; please take this extra sandwich. You didn't eat much that I saw," says Sarah.

"Thanks. Thanks everyone." Johnston departs. Wanda escorts Myron into the Hamilton living room to watch television.

Moments later, Sarah hears a knock at the backdoor.

Thomas answers it. "Hi, Gordie. What can I do for you?"

"Good afternoon, Thomas. I hear you went out to Sand Lake today, to the overgrown property that's next to mine."

"Step inside," Thomas says, and he leads Gordon Oswald to the Hamilton kitchen table still covered with dishes.

"Hi, Sarah," says Oswald. "I'm sorry if I'm interrupting lunch."

"It's okay, we're finished," says Thomas. "Have a seat. Well, what brings you over? Like a cup of coffee?"

"No coffee for me, thanks. I was curious about your trip to Sand Lake. What did you find?" asks Oswald, taking a seat.

"Gordie, Investigator Johnston won't allow us to talk about our visit to Sand Lake. The sheriff has put a deputy at your driveway with orders to stop anyone who shows up."

"Damn!" Oswald's voice booms. "Damn that sheriff."

"Gordie, I'm only repeating what I was told," says Thomas.

"I know. But that sheriff! He's messing with me again. He stationed his deputy at the old factory and almost lost me a good sale. He's got some nerve blocking my cabin entrance."

"Gordie, it's for the best, let me tell you."

"Tell me what?" asks Oswald, placing his hands on the table.

"I'm sorry, bad choice of words. Forget I said it."

"I don't like it one bit; that Sheriff is meddling once too often. We'd all be happy if he would just stay in Winterville."

"Oh, I should tell you one thing," Thomas suddenly remembers. "When we were out there, Myron and I took the tarp you had covering your rowboat. We needed to use it. I hope you'll understand we meant no harm when this is all over with."

Oswald shakes his head. "No, I don't understand this at all. You can bet I'll be going out to my cabin tomorrow, and I hope Sheriff O'Day is there so I can give him a piece of my mind. He's messing with the wrong man." Oswald pounds a fist into his exposed palm.

"Gordie, please be calm. The whole town need not panic. We don't need more gossip. You'll feel better with a good night's rest."

"You're probably right. I'll be going now. Thanks."

"I'll see you to the door," offers Thomas.

Soon, Gordon Oswald's car is heard driving away.

"Thomas, Gordie sure was upset with the Sheriff. I don't know if you should have told him about the deputy."

"Sarah, I had to tell him. What if he would have gone out to his cabin tomorrow and unexpectedly ran into the Sheriff or deputy, who knows what might have happened. I don't know why the Sheriff thinks he has to seal off Gordie's property anyway. You can get to the Peterson land from the township road without ever stepping foot on Gordie's property."

"Either the Sheriff doesn't know that or he distrusts Gordie," insinuates Sarah. "If you ask me, Jonathan's in over his head. All this has given me a headache; I'm going to lie down."

Chapter Thirty-two

S heriff O'Day arrives at Sand Lake as the sun peeks above the horizon. His deputy, groggy from all night duty, welcomes the orders to go home.

At seven a.m., state crime technicians O'Day is waiting for drive down the township road in a panel truck behind Charles Johnston.

"Morning, Jonathan."

"Top of the morning, Charles. Where are these human bones you said you eyed yesterday?"

"Near the lakeside of this overgrown jungle. Best way means walking down the Oswald driveway until we get to the shoreline, turn left, and look for a small gap in the trees after the fire pit."

"Sand Lake has been a burial ground in the past," O'Day offers, "but it's been a watery burial ground with more than one body dumped in the lake. Any reason we're not using scuba divers?"

Johnston waves his arm to the two technicians standing next to their truck as he answers O'Day. "Because the killer didn't have a boat or wanted to confuse us. I don't know Jonathan; truth is the bones were buried on land." Johnston sees O'Day scowl as the technicians bring out shovels, a sifting box, small brushes, a hand trowel, and a body collection bag, in addition to their crime-solving toolkit.

Johnston and the sheriff walk towards the lab duo and offer to help carry the technicians' tools.

The four men find the staked tarp undisturbed except for rainwater pooled on it. Slowly and carefully, the four lift it up by the corners and lower it over the mound of dirt Myron had created. The rainwater is allowed to drain away.

The Sheriff and Johnston from a distance observe the technicians as they set to work. Johnston reaches into a pocket, removes his 35mm camera, and clicks off several pictures.

The four men in the clearing fail to notice the watching eyes of Gordon Oswald. Oswald, upon seeing vehicles in his driveway, had driven further down the township road to another cabin he knew would be unattended. He had parked in the neighbor's driveway and walked along the shoreline toward his cabin. Standing by the lake, he heard voices and hunched down behind a maple tree and saw the four men. The number of vehicles told him the Sheriff had come with friends—official friends, judging by the license plates on the van. The old Chevy 210 indicated Investigator Johnston was also present; more persons than one deputy Thomas had said would be at Sand Lake.

He follows the path past the two bent branches until almost to the clearing. He quietly sidesteps to the east to a position where he can get a glimpse of what is happening in the clearing. He stands perfectly still even as an eastern goldfinch sings above his head. He holds his breath until the songbird flutters away. He remains safely hidden from humans, if not birds.

In the clearing, the technicians are finished removing the dirt from the top of the wooden box. Johnston steps closer to confirm his recollection there is indeed a stamped symbol on one of the boards. "Product of USA" is all that Johnston can make out.

The top of the box itself is now fully visible. A technician is measuring it—sixty inches one way and forty-two inches the other, he announces. With a small crowbar, one technician loosens both ends of the boards constituting the top of the box.

The Sheriff endeavors to see into the hole. He hears Johnston say to a technician, "Do you see what I see?"

"There's more than one body in there," the technician answers.

"I think you're right," replies Johnston.

The second technician, wearing latex gloves, bends over to lift out of the box what the Sheriff recognizes as a pelvic bone. The bone is raised to face level by the technician to inspect all sides.

Oswald double checks to see that all persons in the clearing are focused on the bone before he, as quietly as he can, retraces his steps to the entry path and back to the shoreline. Confident he has not been detected, he jogs parallel to the lake, past his cabin, and to his car. *I need time to think*, he tells himself.

"Sheriff," asks one of the technicians, "can you go back to the van for a second body bag?"

"You betcha."

The technicians follow standard operating procedure: in order, taking pictures, noting the location of each bone in the box, and methodically tagging each bone or bone fragment before placing it in a body bag. They place only two bones in their second body bag.

The technicians replace the removed boards after identifying and removing all recognized human remains to one of the body bags. Oswald's tarp is also staked down over the box still in the hole.

Johnston and the Sheriff are instructed to secure the scene until the technicians can return later in the day with a truck big enough to transport the box without tipping it. Both help carry the two body bags to the technician's van where O'Day gives them directions to the funeral home in Winterville used by the county as its morgue.

"I'm thinking that the two bones the technicians separated out have something to do with the bones found in the old factory near Clinton," suggests Johnston.

"How so?" asks the Sheriff, checking his wristwatch.

"The two seem to match the bones missing from the priest's skeleton. Missing from the cistern were a pelvic bone and one other. That makes two. Right, Jonathan?" Johnston takes out his notepad.

"You're right, Charles. But now we've got a second body."

"I recall that the cistern skeleton had a ring on one finger."

The Sheriff nods. "Yeah, that Anderson boy, Oscar, told me he thought he had seen a ring on one bone. I was sure the ring meant the skeleton was Arnold Peterson's wife, but I was proven wrong when the dental records came back identifying Father Murphy."

"I wouldn't be so sure," says Johnston. "The mix-up in bones could have been someone's deliberate attempt to disguise the identity of the second person. Someone knew the priest was buried here, if he was, and tried to remove the priest's bones before putting in another body. It also would have been easy to miss a bone or two."

The Sheriff watches a car approach, and waits for it to pass before continuing. "That could make sense if it hadn't been for that ring. The second body had to have been fully decomposed before one hand bone was mistaken for another."

"Not if the hand of the second victim had been severed," suggests Johnston." He notices a grimace on the Sheriff's face.

"You may be right. We've got to let the crime boys tell us. They should be able to identify any telltale marks that a hand was chopped off. I'm concerned the second person may be an unreported missing person."

"Let's not go there yet Jonathan; did you see bricks in the box?"

"No, but I didn't get a clear look into the corners of the box as I was staying back and out of the way. Did you?"

"No. I was at more of a disadvantage than you."

"You want to stay here first, or should I?" asks Johnston.

"You stay here," says the Sheriff. "And I'll bring us back food. How much time did you spend yesterday checking behind the tree line around the perimeter of the clearing?"

"Not much. We had to hustle to protect the box from the thunderstorm coming." Johnston feels his pocket for a pen.

"Okay, then. I'll check on the delivery of the body bags to the Winterville funeral home and will stop to get us takeout hamburgers. We can look around this property further. I'll be quick."

"I'll try to put new ideas in my notebook. I'll be here."

An hour later, two vehicles approach him from the west. The second one, a red pickup, slows, but does not stop. He pays no heed.

Johnston continues to analyze what has been found this day, along with what he knows about the bones of Father Murphy. *Perhaps now his boss will give greater priority to the work he is doing to find the killer of the Clinton priest.* The only apparent common denominator between the priest's bones and the current discovery is Arnold Peterson. Peterson owned the non-functioning factory. He and his wife, Esther, owned this property on Sand Lake—his wife may still own it, if she's alive. She was church secretary when Father Murphy was the pastor. There was a little more than a year between when she was said to have disappeared and Father Murphy was said to have left.

Johnston pages back through his notepad for more details. He keeps being stymied by one fact he cannot fit neatly into his equation: the bricks found in the cistern at the factory.

The letters on the one brick could be the initials of Gordon Oswald, Elevator manager. He had access to the factory, his Sand Lake property is next door to the Petersons', and he knew no one ever used the property. There are bricks used in Oswald's lake property driveway pillars that match those found in the cistern. Johnston then realizes the bricks are all too common—Oswald having that kind of brick isn't probative of anything.

What motive does Oswald have? He thinks of only one motive: he must have feared being exposed—he killed one victim, the second victim found out, and so he had to kill the second victim. But Johnston doesn't know who died first. Esther Peterson may have been the first to disappear, but that does not prove she was the first to die. She may have truly run off for reasons unassociated with her husband. She had a relationship with the priest, even if it was only as the church secretary.

A third vehicle attracts Johnston's attention. It is the Sheriff.

"Sorry it took so long," apologizes O'Day, handing Johnston a cold hamburger. "I see your notebook is out. Any new thoughts?"

"Thanks for the burger, and no, not really. The length of time from crime to discovery really favors the killer. After so much time has passed, it's hard to retrace the victim's actions or whereabouts before death. I've concluded we need a better handle on those bones we found today."

"I agree. That's why I have already called the head honcho at the state crime lab and asked him to expedite this case. I also told him today's discovery could be connected with the skeletal bones of the Clinton priest and that they had already examined the factory bones so that should help speed things up."

"Good idea," replies Johnston, taking a bite of his hamburger. "Can we get another look at that buried box?"

"Yes. The two body bags were dropped off at the funeral home. One of the technicians requested analysis equipment and a pickup truck. I offered to drive the truck back here, but it hadn't arrived."

"I'd like to get a look at that box," says Johnston. I keep bumping my head against a wall in this case."

"A brick wall?"

"Good one, Jonathan." Johnston frowns.

"I'm serious. Why choose this property to hide bodies?"

"Every scenario I consider in this case results in some connection to those letters on the brick. I've given more thought to the letters being initials—possibly the initials of Gordon Oswald."

"I know we talked about the backward C being an unfinished letter. Could it maybe be the beginning of the letter R?"

"I suppose it could," says Johnston without enthusiasm.

"If so, that would give us three letters—G-O-R—which would begin the name of Gordon."

"You might be totally onto something there, Sheriff. But what motive would Gordon Oswald have had?"

"I'm stumped on that," admits O'Day. "I've thought about your approach to motive being either sex or money, but that doesn't fit Oswald in any shape or form."

"I agree. Besides which, he routinely has fished Sand Lake for years. His fishing buddies swear he knows Sand Lake like the back of his hand. He must know every drop-off and shallow spot in the lake. If he wanted to hide a body—or two—I'd have guessed he would have tossed them into the lake." Johnston shoves the wrapper from the devoured hamburger into his pocket.

"You're right, Charles. Why would he take a chance on burying a body when someone might find the makeshift coffin—as we did?"

"I don't know that the box was a makeshift coffin. We need to look again, carefully, at its construction," suggests Johnston. "It could have been designed to hide someone until a ransom was paid."

"Are you saying the motive was *extortion?*"

"Until it's ruled out, it could be a possibility. Do you think that Oswald needed money?" asks Johnston.

"Not that I know of." The Sheriff waits while a red pickup zooms by. "His lifestyle has been consistent with folks around here."

"What about illegal debts, like gambling?" questions Johnston.

"None show up. There might be a secret poker game in Clinton every now and then, or a bet between citizens on the outcome of a baseball game, but that's peanuts."

"If not money," Johnston poses the question: "What about sex?"

"You've got to be kidding. Have you met Oswald?"

"Yeah. You're right. Money has to be the motive unless he was motivated by a secondary factor such as revenge."

Sheriff O'Day's attention is diverted by the sound of a pickup truck approaching from a distance. "Do you hear that?"

"Yeah. I hope it's the truck ready to haul away the box so that I can get a good look inside." Johnston's hopes are realized. It is indeed the crime lab technician returning to collect the box that held the newly discovered bones.

A green pickup with oversized winter tires backs into the Oswald driveway. It's similar to other trucks with but one difference—a tarp and plastic sheathing laid completely over the truck bed.

"Okay, let's get this done," Jonathan calls out, sounding official. "Back up the pickup as far as you can into the driveway. I don't feel like carrying anything farther than need be."

In the clearing, the three men slowly lift the tarp to again expose the excavated box. Johnston makes sure he's up front and nearby when the technician begins to set aside the top boards of the box. Bending over, Johnston takes a good look in the box—it holds only one brick. Signaling the technician, he asks if the brick can be lifted up to see if there is any writing on it. The technician shows Johnston all four sides—no letters of any kind.

"What strikes you about the brick?" asks O'Day.

"That it matches the two I found in the cistern. But again, we're back to the fact that this county has millions of bricks. It tells us nothing and there's nothing about this brick that could be used for interrogation purposes. There are no leads to a suspect." Johnston sighs. "Worse, if crimes continue to be unsolved in this county, no one will want to live here."

"Do you think the bricks are merely a decoy?" asks O'Day.

"No, absolutely not. I'm convinced the priest made the brick scratching. He was trying to say something. It had to be important."

O'Day notices that the technician is ready to lift the box from the hole. "He probably needs our help," he tells Johnston. "Anything else you want to check in the box before we send it on its way?"

"Let me look." Johnston examines the box once more. "Wait ... see those two large, maybe forty-penny nails? Save those, definitely."

"Okay," replies O'Day. To the technician, he says, "Put those two nails in a separate evidence bag. Please photograph and mark on the inside of the box where they were located."

After marking the nails' location, the men lift the box out of its hole. The threesome slowly walk down the path, now widened, previously used to connect the clearing with the lake shoreline. Once clear of the trees, it is easy to carry the box to the pickup truck.

Sheriff O'Day recognizes a faint smell of urine. Maybe, he thinks, an animal dug through the dirt after the box was buried. He's sure that the lab will check it out. In the pickup bed, on top of the protective plastic, the box is tethered to the sides with wideband cloth straps and covered with Oswald's tarp. The tailgate is closed.

"You take the box back for examination and testing," O'Day directs the technician. "We'll notify you if we find anything else."

The Sheriff, carrying unused evidence bags from his car, joins Johnston to take a third look around the clearing while daylight lasts.

Chapter Thirty-three

Sarah returns from early Sunday mass. She finds Thomas slouching around the kitchen.

"You look very nice," flirts Thomas.

"You look like … er … you need to find your razor," replies Sarah. She doesn't comment that Thomas needs a new robe. The plaid brown one he's wearing is more than faded from repeated washing. Sarah had sewn the belt loop back on and stitched one shoulder seam. Still, Thomas prizes it like a child's security blanket.

"I'll get cleaned up here shortly. I was going to check something. Now, I don't remember what it was."

"Thomas, it's Sunday. Relax. You tossed and turned in bed all last night." Sarah opens the refrigerator.

"I guess I'm worked up over what happened yesterday. I hope Gordie didn't charge out to his Sand Lake cabin like a raging bull. He was really upset last night. Maybe I should have kept my mouth shut about the sheriff putting a deputy near his property."

"Dear, you told me last night you had to do it. Trust your first instinct. You can't be responsible for what Gordon does. He's an adult. He knows right from wrong. Sure, he may yell, but he didn't do anything but complain at the old factory, did he?"

"No. You're right, Sarah."

"Then, you've got nothing to worry about. Get yourself shaved; I'll boil some water for poached eggs and plug in the toaster."

Thomas hugs Sarah. He needs to relax. A hot shower will help.

Sarah hears her daughter's clunky slippers approach the kitchen. "Good morning, Wanda."

"Morning, Mom," she says sleepily.

"How are you this morning? I was asked about you when leaving mass this morning." Sarah sees Wanda rub her eyes.

"Oh, yeah?" Wanda helps herself to a piece of toast.

Her mother has the refrigerator door open, reaching for a carton of eggs. "Don't you want to know who?"

"Doesn't matter. If it's important, I'll probably hear about it."

"Going anywhere today?" asks Sarah.

"Probably going to visit Myron at the old factory." Wanda turns the dial on the kitchen radio. The room is filled with music—the song, "The Twelfth of Never." She quickly turns down the volume.

"Probably just hang out. Did Dad say anything this morning about what we found at Sand Lake?"

"No. He's more concerned about what Mr. Oswald might do if he found the sheriff blocking his Sand Lake cabin driveway." Sarah drops bread slices into the toaster. "Your dad and I are going to go next door to have a second look at what's inside the Peterson home."

"I bet the place is a wreck."

"It's dirty all right, but with effort it could shine."

Wanda finishes spreading butter and strawberry jam on her toast, sets it down, and pours a glass of orange juice. Not wanting to disturbing her mother at the stove adding eggs to the boiling water, she waits to say, "I'll be in my bedroom until the bathroom is free."

"Okay, Wanda." Sarah finishes poaching the eggs and adds two glasses full of orange juice next to them on the kitchen table. While waiting for the toaster to pop, she reaches over to turn the radio dial back to the PBS news channel.

Thomas, having changed his robe for khakis and a black-and-red plaid shirt, returns to the kitchen, showing off his clean-shaven face.

"You look much better," praises Sarah, glancing up at him.

"Thanks. Did O'Day by chance call? I'm hoping for details on the bones we found at the lake, assuming he's out there today with Investigator Johnston. I guess it would depend on whether or not the state crime lab had available manpower."

"Don't they always have someone available?" asks Sarah.

"Yes, but they might not judge it's important enough to rush."

"I wish we'd rush ahead to quiet times."

"Many persons in Clinton would agree with you," says Thomas. "What say, as soon as we finish breakfast, we go next door to keep our minds busy? After the garage, I might want to inspect those first papers again."

"That's fine. I saw Clinton did not merit any area news mention in our regional Sunday paper."

"Good. I'm positive the Sheriff would not be releasing any news about yesterday. I need to get a quote from him for our next *Pioneer Ledger* edition. There's bound to be gossip."

"Nobody said anything in church this morning," says Sarah. "Have you seen the patch over Rosie Klempler's eye?"

"No, what happened to her?"

"I saw her yesterday afternoon in Goostree's. She had a gauze patch taped over her right eye. She said it was because she had a sty. I would disagree."

"Why?" asks Thomas, finishing his eggs.

"Well, I'm sure I saw discoloration under one edge of the patch—like she had a black eye."

"Why would she lie?" asks Thomas.

"I don't know. I didn't say anything—I just wished her a speedy recovery."

Thomas gives Sarah his empty glass and small plate, and she takes them to the sink. He thumbs through the Sunday paper on the table. He's more interested in who's advertising than in the news.

Thomas slides the key into the front door lock of the Peterson house. Nothing inside looks different. Behind him, Sarah asks, "Should we just start with the garage?"

After walking through the kitchen, he opens the door into the single-car garage. A four-door white Ford Fairlane sedan takes up most of the space. "I didn't think Peterson's car would still be here," says Thomas. "The doors are unlocked."

"It probably made good sense to leave it here," says Sarah. "Who would take it? Let's take a look around."

Ten minutes later, Thomas says, "I haven't found anything of value. We need to look in the house to see if there is a second set of keys. This key I have doesn't fit the side door from the garage to the outside."

"Nothing in the car, either," says Sarah. "I found the ignition key under the front floor mat. I'll leave it there for now. Let's recheck the basement. I found a flashlight in the car trunk that we can use."

As the two head downstairs, Thomas says, "I don't recall anything special about the basement from our last visit."

"It's musty. Remember the receipt for concrete. Perhaps there was some repair made to the house foundation or the floor."

"Sarah, I have gone over the entire perimeter of the basement and found nothing but a hairline crack near the utility hookups. The musty smell must have been something that was left wet down here."

"What about the floor?" asks Sarah.

"There's a pencil-line crack on the unfinished side concrete floor, but it's never been fixed. I don't see a problem."

"That only leaves what's under the carpet in the finished area."

"I'm not ripping up any basement carpet today. There's nothing behind any of these pictures on the wall."

"Okay, we can go back upstairs, and check the kitchen cabinets and the second bedroom. Maybe we'll find those keys you mentioned in the garage." They both ascend the basement stairs and stop at the broom closet between the garage door and basement stairs. Opening the folding closet door, Thomas sees a stack of assorted cardboard boxes, all indicating they were filled originally with produce.

"What are those?" asks Sarah. Thomas pulls down the top box and opens the folded-over cardboard flaps.

"Woman's clothes," replies Thomas.

Sarah steps over to take a look. "How odd," she says. "I remember Esther Peterson wearing that red floral dress. The huge collar did nothing for her but accentuate her slim shoulders."

Thomas looks quickly through the contents of the other boxes. "Same thing—dresses, handbags, shoes, scarves, coats, hats, even lingerie." He turns to face Sarah, looking perplexed. "If she ran away, why would she leave her entire wardrobe here? Sarah, please look in the main bedroom closet."

Dropping the handbag she's holding, Sarah moves quickly through the kitchen and into the main bedroom. The closet still has some women's clothes scrunched behind a garment bag at the far end and two pairs of women's shoes on the closet floor. A yellow suitcase stands against the back of the closet. She returns to report her findings to Thomas.

"It looks like Esther Peterson did not run away. She surely would have packed at least one suitcase. I don't get that impression here."

"Why would Arnold have kept all this?" asks Thomas.

"Well, he would know he could not just give this stuff away—that would raise many questions. And, he couldn't sell it either."

"Where's her jewelry if she left everything?" asks Thomas."

"Good question, I remember her wearing several different rings, brooches, and necklaces. It seems unlikely she'd take all her jewelry with her if she really only went away on a trip."

They both go back to the large bedroom and begin searching through the dresser and nightstand.

"Thomas, I've found a jewelry box in this drawer," says Sarah. "It was tucked under Arnold's shirts."

"Let's see." Thomas removes it from the drawer and the two begin poking through its contents. "Looks like it could be hers—it's certainly not male jewelry or what I would wear."

"I don't see the rings she wore most often—the quartz one, a red-colored gemstone ring, and one with a green gemstone."

"The quartz and green stone rings are here. We're missing the red-colored gemstone," reports Thomas.

"Let's keep looking." The search through the bedroom continues, but they find no other jewelry. A thorough search of the second bedroom and the kitchen cabinets and drawers also uncovers nothing unusual.

"I think we've exhausted all the places to look," says Thomas. "No more legal papers. No keys. The only find unexpected was Esther's clothes."

"What are we going to do about the car?" Sarah asks. "It's not part of the real estate that is the house."

"I have no idea. It strikes me as a decent car. I'll try to remember to talk with Windhurst on Tuesday. Also, we should change the lock on that side garage door if no key shows up."

Thomas and Sarah had long since locked up the Peterson house, while Johnston and O'Day were still at Peterson's lake property.

"Sheriff, there's nothing but weeds. No sign any human being ventured through here."

"Charles, you're right. Haven't seen one old beer can."

"Jonathan, when will you release a statement on the bones?"

"I want to keep this mum until I get an updated report from the crime guys. Right now, we got a molehill of verified information when there should be a mountain of details."

"We're dealing with a decomposed body to bones. That takes a long time. The crime lab previously noted what they described as the trace mark of a bullet on the priest's skull. I'm sure you saw the report." O'Day nods as he continues to listen to Johnston. "The lab went on to state the wound was not life-threatening. Obviously, no lab technician can say if the bullet was deliberately or accidentally fired. And, Jonathan, we can't identify any instrumentality inflicting any fatal puncture wound because the passage of time allows natural body bacteria or invading insects to destroy the body tissue. Specific poison residue could reside in the bones. Who knows if the killer has remained in Clinton, or the county, or is even still alive?"

"So you disagree with my idea to keep this quiet?" asks O'Day.

"I think if the killer is still around, we should alert citizens to be vigilant. Any information may help us. Yes, maybe even from a crackpot. If the killer is already dead, it won't hurt to alert people. We can post a couple "beware of dog" signs along the road and stretch some crime scene ribbon across the shoreline side. We can ask Gordon Oswald to call you if he sees anyone. We could issue a statement that we're investigating; if we give the story to Thomas Hamilton, it won't be in the newspaper until Wednesday at the earliest. That'll give us time, although people will begin to gossip about having seen the deputy parked out here."

"Charles, you're right. I'll speak with Hamilton tomorrow. Anything else you want to do today?"

"It's been a long day. I need to retrieve the shovel or other tools left near the box hole."

"I don't have any dog warning signs, but I have some "No Trespassing, No Hunting" signs. People in this county respect those. I'll have the deputy post them and string crime tape by tonight. See you back in Winterville." Johnston nods.

"Damn cockleburs," O'Day curses as he glances at his uniform cuffs while sliding into his car. He answers a radio call and then points his car south toward Clinton. Nearing the town limits of Clinton, he sees a faint light at the old factory. He has no time to stop.

Inside the factory, Wanda complains, "Myron, you've been at this all day. You didn't even eat your lunch. You need to call it quits."

"Wanda, not now. This one piece doesn't quite fit as the diagram shows it should. I've checked all the other parts, and this is the closest one to the diagram. Just bear with me."

"Okay. I'm tired of sitting on this old chair. I'm going to walk around. I think I'll see what's upstairs."

"Go ahead. You'll just get dirty," advises Myron.

Wanda shrugs. Appearing tired and bored, she nevertheless climbs the stairs at the far end of the first floor, two steps at a time. The old light switch works, as do two of the three bulbs that are strung across the second floor ceiling joists. It resembles a cornfield maze built out of sacks of fertilizer, feed supplements for cattle and hogs, and even a few bags of dog food.

Wanda begins to wander through it and finds what could be a small room. She turns away from the room and walks down the middle aisle until she reaches another open space. On the far end is a sliding door that opens directly to the outside. Myron once explained the door is used to load bags onto the second floor.

She stands quietly to listen to Myron sanding below, and suddenly an unexpected whoosh of air hits Wanda on the back of her neck. She lets out a shriek. Her right foot slips on a small pile of feed pellets escaping from a broken bag. She tries to brace herself against a wall of bags, eight high. A bare light bulb swings, casting wavering light into the rafters and creating spooky ceiling patterns. Holding her breath, Wanda dashes toward the open stairway light. Bumping into a stack of bags, she runs to the stairs and bounds down them.

"Hey, what's going on?" Myron asks. "I was coming to check on you. Are you okay?"

Wanda stops in Myron's arms to catch her breath. "I'm okay. Upstairs scared me. I felt a weird sensation on the back of my neck."

"You likely disturbed sparrows or a grackle family."

"I don't know, and I'm not going back to find out." Wanda takes a deep breath. "I'm just going back to turn off the lights. Whatever is up there can fall back to sleep."

"You moved quickly. I heard you running across the floorboards up there. You didn't tear a hole in your jeans again, did you?"

"No, I didn't." Wanda pouts, but Myron can tell she's teasing.

"I figured out the sailplane piece. I'm about ready to go."

"Me, too," says Wanda. Looking around, her eyes come to rest for a moment on the cistern barricade. "Myron, do you think that box out at Sand Lake could have come from here or the Co-op?"

"I don't know. The Elevator receives boxes and crates of all sizes but the Sand Lake box was not a size I've seen since working there. Sometimes it's parts; sometimes five-gallon pails of solvents are put in a crate. One has to read the label stapled to the outside. I think the box at Sand Lake originally held something with small parts, like nuts and bolts. But, of course, other stores get wooden boxes, too."

"Like a grocery store?"

Myron turns pale. "I guess so," he says weakly.

Wanda instantly recognizes she's caused Myron's anxiety. "I'm sorry. I didn't mean anything, really."

"That's okay, Wanda. Once people learn about the bones at Sand Lake, there will be talk. People might jump to the wrong conclusion because my father uses wooden boxes in his store. That would be plain awful."

"I wasn't thinking about that, honest," says Wanda.

"I know. I'm positive Investigator Johnston will try to fit the box at Sand Lake with its imprint together with the brick and its initials. He's sure to wonder if there is a connection to my Dad."

"Myron, you're worrying too much. I'm sorry I opened my mouth about the box and where it might come from. We have to have faith."

"I keep telling myself something like that. I was fearful when I first found the brick, then somewhat relieved when we talked to your father. Now, I'm getting the worry back. I could have believed in the idea the bones belonged to some tramp, or that Father Murphy's killer was a tramp—someone long since gone. But with finding these new bones, I've discarded my tramp theory. One murder, maybe, but not two—or more, for all we know. I now believe more than ever that Father Murphy scratched those letters on the brick. How he did it or where he did it, I don't know. God may be trying to tell us something. I've prayed my father was not involved in all of this. I've prayed it was not someone else in my family. Father Murphy had to know something he could not directly tell."

"Myron, you're right. No priest can tell anyone what he hears from a person's confession. Not even a judge can make him tell. There's a sacrament—a sacred trust. In confessing to the priest, you're speaking directly to God. We don't know His plan; we have to trust that it will work out. It has to. It just has to."

Myron puts his forefinger to Wanda's lips to quiet her plaintive words. They hug each other in silence.

A light flashes momentarily into the factory through a far upper window. Wanda catches a glimpse, but then it's gone. "Myron. ..."

"Shush, Wanda. Hug me for a minute. Then we'll go. We can let Sheriff O'Day worry."

Chapter Thirty-four

Lies will not support the past
False fronts created will not last.
In this world of gloom and woe
In wisdom, faith, and trust we grow.
For all that we carry in our heart
Or that our words will impart,
Memories in our hearts still glow
Showing us paths on which to go.

"Thomas, that's beautiful. Where did you obtain or find that wonderful poem?"

"I wrote it, Sarah, many, many years ago."

"I've never seen it."

"Oh, it was a time when I envisioned my skill to mechanically create printed words meant I could become a poet. I would scribble random thoughts on pieces of paper from time to time. When I realized how hard it would be to write enough poetry to fill a book, I thought I could adapt my verse to unique cards of thanks or memorials in the *Pioneer Ledger*, but it never happened. People either wanted to copy what had been printed before or add their own personal thoughts. I tossed out most of my scraps of paper. This poem was my longest. I stuck it into a book as a bookmark and forgot about it."

"What were you thinking about when you wrote this poem?" Sarah tries not to tip Thomas to the fact she is anxious that he may perceive more about her than she thinks he understands.

"Oh, nothing. It was just my imagination." Thomas changes the subject. "How many items do you have for this week, Sarah?"

"I have ten to twelve. The fall bazaar season is going strong."

"I hope you have something on the Lutheran Ladies Aid bazaar. They have a two-column ad running. I'd like to see them succeed. Others may then realize that it pays to advertise. I also need your help to find something for the opinion page."

"I've received the Lutheran Ladies' details. How much page one space are you saving for the news about finding the bones?"

"I'd like to tell the whole story of what happened, but I'm not convinced the sheriff would be happy. I'll call him this afternoon to determine if he has more information and what I can print."

"Remember to tell him about Esther Peterson's clothes in the house next door."

The telephone rings; Thomas listens as Sarah answers. He can tell by her comments he isn't needed, so he proceeds to the linotype to set ordered classified ads.

After she sets down the phone, Sarah looks at Thomas' poem again. The words touch too close to her heart and soul. She remembers Melissa and the unborn child reclaimed by God. A tear wells behind her eye. She is confident her secret is still safe. Thomas' poem probably indicates that he'd been dwelling on some character in a book, nothing real. She feels temporarily relieved.

"Mom?" Wanda calls out. "Hey, Mom."

Sarah wipes her eye with a tissue. "Wanda, you surprised me, although I'm glad you didn't let the screen door slam."

"I'm home for a sandwich," replies Wanda.

"Wanda, would you like to go with me to Winterville Wednesday? Ladies from St. Mary's are going to a St. Barnabas circle function. The church function shouldn't be long, and then I'd like to go shopping for new sneakers."

"I'd rather not. Shopping would be okay, but sitting with your church ladies is not exciting."

"Okay. I was only asking. I have to drive if I want to shop."

Wanda nods and hurries off. "See you later, Mom."

It's nearly three p.m. before Thomas finds time to telephone the Sheriff. He pulls a blank sheet of paper out of a kitchen drawer and dials the nearby telephone.

"Good afternoon, Sheriff," Thomas greets him. "I think you know why I'm calling, but I also have something new for you."

"What's that, Thomas?" asks Jonathan.

"You know, I'm renting Arnold Peterson's home next door. Sarah and I were in the house yesterday afternoon, and we found boxes of Esther Peterson's clothes in a broom closet. Plus, we discovered there are still women's clothes, shoes, and a suitcase in the larger bedroom closet."

"What kind of boxes?" asks O'Day.

"Ordinary cardboard boxes—that's not the point. The boxes were full of Esther's clothing."

"What color of box?" Thomas chafes at O'Day's question. He seriously doubts the Sheriff can decipher what is important.

"Anything other than clothes?" asks O'Day.

"There was a jewelry box in the bedroom dresser. Lots of jewelry in it, but Sarah said Esther always wore a red gemstone ring, and that wasn't there. I believe she also wore a wedding band, but it wasn't in the jewelry box either."

"A wedding band? Was that gold?"

"Yes, as I remember," says Thomas.

"And a red gemstone?"

"Yes. Sarah definitely remembers Esther often wore such a ring."

"Do you know what size the rings were?"

"Well, no, although Sarah estimates about a size six."

"A size six—that's smaller than normal. Did Esther Peterson have small hands?"

"Yes, she did, Sheriff."

"Did you check any of the clothes for marks or stains?"

"Well … no. We didn't think of that. Once we determined the boxes held clothes and nothing else, Sarah and I closed the boxes."

"I'm going to send Mr. Johnston to inspect those boxes of clothes tomorrow. Can he obtain the house key from you?"

"Certainly," Thomas agrees. "It may be nothing; Sarah and I found it odd. Any woman who plans to leave her husband for good would, I'd think, take some of her clothes, if not all of them."

"Yes, that would make sense," agrees O'Day. "I'm assuming the issue with the clothes was not your entire reason for calling."

"Correct. What can you tell me about the box contents found at Sand Lake? Any news I can print?"

"There's not much I can tell you. You already know we found bones. I've asked the state crime lab to have a good look at them. And, to do it quickly," says O'Day.

"Did the box remain at Sand Lake?"

"No. We've removed it for safekeeping. You could print that so your story does not start a stampede of curiosity-seekers to Sand Lake. We've posted 'no trespassing' signs on the property, along with stringing crime scene tape."

"How many bones were in the box, Jonathan?"

"Between you and me, indications are more than one skeleton. You can't publish that."

"Any connection to Father Murphy?"

"Thomas, we don't know. Can't rule it out, but please don't speculate in print. As you can understand, we need to get answers that are strong enough to stand up in court."

"Jonathan, I fully understand. Are you going to have a news conference or send out a statement to the press?"

"Thomas, I'm not planning either at this time. You can print a story in your newspaper—that will be enough to get me bombarded with calls."

"Thanks, Sheriff, I'm glad you trust me. In my story this week I'll quote you only as saying you're working on the investigation and can't comment on specific details."

"That would be fine," affirms O'Day.

"Can I mention the state crime lab?"

"As I mentioned, you could say they have removed all evidence from Sand Lake. It would help if you were not specific about the location—just that it was Sand Lake."

"Anything else I should know?" asks Thomas.

"No. That's about it. Charles will come to Clinton tomorrow to have a look at those clothes."

"Thanks again, Jonathan. Give me a call if I can help with anything else. Bye, now." Thomas hears the other end of the line click. He eyeballs his notes. Not much there—but enough. Having an exclusive was nice from a journalistic standpoint; that a person may have met a violent death was not.

Sarah walks toward the kitchen sink, arms outstretched, fingers pointed upward. Thomas turns on the water.

"Thanks," says Sarah. "Hot water and soap can't be beat for ridding the hands of cleaner used to dissolve printing ink."

"Just finished talking with the Sheriff. *Pioneer Ledger* has an exclusive this week on the bones found at Sand Lake."

"Any new information? Like whom the bones belonged to?"

"No, it's too early. And, we are still gagged on speculating. Johnston is coming back tomorrow to look at the clothes and jewelry box next door. I said we'd give him our key," says Thomas.

"People will start new gossip, seeing him here every week."

"No reason to worry about that. We're a newspaper in a small town, and he's a known investigator. The thing that bothers me is that Jonathan O'Day is relying on somebody else—Johnston—to do the work and make a decision about evidence. He should have personally checked out the house before Old Man Peterson was accused of murder. And, O'Day should have been at Sand Lake on Saturday and known it was Arnold's property a long time ago. Ten years ago, when the person responsible for money at St. Mary's went missing, the church accounts should have been audited."

"What if people think we know more than we do?" asks Sarah.

"What's new about that? People in this town understand we haven't printed all story details if it would adversely affect someone. Why would they think we changed?"

"I guess you're right. The whole town is probably unsettled over the discovery of Father Murphy's bones. Finding more bones, especially at Sand Lake, likely will unsettle them even more. Did the sheriff say anything else?"

"Nothing about the identity of the newly discovered bones, if that's what you mean. I don't think he knows," says Thomas.

The front screen door slams, announcing Wanda's return. Thomas calls out to her. "Wanda, I need to talk to you for a moment."

"Yes, Dad. Sorry about the door slamming."

"It's not about that," Thomas assures her. "I spoke with the Sheriff this afternoon. The paper will run a story this week. I promised him that we would not talk to anyone about finding the bones at Sand Lake. I need you to promise me that you—and Myron, too—will keep silent."

"No problem," promises Wanda. "I really don't want to be involved. It's gruesome. It upsets Mom, too. Will those other newsmen be in town again?"

"I would say so, once the news gets out."

Wanda frowns. "So what happens now?" she asks.

"Investigator Johnston is coming tomorrow to look at the house next door. He's the same fella you and Myron met out at Sand Lake on Saturday."

Wanda nods and goes into the kitchen. Finding his printer type stick, Thomas opens the California job case to find the right sized type font for a story headline.

MORE BONES FOUND

At Sand Lake

Exclusive

More human bones were found this past weekend near Sand Lake, northwest of Clinton. Sheriff Jonathan O'Day confirmed the discovery in an exclusive story for the *Pioneer Ledger*.

Specific details were not available at press time. Sheriff O'Day said he was investigating and had called in the state crime laboratory for assistance.

Readers will recall the identification of the skeletal remains of Clinton's Father Murphy, late of St. Mary's Catholic Church.

No authority contacted by the *Pioneer Ledger* would have any other comment.

The Sheriff said that persons should stay away from trying to do their own investigating at Sand Lake, as that would hinder authorities.

In addition, he said, the human remains found have been removed from Sand Lake. No timeline for release of any further details could be obtained.

The *Pioneer Ledger* will try to have more information next week.

Thomas is rereading his story when Wanda comes back into the newspaper production area.

"When this Mr. Johnston comes back," she begins without preamble, "would he also be investigating the unexplained footprints outside and the lights that have been shining into the old factory?"

"I don't know. You could ask him, but that's the sort of thing that often normally happens," answers Thomas.

"I thought I saw a strange light again last night."

"It could have been be one of those curiosity-seekers the Sheriff is always upset about." Thomas closes a type drawer.

"I suppose. Still, it makes me nervous. I'm only going out to the factory if I know Myron is already there."

"Good idea," acknowledges Thomas.

Both Sarah and Thomas are lost in their own thoughts at supper, and neither converses much with the other. Finally, as Sarah begins clearing away the dishes, Thomas says, "I think I might turn in early and read for a while."

"All right, dear. I plan to finish cleaning up here and watch some TV. Wanda is starting on a new dress. I hope the sound of her sewing machine won't bother you."

"Even if it did. I wouldn't say anything. I agree with you she needs to do something besides sit out at the old factory every night."

Thomas decides to publish his story on the discovery of the bones at Sand Lake, exactly as he'd promised Sheriff O'Day.

At mid-morning on Tuesday, Charles Johnston arrives.

"Sheriff said you'd be by this morning," Thomas greets him. "I have the key for you to the Peterson house."

"Thanks, Thomas," says Johnston. "Sheriff said you found Esther's clothes packed away in the kitchen closet. Is that right?"

"Yes. And there are a few female clothes in a bedroom closet. Check out the whole place if you want."

"Okay, I'll be back with the key when I'm done." Johnston sidesteps a box on the floor on his way out. An hour later, he returns. "I looked at everything that I thought necessary," he tells Thomas. "The fact so many clothes are there is suspicious, but I was more interested in what was not there, frankly. I saw one dress with dried bloodstains on it. It could be nothing, but I'll let the Sheriff know."

"I talked with the Sheriff yesterday. The *Pioneer Ledger* will have a story on the bones we found at Sand Lake. Nothing specific."

"Thanks, Thomas. Difficult thing. I'm staying away from Clinton tomorrow so I can avoid repeating 'no comment' to every question." Johnston excuses himself and wonders if he's said too much. He suspects there was a second pair of interested ears listening.

Johnston's Chevy is on its way, nonstop to Winterville. With any luck he'll make it to the Sheriff's office before Jonathan leaves for lunch. For some reason he never realized how many trees line farm fields along the highway. Nothing slides off his full backseat as this time he brakes less aggressively in the county parking lot serving the Lake County Sheriff's Office.

"Rebecca, Sheriff O'Day in?" asks Johnston.

"Sure is. Walk on in."

"Good morning, Jonathan." O'Day is facing away from his office doorway that Johnston stands in. He waits for an invitation to enter.

"Sit down, Charles. Tell me about Peterson's house."

"Not much there. One could theorize that Esther Peterson did not leave of her own free will, based on the amount of belongings left there. Or, she left in a huff. I found one dress with what could be bloodstains. It's surely a dead end. I'm going to send it to the state lab, just in case, but I'm not going to put any priority on it. Have the state guys said anything about what we dug up at Sand Lake?"

"Yes. Half-hour ago state lab called with a preliminary finding that one of the two pelvic bones we found Sunday matches the skull and other bones identified to be Father Murphy."

"What about the other pelvis?" Johnston asks.

"Don't know yet. They think it may be female. I told them not to tell me anything like that until they know for sure. No reason to again cause us embarrassment with a mistake."

"What about the detached hand bones?" asks Johnston.

"Father Murphy." O'Day reaches for a paper with notes.

"How could that happen?" asks Johnston.

"Remember, in addition to the missing pelvic bone, we were missing a forearm bone. The ligaments that hold bones together would be gone—the body had decomposed."

"I understand ligaments being missing after a decade. So I gather what you're saying is that the bones found with Father Murphy's skull included two wrist bones, but only one wrist could be matched to Father Murphy."

"Correct. First time around, lab only tested the hand with ring and fracture. They did not want to destroy the entire skeleton. The hands appeared to be similar in size and structure."

Johnston scratches his head, thinking. "So we still have an unidentified wrist bone or hand from the old factory cistern. Let me guess: the missing forearm bone of Father Murphy was in the bone collection we dug up at Sand Lake."

"You're two for two," O'Day tells him. "While the state lab is still analyzing everything from Sunday, one technician thought one lower arm bone didn't fit. She made the conclusion quite naturally because in reconstructing the skeleton, she came up with three lower arm bones, and one looked larger than the two others. Since her colleague was trying to match the extra pelvic bone to Father Murphy, she gave him the extra arm bone as well. It, too, matched Father Murphy's skull."

Johnston looks perplexed. "Seems like at some point, Father Murphy and this second person were in the same hiding place. While that could happen, why was one moved?"

"You're the investigator," O'Day responds. "You tell me."

Johnston pulls out his notepad, flipping through pages before meeting the Sheriff's gaze. "Somebody got scared the bodies would be found?"

"I would agree that's a likely scenario if two bodies were moved. But that doesn't fit the facts we know."

Johnston tries another scenario. "Okay, how about ... somebody got scared that the bodies would be found at the lake and got interrupted before both bodies could be moved to a new hiding place."

"I don't like that scenario either," says O'Day. "The bodies would have had to be decomposed to a skeleton and in such a state neither body would have weighed a great deal. They easily could have fit into a gunnysack. Someone most likely would not have taken the chance on making two trips if all the bones were going to be relocated. That box at Sand Lake was in a clearing well protected from casual passersby."

Out of skeleton-moving ideas, Johnston asks, "Sheriff, when did the lab say they would have more results on the second skeleton?"

"They didn't."

"I would suggest we give them the name of Esther Peterson as a possibility. Perhaps we can get lucky and medical records still exist that would help us determine if one of those skeletons is her."

"I think you're right," agrees O'Day. "If you are, and both Father Murphy and Esther Peterson were initially buried at Sand Lake, they would have had to have been buried at two separate times, since they went missing a year apart."

Johnston lets his eyes gaze out the office window. His mind is churning. "Jonathan, what if we were dealing with two killers.

"I wouldn't dismiss a more than one killer theory."

"I have this crazy thought …" Johnston begins.

"What is it?" O'Day encourages him.

Johnston shrugs. "It probably makes no sense, but … since Esther Peterson was church secretary and disappeared first, Father Murphy may have been her killer. And then, someone—maybe her husband—discovered that and killed Father Murphy for revenge."

"I agree; your thought is crazy. What would be Father Murphy's motive for killing Esther?"

"Money. Missing money. The money the priest was hiding from the diocese. The priest found out that Esther was helping herself and became enraged. He might have struck her, or enraged, accidentally pushed her, and she suffered a fatal injury. If it happened at the rectory, her body could easily have been put into the car trunk while the priest's car was in the garage with the door closed."

"Why bury her at Sand Lake?" asks O'Day.

"The priest knew the land was owned by the Petersons. Arnold's jealousy over Esther's spending so much time at the church was well-traveled gossip—he'd be the perfect murder suspect. No one would finger a priest as the killer."

"What about the land survey with the initials?" asks O'Day.

"Arnold Peterson was selling his factory and his home, but he couldn't let it be known where he buried the priest, so he kept the survey without identifying parts. He placed the initials on it, either to lead authorities astray or to help him recall its location."

"Charles, that's getting too complicated."

"I know it is, but it's beginning to make sense. Remember, Peterson forged the postcard from his wife. The two skeletons were found on property he owned at the time."

"Yes, but he was not the only one with opportunity for access," O'Day argues. "Anyone could have been to Sand Lake. The old factory cistern was available to anyone who would have made the effort to get to it."

"How about the question: Why didn't Arnold have his wife declared legally dead after she had been missing for seven years?"

"He didn't need to," insists O'Day. "The property was in joint tenancy. He had right to sell it as owner in his own right."

"Not completely so. He would have needed her signature on any warranty deed if she were legally alive. No death certificate is on file."

"Okay, I give up. Does it matter? He died before that bridge had to be crossed. Let's wait until I talk with the crime lab again before we try additional assumptions. I'll mention Esther Peterson as the possible second skeleton. Oh, and have you thought about the brick with its letters? How does it fit in with what we have confirmed?"

"We know no inscribing tool was in the factory cistern when the skeleton was found. If Father Murphy scratched the letters in the cistern before he died, we're missing the tool he used."

"What about the two nails in the Sand Lake box?"

"One of those could have been used," says Johnston. "I would lean that way." He shifts around in his chair.

"Then that puts Father Murphy in the box at Sand Lake—while he was still alive."

"That's right, Jonathan. And, it would most likely put him in the box with the other body—the second skeleton."

"Do you think the killer forced Father Murphy into the box alive, to scare him into telling where the diverted money was?" asks O'Day.

"Hadn't thought of that. I'll add it to the scenarios to be further explored later. Let's go grab some lunch."

"Good idea. Later, we can talk about how we'll respond to the flurry of questions we're going to get, starting tomorrow when the Clinton newspaper announces the discovery of more bones."

"I'll let you handle the questions," Johnston says. "I plan to find tasks to do tomorrow that are not in Clinton. I'm ready to eat."

Before leaving the building, Sheriff O'Day tells Rebecca where the two are headed. When they reach the café, O'Day holds back, his hand on Johnston's arm. "Listen, if it was Father Murphy who killed Esther Peterson, and Arnold Peterson killed Father Murphy, and Arnold is now dead, one thing is certain."

"What's that?"

"We shouldn't be finding any more skeletons."

Chapter Thirty-five

"I see you brought with you beautiful additional help this morning, Thomas."

"Yes, Virgil; yes, indeed. Sarah volunteered to help me transport these *Pioneer Ledger* bundles to your post office station."

"Wow," exclaims Virgil, reading the headline on a bundle set on the counter. "More bones! Jesus, Mary, and Joseph. What is this all about, Thomas?"

"Can't really talk about it, Virgil. Story says everything I can say."

"All right; I understand," responds Virgil. "I'd better get these in the boxes. If someone sees it and goes to the café, I'll get a flood of people in here clamoring for me to hurry up."

"You've got every bundle, Virgil," says Thomas. "See you next week. Did you contact the sheriff about what you told me last week?"

"No. I decided not to get involved."

Outside, Thomas advises Sarah, "We'd better get back to the newspaper. I'm sure our telephone will be busy today."

As he predicted, the telephone is ringing as Thomas and Sarah enter through the backdoor. Thomas answers and speaks with the caller for a few minutes, and then says to Sarah, "You won't believe it? The caller was offering to tell me where *more* bones are buried and wanted to know if there was a reward for his information."

"It will be like this all day. Do you have any plans?" asks Sarah.

"I was going to put on my super-hero cape and fly over the county, looking for bad guys in black hats," jests Thomas.

"Thomas, you're being silly. Remember I'm going to St. Barnabas tonight, so I will need the car at six o'clock."

The day is as predicted—one phone call after another. Thomas tries to work, but Sarah repeatedly calls him to the phone. The commotion dies down by late afternoon. Sarah, although exhausted from the day's events and wishing she could stay home, prepares for her trip to Winterville.

Her drive to Winterville is unremarkable, except for a white Ford passing her from behind, pulling off, and speeding to pass again. On this highway any speeding car causes her consternation. Sarah does not stop constantly checking her rearview mirror until she drives into the St. Barnabas Catholic Church parking lot, one block off the main highway.

Sarah enters St. Barnabas through its backdoor with inside stairs to the lower-level social hall. She steps into the hall and recognizes Hilda and Sharon Swanson from St. Mary's; she strides across the room in their direction and greets them. "Hello, Sharon … Hilda. I didn't expect you'd both be here."

"Hello, Mrs. Hamilton," replies Sharon. "My mother and I wanted to do some wedding shopping here in Winterville. We made an afternoon of it. Is Wanda with you?"

"No, she's busy, sewing a new dress," explains Sarah.

"Hi, Sarah," says Hilda. "Terrible thing, wasn't it, the finding of another skeleton at Sand Lake?"

"Yes, totally gruesome," replies Sarah.

Several ladies approach Sarah, and she becomes the center of attention. All conversation turns to the Sand Lake discovery. Sarah says she can report no more than what is printed in the *Pioneer Ledger*, but the women don't believe her.

"Ladies," chastises Sarah, "we've got to let the authorities solve this mystery. We may have our own thoughts, but what is really needed is evidence, strong reliable facts that can be verified as proof. I'm sure the sheriff knows what he's doing. We have to trust that he and his deputies and the other law enforcement officials will succeed in their work to capture the killer." A majority of the assembled women nod in agreement. She continues, "Now, I see our meeting is about to begin. I suggest we all direct our attention to the podium. I'm ready to do something constructive."

The meeting adjourns at nearly eight-fifteen p.m. At its conclusion, Sarah offers quick good-byes and drives to the shoe store across town, hoping she has time to shop. The door placard states the store is open until nine p.m., giving Sarah ample time to try on several pairs of sneakers. She finds a comfortable pair and buys them.

Her new sneakers are on the backseat as she starts her trip south toward Clinton. The highway is dark—tonight there is no moon and few stars.

One to two minutes outside of Winterville, Sarah becomes acutely aware of a car, racing at high speed and with its headlights on high beam, approaching from her rear. *This driver better pull out to pass me quick*, thinks Sarah. *I shouldn't have come to St. Barnabas tonight. I should have trusted my feelings that I was too exhausted and stayed home.*

Sarah prays the speeding car will pass her. She's agitated and still slightly annoyed that the ladies at St. Barnabas wanted to talk about missing bodies and the bones at Sand Lake. Moreover, she was upset she had been put in the position of having information she was not allowed to share—she should have realized the women would want to share gossip.

Suddenly, the speeding car strikes Sarah's car hard from behind. "Oh, my God!" screams Sarah. Her body is jolted forward, but she's held tight by her seat belt. A second jarring collision reverberates from her car's rear bumper forward. She thinks she hears glass breaking. Again, she is bounced towards the steering wheel but held back by her seat belt. Sarah keeps the steering wheel pointed straight ahead, wheels on the road. She speeds up. Her pursuer does likewise. The distance between them narrows.

Why me, Lord? I've already had one terrible accident on this road. Please, not again. Sarah prays that she can get home safely. She needs to get home—to Thomas and Wanda. They've done nothing to deserve losing her. She needs to be home, to have it as her mother wanted.

Her antagonizer races his car up beside her. He turns his front wheels toward Sarah's car, to a spot behind the front bumper. Sparks from metal flash on contact. Sarah's car is pushed toward the ditch, parallel to the highway. She jerks her steering wheel to the left, and returns a crunching blow to her attacker's front side. Again, the sparks of metal on metal spray into the air. This time she knows she hears the sound of breaking glass. She loses her left front headlight.

She hears the other engine roar, sees headlight beams crisscross in front of her, and is rocked by the resulting crash that seems to momentarily lift her front wheels completely off the road.

"What do I do next?" she screams aloud. "I'm losing this battle! I'm losing control of my car!" Her front wheels are facing right, not straight, and she can feel the looseness of the gravel on the shoulder of the road. Her right-side tires are spitting gravel pebbles backward and sideways. Her car is losing traction as she slides sideways; her rear wheels are spinning. "Dear God, why? Thomas, Wanda, Melissa! I love you all!" Sarah cries, and she expects these to be her final words.

Sarah's car leaves the highway shoulder and flies twenty feet over the bottom of the highway ditch. The turned front wheels strike the top of a perpendicular embankment created for a farmer's entry road to a cornfield Her car bounces a second time as the rear wheels collide with the entry road; it lurches almost sideways as the rear tailpipe and hanging rear bumper gouge into the field road.

Sarah's head strikes the car's roof with punishing, terrific force. She feels her neck compress before she loses consciousness. It's all happened within seconds. Sarah and her car come to rest on top of the entrance road embankment, facing away from the highway.

Her attacker promptly applies the brakes, slows down, turns around on the highway, and drives back. He turns off his headlights and swivels to see if there is any other traffic, and then opens the driver's door. One man emerges from the car; he stands there on the highway, alone in the darkness. Slowly he walks around to the passenger side of his car, checking for dents. He rubs his hand over the front wheel to see if the fender is touching the rubber tire tread.

Satisfied with what he finds, he retraces his steps to the driver's side. He reaches into the backseat for a brown paper bag that holds a pint of expensive whiskey, a small roll of black tape, and one pair of leather racing gloves. He tucks the whiskey bottle and tape into the front pocket of his sweatshirt, pulls on the racing gloves, and slowly walks over to Sarah's car.

Peering in a window, he sees Sarah's body slumped sideways on the seat. Her head hangs toward the passenger door. He walks slowly around the car to again look inside. Sarah is not moving. With deliberate movements, he opens the passenger door and leans in. He removes one glove and feels Sarah's neck. There is a pulse, but she remains motionless. He puts his glove back on.

Ever vigilant, the man looks up and down the highway. No vehicle lights are visible. He turns off the ignition in Sarah's vehicle and pushes the headlight switch to the off position. He sticks a piece of heavy black electrical tape over the dome light pushbutton switch to keep it depressed so that the car's interior will be dark.

Walking back to his car, he puts on a raincoat, and then reaches for a coil of rope and medical adhesive tape. He spreads out a tarp and blanket inside the car's trunk.

Sarah is still unconscious when the man returns. He reaches to unlatch a stretched seatbelt, and twists her body so that she is lying on her back on the car's bench seat. Her wig is matted with blood. He clutches her to his chest before drags her, face up and head first, out of her car. The heels of her shoes leave almost imperceptible marks on the surface of the entry road and shoulder of the highway as her attacker drags her to his Ford Fairlane, only once having to readjust his grip of her. He again looks up and down the highway.

Satisfied that he has enough time, he binds Sarah's hands and feet with the rope. He lifts her bound body from the ground into his car trunk, ties a folded bandana across her eyes, and places one piece of medical tape across her mouth. He feels her pulse. It is still weak. He presses a second bandana against her skull and wraps medical tape under her chin and over her head to hold the cloth against her head laceration. He closes the trunk.

Walking back to Sarah's car for the third time, he turns on the ignition and the engine hums. He places the manual transmission into drive, leaves the driver's door open, and with his body half in and half out of the car, he guides it straight ahead about twenty feet, leaving it less visible to vehicles that will pass by on the highway.

From the pocket of his sweatshirt he takes out the whiskey bottle, twists off the cap, and liberally sprinkles the whiskey over the car's interior. He tosses the bottle cap into the front seat foot well and the bottle onto the backseat—watching as it bounces to a final resting place. He removes the tape strip from the dome-light button, closes the passenger door, leaves the keys in the ignition, and closes the driver's door enough to turn out the dome light but not enough to fully close the door. Believing he has done all he needs to do, he returns to his four-door sedan.

Rechecking his own car for damage, he decides it's drivable, and time to proceed south to Clinton. He hears no noise from his trunk—his car's engine being the only sound heard. Within minutes, he sees the lights of Clinton up ahead.

He leaves the highway before he reaches the town and dust swirls from the dirt road to the old factory. Before his headlight beams can be seen by anyone in the factory building, he turns them off and continues on in the dark. As he observes no light from inside the old factory, or no cars parked outside, he decides to turn his headlights back on. He believes good fortune is his this night; the old factory is deserted. He pulls over to park several yards from the factory's sliding entrance door.

He reaches into his front pants pocket, from which he pulls out a key ring with three keys. He listens for any noise from the trunk; there is none. He again dons his leather gloves and exits his car.

He slips his key into the padlock that secures the sliding entrance door, unlocks it, and quickly removes it to allow him to pull the door six feet to the left. After jogging back to his car, he opens the rear passenger door and unfolds his raincoat. Next, he mentally rehearses his preplanned factory-entrance sequence as he buttons his raincoat, checks for extra tape and rope, and lifts the trunk lid.

Sarah groans softly but does not move. He reaches into the trunk and picks her up as gently as he can, careful not to let her head sag forward.

Tightening his grip on her, he pushes on the trunk lid with his elbow to close it, and carries Sarah through the open factory door. Once inside, he lets out a groan.

He has debated with himself whether or not it is worth the risk to turn on the factory's interior lights. He decides it is. He cannot afford to injure himself by tripping over parts of a sailplane. If no one is at the old factory, he reasons, there is no one within miles—he knows this from his observations on previous scouting trips. At night, either the two young kids are there with the lights on, their cars parked in front, or the building is unoccupied. Only one time was there a person in the building after the two teenagers had driven off. Turning slightly, his right index finger flips the lights on.

He leaves the sliding door in place and walks as fast as he can around the sailplane and toward the far side of the first level to the stairs that lead to the second floor. He turns on the second-floor lights. Sarah is becoming heavier and harder to balance and carry as he proceeds up the stairs, trying to maintain his equilibrium.

He is not familiar with the layout of the sacks on the second floor. He knows stored contents and bags are shifted around from time to time. Because it is now autumn, the Elevator has not re-stocked bags of seed corn. Nevertheless, his plan is intact, as he moves around some bags, searching the second floor for the stacked bags of seed corn that he knows have been saved from spring. These unsold bags are unlikely to be disturbed for the next day or two—he only needs that long for his plan to work.

The seed corn bags are halfway down the length of the building, off to the right. There is a single-file access that jogs to the right, go-ing to the exterior wall of the building. Someone has decided to clear out the center of what had been a solid stack of bags—it looks like a child's fort but without any signs of youngsters' visits. He carries Sarah down the second-floor aisle toward this fort as he searches for the nearest unobstructed vertical support post. These posts, ap-proximately 10 inches square, are made of strong timber and are strategically spaced to hold up the building's roof.

He places Sarah on the exposed floor near the bag fort, while he prepares a spot in front of the support post. Three seed bags are placed on the floor, perpendicular to the post. He places Sarah in a sitting position; feet thrust forward and her back against the post. He unties her hands, pulls her arms behind the post, and rebinds her hands. For extra measure, he ties one piece of rope around her waist, with its nautical knot behind the post. For one last detail, he places a seed bag over her still-bound feet.

Confident that Sarah is not going anywhere, he holds two un-gloved fingers against her wrist to check her pulse. It is stronger now. Her breathing sounds more regular. She is making sounds in her throat and moving slightly to indicate she may be coming around.

He looks over his handiwork, but he knows he needs to get out of there. Near the building's exterior wall, he reaches up over his head and takes down ten to twelve corn seed bags. He stacks them to fill in the entrance to the cavity that now houses Sarah.

He plans to be back in a few hours. To exit, he slips on a pair of blue cloth surgical shoe covers. He walks backwards and swings his left covered shoe to disguise or obliterate any footprints he may have left when he entered the factory. He slightly unscrews the light above the second floor stairs until it goes out.

At the front sliding door, he slips off both shoe covers, takes off his raincoat, slides the factory entrance door closed, and locks the padlock in its proper position. As he walks back to his car, he takes off his gloves and tosses them along with his other used apparel into his trunk for later disposal. He puts his key ring into his pants pocket as he checks the appearance of the trunk. A moment of panic arises when he does not see Sarah's wig in his trunk. He knows it's not in the factory, and he has no time to retrace his steps.

He slowly backs up his car until he can make a U-turn. He must return this Ford to a driveway near Sand Lake and retrieve his own car. So far, the riskiest part of his plan is a success. Yet, caution is still required, as Sarah has not disappeared.

At the start of the ten p.m. local television news, Thomas already fears that something may have happened to Sarah. By the conclusion of the half-hour program, he has convinced himself that Sarah is in trouble—she should have been home long ago. He is guilt-ridden that he didn't insist she stay home when he saw that she was ex-hausted after all the commotion over Sand Lake.

"Wanda!" he calls out to his daughter. He wonders what he will say to her. He doesn't want to overly alarm her.

"What is it, Dad?" she asks as she comes out of her bedroom.

"I'm a little worried. Your mother is not home yet. She is never two hours late without calling."

"Wow, I didn't realize it had gotten so late," says Wanda. She sighs. "I should have gone with her. She asked me to go with her. I said "no."" Wanda's eyes begin to get teary. "I should not have been so selfish." Wanda wipes her eyes.

"I feel terrible, too," says Thomas. He reaches out for her hand and leads her into the kitchen. "Sit at the table with me. We need to figure out what to do."

"Should we call someone?" asks Wanda.

"Good idea," agrees Thomas. "I have a Winterville telephone book in the front office." Within a minute, Thomas is back at the kitchen table and paging through the phone book, looking for churches.

"Here it is. St. Barnabas Catholic Church. I'm going to call." His breathing is ragged as he waits for someone to answer the phone. "Hello? St. Barnabas Catholic Church? I'm Thomas Hamilton in Clinton, and I'm so sorry to disturb you at this late hour. My wife, Sarah, left Clinton to attend a lady's social function at your church tonight. She is still not home, and I've had no word. Is she possibly still there at St. Barnabas? Oh, I see. Yes, I'll hold on while you check." Thomas talks across the receiver to Wanda. "The priest is checking the church to see if anyone is still there. He doesn't think so but is willing to make sure."

"Dad, if Mom's not there, I want to call Myron."

Thomas puts his index finger to his lips as a signal for Wanda to stop. "Yes, I see," he says into the phone. "The church is empty? No cars in the parking lot? Thank you; you've been extremely helpful. I appreciate your prayer. Good night." He hangs up the phone and turns to Wanda. "Okay, honey, you want to call Myron, why?"

"Myron and I can go drive the highway to Winterville to see if we can find Mom. Maybe she's stuck somewhere along the road."

"Wanda, I don't think that is a good idea."

"Dad, you can stay here, in case she calls. We can always find a payphone in Winterville to call you."

Thomas is reluctant, but he agrees.

Wanda immediately calls Myron and fills him in on the details. "Could you pick me up at my house and drive to Winterville with me?" she asks. "Great. See you soon." She hangs up the phone, telling her father, "Myron will be here in ten minutes."

In less than ten minutes, Wanda hears a knock at the backdoor and Myron is welcomed into the Hamilton kitchen.

"Thanks for coming to help," says Thomas.

"You're very welcome, Mr. Hamilton. I'll go with Wanda to check the highway to Winterville, and we'll also drive by St. Barnabas church."

"I'm ready to go Myron," says Wanda. "Let's take my car; you drive."

"Please call as soon as you find out anything," says Thomas.

"We will, Dad."

Myron and Wanda start out immediately in Wanda's car. Wanda is fidgety and keeps turning her head in every direction, hoping not to miss anything.

Northbound on the highway to Winterville, Myron keeps his speed ten miles per hour under the posted speed limit. There are no cars stopped along the road. Oncoming traffic totals only two vehicles, both trucks.

"Wanda, we're almost to Winterville. There's nothing. Where could she be?" Myron taps his fingers on the steering wheel.

"We need to keep looking. I've never seen my Dad so worried; I'm worried, too."

"We're at the Winterville city limits. Let's find the church."

"This is probably useless," Wanda moans. "Dad called the church and was told that all the women had left and the parking lot was empty."

"There's the church on the left," Myron points out. "Yeah, I don't see any cars, and the church is completely dark. I'll turn at the next intersection so I can get to the parking lot. "

"It's empty," Wanda sighs, "as Dad was told."

"Was your Mom going anywhere else?" Myron asks.

"Yes, she was going to buy shoes, but that store must be closed by now."

"We can still check," says Myron.

Wanda nods. "Take the next right turn; follow the curve. There—that's it up ahead. It's closed; I notice only a night-security light. The parking lot is empty. There is a payphone near the front door; I should call Dad."

Myron parks the car and Wanda gets out to make her call.

"Dad, we haven't seen any sight of Mom or the car."

"There's been no contact here, either," Thomas says. "I'm going to telephone the Sheriff. You and Myron come back home."

"Yes, Dad. We'll be home soon."

Wanda tells Myron to drive back to Clinton, as her father is contacting the Sheriff.

"We can keep looking on the way back, Wanda. We'll find her. She'll be okay."

Neither Myron nor Wanda observes anything along the highway during the return trip to Clinton.

Nearing Clinton, Myron asks Wanda, "I don't want to be selfish; I know you need to get home. Would you give me a minute to stop at the factory? I forgot my mother's birthday present there. I couldn't wrap it at home. Maybe your mother, like the other night, stopped at the factory on her way home and had car trouble. It's a long-shot."

"I really should be getting home. I'm starting not to feel very well. I'll look everywhere to find my Mom. Okay."

"I understand, Wanda. I won't dilly-dally; trust me." Myron turns off the highway in the direction of the old factory. The building is dark, no vehicles. After parking in front, Myron takes out his key and opens the padlock, then pushes open the old factory door.

Flipping the light switch, Myron and Wanda enter the factory; it looks exactly like any other visit.

"Sorry, Wanda. I guess my long-shot fails. I thought she might have come here, as she did that night once before—to check on us. Let me retrieve my present."

Wanda cups her hands around her mouth and shouts: "Mom, are you here? Its me, Wanda."

On the second floor, Sarah is groggy and disorientated. Her head aches something fierce, and she's lost feeling in her hands. Her world is black, and she doesn't know where she is. She thinks she is hallucinating when she hears Wanda's voice. She tries to speak, but she can't. Her entire body is constrained. She tries to lift her feet but can't do that either.

Please come upstairs. I'm here! Sarah screams inside her head. *Please help me; please help me.* The words do not disturb the silence of the factory's second floor.

One floor below, Wanda calls her mother's name twice more.

"I'm sorry, Wanda," Myron says again. "I don't think anyone is here except us."

"Maybe with these high ceilings I can't be heard upstairs."

"Give it a try. That's all we can do."

Wanda flips on the light switch by the second floor stairs; at the top of the stairs, only one bulb at the far end glows with light. She shouts back to Myron, "Another bulb has burned out. There were two good ones out of three when I was up here the other day." Cupping her hands to her mouth again, she yells: "Mom, are you here? Please answer."

Wanda hears no response. She steps ten paces forward, but then turns around, disappointed, when another call goes unanswered. She is more disheartened as she descends to the first floor. She hesitates near the barricaded cistern and looks into its shadows. After reciting a rare prayer to herself, she rejoins Myron.

"Wanda, I took a quick look outside around the sides of the factory, and there's nothing out of the ordinary. Car tracks look like your Fairlane and mine. We should go."

Wanda reluctantly nods her head.

Myron turns out the lights, padlocks the factory door, and the twosome returns to Wanda's car to begin the ride back to the *Pioneer Ledger.*

All the lights are on in the *Pioneer Ledger* office and living quarters. Thomas looks completely disheveled. Three coffee cups with varying amounts of liquid sit in random order on the kitchen counter. A half-eaten jellyroll is perched on top of one of the cups.

"Dad, we're home," Wanda cries as she comes in with Myron via the backdoor. "We couldn't find anything, Dad!" Wanda wails, tears streaming down her face. "I'm really scared."

"I am, too," Thomas admits, trying to remain calm. "Sarah has never been extra late without calling. But we must not get too upset. I called the Sheriff, and he's notified the investigator, Mr. Johnston, who'll be in Clinton tomorrow. You both need to try to sleep."

"Wanda, I'm going home but I'll be back at daybreak," says Myron, giving her a hug. "We'll look for your Mom as soon as it's light out—if she is not already home."

Wanda gives him a kiss as he is leaving, and then says to her Dad, "I don't think I can sleep, but I'm going to lie down. Call for me if you need anything."

Thomas is left alone at his kitchen table. He reaches for a cup of coffee but spills half of it, as his hand cannot stop shaking.

"Sarah will be all right. She is safe," he keeps saying over and over again. "God, I've seen enough horrible death uncovered this weekend. I don't need to experience any more."

Chapter Thirty-six

Sarah is having difficulty mentally trying to determine if what she believes happened is real, or if her mind is playing tricks on her. Her jumbled thoughts slide from conscious to unconscious. The physical pain she is experiencing feels real. Her mind mimics an uncontrolled slide projector where she visualizes a car careening in front of her; with a click, an image of headlights in her rearview mirror blinding her; another click, Melissa's name on a gravestone.

Oh, God, help me. You are the resurrection and the life. Help me realize the hope of your prophet Jeremiah. Please help me. Oh God, don't forsake me.

Sarah thinks she hears footsteps. *My nose tells me I must be on some farm. I hear birds above me.* She feels a chill, whether it is from fear, lack of body heat, or exposure to the elements, she cannot comprehend.

She hears a voice: "Good morning, Sarah. I told you I would be coming back." The voice sounds familiar, but ominous.

Sarah wonders what time it is—how long has she been here? She heard birds chirping earlier but now, all is silent. She hears the voice again. "I brought you a drink of water and a bite to eat. I can give them to you if you promise you'll not yell or shout. Just nod your head 'yes.' I'm not going to hurt you. You still need to be quiet if I remove the tape. Can you do that for me today?"

Sarah thinks she recognizes the voice, but isn't sure. She needs to drink; and nods her head.

"Now that's a good girl. Just a moment. I'll loosen the tape. Stay still; it may hurt a little. Good. Stay quiet. Open your mouth. Here's water. Drink slowly. Slowly, now. You can have as much as you want, just don't choke. Good. Let me pull forward the tape that's under your chin. Here's a bite of a peanut butter sandwich. Take it easy. That's good. Take another sip of water."

Sarah feels the dryness of her throat temporarily disappear. She does not feel hungry, but she eats the sandwich unaware of when next or if she would be offered food. With the tape removed from across her mouth and loosened under her chin, she can partially separate her lips, but not completely.

She has to speak.

"Why are you doing this to me?" asks Sarah, the words barely audible.

"I have to protect myself."

"I am no threat to you," she insists.

"Yes, you are. You know more than what your husband prints in his newspaper. I've seen the investigator come to Clinton several times. He's tried to have me disclose things. I saw Mr. Johnston visit the *Pioneer Ledger* earlier this week, the day before the story on finding bones at Sand Lake was printed for the entire town."

"The investigator doesn't confide in me. I've heard gossip, but everyone in town hears the stories, listens to the same lies."

"Your daughter has been out to the old factory on several nights, looking around."

"She's only there because her boyfriend is." Sarah catches herself trying to breathe though her mouth and almost coughs. "She's not searching."

"I don't believe you. She doesn't need a flashlight to visit her boyfriend. That plane, or whatever it is, is on the first floor. I've seen the lights go on ... on the second floor. There's no reason for her to be on the upper floor unless she's searching for something."

"You're wrong. You're wrong." Sarah feels a sharp pain that starts in her hand and shoots up her left arm. "Please loosen the rope on my hands. It's hurting me."

"When time is right. You can't tell me you were not good friends with Father Murphy."

"Father Murphy?" Sarah twists her head back and forth. She needs time to think. Her conscience tells her she should not talk about Father Murphy. Her past is overtaking her, filling up her mind. *Melissa, oh Melissa. Sweet Melissa. Honey. I'll join you in heaven if God will forgive me. Our father who art in heaven, hallowed be thy name. I should have obeyed, listened to my mother, the commandments. I feel so worthless. I have failed in the values all women need to lead a proper life.*

"You can't tell me you were not good friends with Father Murphy," repeats the voice.

"He ... he was the priest for St. Mary's Church. The whole town of Clinton knew him," Sarah says slowly, haltingly, trying to endure the pain in her left arm. Her hands are throbbing with each quickening heartbeat.

"You knew him better than others."

Sarah gasps. "No. That's not really true."

"You stayed late when he had all those fund-raisers. All the other ladies would go home. You stayed. You stayed there with Father Murphy."

"Not … all the time."

"Father Murphy pleaded for your life and two other women before he died. He said he would absolve me of sin if I repented. I've led a respected life for years. The three of you never understood how safe you were as long as I believed Father Murphy would keep his word and not tell on me."

Sarah freezes in shock. She shivers. She discerns the shiver as one of fear, not cold. How would the voice know Father Murphy pleaded for others unless he killed Father Murphy, or was there? This new fear causes her to shiver uncontrollably. Panic rises in her chest. "You … you killed … killed Father Murphy," the stuttering words are barely audible from Sarah's lips. She bites her lower lip as she realizes she has spoken aloud.

"Yes," the voice replies smoothly, "he knew too much."

"Father Murphy was a kind and generous soul. He wouldn't hurt anyone. He wouldn't; he just wouldn't," Sarah says, feeling numb.

"Oh, you know different, do you? He was very attentive, shall we say, to parish women, older women at St. Mary's, especially the woman who was going through a crisis in her life. I'm sure he did more than listen."

"I don't know if I can say I… understand," says Sarah, trying not to rile her captor while at the same time hiding her Father Murphy secret. "Father Murphy was doing what priests do. He's supposed to console, offer comfort to all parishioners. I'm sure he was only doing that. To those in despair, he tried to offer hope, that's all."

"He deserved to have his hopes taken away."

"No one deserves to have their hopes dashed. Killing Father Murphy does not extinguish God's hope."

"Father Murphy wasn't killed for God's hope. His hope was secular. His hope was to build that gym for the kids at St. Mary's. I made sure I took that away from him."

"You couldn't take the gym away. It wasn't even built."

Sarah hears the shuffling of feet. Then, the voice is back.

"Yes, I could. Father Murphy needed money to build the gym. I knew the diocese refused him financial help to build his gym. The bank refused. He had to go back to his favorite church ladies. He had to take money from the Sunday collection plate. He had to hide his transgression."

"Father Murphy would not steal church money," mumbles Sarah.

"Well, not steal exactly, but divert money to his purposes and realize both of his earthly desires. Create times to lure and gain the affection of his most favored church ladies, and have them toil for a growing money pile."

"You're wrong. You're wrong."

"Father Murphy must have worked his magic spell on *you* for you to be so convinced. You can't swear on a Bible that Father Murphy did not try to get you alone with him, touch you in forbidden places, stimulate the warmth of your desire, utter sweet words only lovers would say. You can't! I saw the signs. I saw *all* the signs. Rosie told me it happened to her, too!"

"Mr. Klempler. That's you isn't it. You said Rosie. I know your voice. Now, I know why the blindfold."

"You shouldn't have said that! Shouldn't have spoken my name."

"Why me? Why now?" she implores.

"It didn't have to be. Rosie told me last week that she heard in the grocery store that you were investigating and had information to solve the death of Father Murphy. I couldn't let you do that—ruin my life. I have been content for many years. The guilt went away; what I did was right."

"Having revenge on Father Murphy was not to kill him?"

"No. When I suspected Father Murphy had touched— *violated*—my wife, I confronted Rosie. She denied it at first. My verbal threats did not work. It was only after I physically twisted her arm enough—I nearly broke it—did she tell me the truth. She had been tempted by Father Murphy one Sunday afternoon, but did not drink the wine he offered or succumb to his lustful, lurid advances. I believed her only after she passed out from the burning cigarettes I crushed out on her arm and she had not changed her story. Burns are such ugly scars. She had to give up wearing her favorite sleeveless summer dresses."

"Oh, my God."

"He can't help you now."

"But ... but Father Murphy did not deserve to die."

"No, and I wasn't going to kill him. I had a different idea on how to disgrace him. I saw my revenge in taking away his church gym dream. I had the account at the bank. The majority of the money was deposited into interest-bearing certificates under a fictitious name to keep the bank examiners from suspecting. When it came time to build the gym, I was going to tell the diocese of Father Murphy's scheme to hide church offerings with false overseas gifts. He would have been defrocked. I would have had my revenge."

"But you killed him, you did more than disgrace him."

"I'm afraid I had to. For a few months, I deposited the money and carried out my plan. Then Esther became suspicious."

"She ... she was merely the church secretary."

"Yes, but she became suspicious. She came to the bank, wanting to see records for Father Murphy's special account. She did not dare talk to anyone but me. She liked Father Murphy but she was sure Father Murphy was taking bake sale money and hiding it in a special bank account. She may not have realized it was Sunday collection money. I knew, because the amount given to me was too large, and Sunday offerings were the only place where Father Murphy could obtain such monetary sums. There also had not been a bake sale that entire month."

"You could have lied to Esther."

"No, I couldn't. She had deposit copies only Father Murphy should have had. She was threatening to expose everything. She said it was not Christian to lie to the members of the church. In addition, she feared she would herself be accused of stealing church money. She said, all you need to do is be honest, explain, and the parishioners would gladly support building a gym for their kids. I couldn't let that happen. If Father Murphy's secret account became public, then my diversion would be exposed. Even if I returned all of the money, I could be found guilty of creating false bank records. Creating an account with a fictitious name—that's worse than stealing money from the cashier's cage."

"You threatened Esther?"

"Yes, one day she called the bank. She claimed she was alone at the rectory and could not bring the special deposit to the bank. She asked me to pick it up?"

"So you agreed to do that?"

"Not at first, then I did. I turned my car into the rectory driveway. Esther opened the overhead door; I drove into the empty garage. We met at the garage doorway entrance to the kitchen. She said this was to be the last secret deposit. She planned to tell Father Murphy she knew of the hidden money when he came back home that evening. I couldn't have that. I grabbed her arm, swung her around, and put my hands on her throat, like this." Klempler clutches Sarah's throat.

"Please, please stop. You're hurting me!"

Klempler releases his thumbs from Sarah's throat. "I choked her until she was limp. I took the deposit from the kitchen table, and put Esther's body into my car's trunk. Since I was in the rectory garage, no one saw a thing."

"She's the second skeleton at Sand Lake, isn't she?"

"I warned you. You know too much," Klempler growls. "I found a wooden box in my garage, left over from when I bought my boys a swing set. I checked it and there were no special markings on the box. It was large, but it was all I had."

"You, it was you who buried her at Sand Lake."

"I had heard all the stories about Sand Lake. I was going to dump her body in the lake and have it appear she drowned. But I didn't have a boat. I remembered Gordon Oswald at the café always complaining there was neighboring lake property where he never saw the owner and I needed a remote location. No one would be surprised by a dead body at Sand Lake or by the time found it would be a body gone to bones."

"With Esther gone, you were safe." Sarah tries to rub her hands.

"I thought so. Father Murphy believed she had runaway. The gossip in Clinton helped. Arnold Peterson said he received a postcard from her in another state. Anita took over as church secretary and she didn't have a clue as to what Father Murphy was doing."

"But Father Murphy did something, didn't he?" asks Sarah.

"Yes, he felt guilt pangs. He fretted he would be discovered; his secret would be revealed. People at St. Mary's, he thought, would be so mad they would never build the gym, even if he had the money. He came to me at the bank one day, asking me to put together a record of deposits, interest earned, and the total amount that was in his special account. He was very pious, contrite. I knew that if he turned himself in, he would only ruin me. I could not let that happen."

"So you killed him." Sarah tries to move her legs; her effort fails.

"Well, not exactly. He laughed at my attempt to scare him. Esther's running off was to him a hoax. I denied knowledge. He said he didn't believe me, nor respect I was being serious."

"Why are you telling me all this now?" she whispers.

"I don't envision you telling anyone about me."

Sarah gasps. She hears feet shuffling again, then silence.

Minutes pass. She hears the tinny echo of metal underfoot, ever louder, and approaching her.

"Someone will find my car," she argues desperately. "They will search for me."

"I've planned for that. Your car is abandoned like it ran off the road. With the smell of alcohol, they'll think you were drinking, had an accident, and wandered off trying to find help. They'll see some blood, maybe a wig in the ditch."

"But I wasn't drinking. I don't drink alcohol."

"I helped with that. Who's to say you're not a closet alcoholic? Rosie has been since Father Murphy disappeared. I've found her hidden bottles. Who's to think you don't secretly take a drink or two of whiskey when no one is looking?"

Sarah suddenly becomes irate. "You going to strangle me like you strangled Esther and Father Murphy? Leave my body to decay to a collection of bones, like Esther at Sand Lake! And Father Murphy in the old factory cistern!"

"No. I took him and a small-caliber pistol to Sand Lake realizing I could not strangle him, as I had Esther. His hands were tied and he was alive when we arrived at Sand Lake. He kept trying to reason with me until I taped his mouth to stop his talking. I released his hands and made him carry a shovel, pickax, and a gunnysack with six bricks and two nails. I was going to clobber him with the brick-filled sack; that would not alert a lake fisherman while a gunshot might. First, I made him use the shovel to scrap the dirt off the box hiding Esther. Second, I made him use the pickax to remove the nailed-down cover boards. When he saw Esther's decomposed body, he dropped to his knees and tilted his head to the heavens, praying I thought. All of a sudden, he began to run. I fired a shot, which graz-ed his head and caused him to fall. I dragged his body to the box and rolled him into it next to Esther's remains."

"You killed him; shot him dead. May God have mercy on your soul." Sarah silently prays one Our Father.

"I didn't know if he was dead or not. I thought the bullet killed him. Then he groaned. I grabbed the pickax and swung. It opened a large gash in his side. I had brought along two large nail spikes. I had had thoughts about scaring him and, to show him I was serious, I had planned to drive one of the nails through his hand. But seeing the blood on his head and side, I figured he would die if I nailed the boards back to the box and reburied it in the dirt. So I did."

"What about the bricks? The nails?"

"I tossed them into the box. They were of no use. I had wiped the nails with the gunnysack and I had no fear I could be traced through them or the bricks."

"But Father Murphy's bones were not found at Sand Lake. He was found at the old factory." Sarah's arm pain eases slightly.

"True; right. Three years ago, I learned Arnold Peterson had purchased the property at Sand Lake. Windhurst had told me one day when we met in the bank hallway that Arnold Peterson was selling his house, factory, and land he owned at Sand Lake. I knew about the house and factory, but I was unaware of Sand Lake. I offered to spread the word and asked Windhurst if he knew where the land was located. He said adjacent to a Sand Lake cabin owned by Gordon Oswald. I knew where that was and inquired if Esther had to sign the deed to permit Arnold to sell the property. He said Esther had disappeared seven years ago and Arnold could have a court declare her legally dead and sell the property himself."

"You were going to be found out; isn't that right?" asks Sarah. "But there were two bodies in the box at Sand Lake."

"If Esther was found, no problem. Father Murphy was the problem. I was convinced that if there were court proceedings to have Esther declared legally dead, then there would be a full search for her, including at Sand Lake. Or, if not found by a search, surely a new owner would want to build there and the most desirable location for a cabin would be in the clearing. Either way it was, in my mind, only a matter of time."

"You could have moved both Esther and Father Murphy."

"I could have, however, I saw a better opportunity: Arnold Peterson would be the perfect patsy. He owned the old factory and he had this land at Sand Lake. The connection to him would be obvious. Even if Esther were found, she wouldn't be a link to Father Murphy. I've said enough."

"What if I said what you claim about Father Murphy is true? You had provocation. There were good reasons for your actions."

"I don't think so. Daybreak is almost here. I must go. I'll be back to deal with you later."

Sarah feels new tape under her chin, across her mouth, and the bandana blindfold tightened across her eyes.

She feels cold water being poured over her stomach, lap, and thighs. It feels like she is soiling herself, as she had earlier, but Klempler is diluting the odor. *As if anyone could smell anything with the stench in this place.*

Sarah is more fearful than ever. She has to free herself.

Wait a minute until he's gone, she tells herself. *Then try.* She hears heavy bags being tossed against each other. She counts the soft bag thuds, five total.

The chirp of a bird is all she hears in her realm of intermittent silence and total darkness. She winces in pain as she tries to twist her hands free. She cannot move her feet.

Chapter Thirty-seven

"**D**ad, you should eat something. I've made scrambled eggs," says Wanda.
"There's wheat toast in the toaster."

"Honey, I appreciate your effort and kindness, but I can't eat anything. I've been up all night. My stomach's not ready for food." Thomas is fretful. A hot shower is soothing under the spray, but its effect is not long lasting. His hands have been wrung so hard and often, they are chafed.

Wanda walks back to her bedroom. There is a knock on the front door of the *Pioneer Ledger*. Thomas finds Johnston standing there.

"Charles, come in. Let's walk back to the kitchen."

"Thomas, I'm sorry to hear about Sarah. I've been here in Clinton since daybreak. I suspect Sarah's disappearance is related to the bones we've found. Based on that, I interviewed three people with a G and O in their names. Myron Goostree said he was home last evening. His wife and Myron, Jr., attest to that. Gordon Oswald said he was also home all last night. As he lives alone, there was no household person to verify. A neighbor gent across the street said he and his wife both saw Oswald's car parked outside his house at different times of the night. Godfrey Klempler said he was home. His wife, Rosie, was there to back that up."

"What about anybody else?" Thomas motions for Charles to sit.

"That's everyone I was able to talk to. I don't know how to treat that third letter, the backwards 'C'." Thomas joins him at the table.

"You should be apprised Wanda drove to Winterville last night following the main highway and did not run across anything."

"Probably couldn't see much in the dark. The tree windbreaks along parts of the highway limit visibility to the shoulder and ditch."

"I called St. Barnabas. Talked to a priest there who walked to the church and parking lot. There was no sign of either Sarah or our car at about ten-thirty p.m., he said. Wanda struck out at the Winterville shoe store she thought her mother might have gone to and even stopped at the old factory. Still no Sarah. Not one clue."

"We'll find her. Sheriff has made finding Sarah his top priority. You must hang in there, Thomas. We're doing everything we can."

"Thanks, Charles. I trust you are."

The telephone rings. Wanda rushes into the kitchen to answer it. She looks at Charles and says, "Mr. Johnston, Sheriff says he needs to talk to you."

"Thanks." Johnston moves to the Hamilton kitchen phone.

"Hello, Charles Johnston. What can I do for you, Sheriff?"

"Charles, we found the Hamilton car. No driver; vehicle was empty."

"Where was it?" Charles asks.

"Deputy, responding to an accident call, found it south of Winterville on the highway to Clinton. I went out there myself. Car was heavily damaged on the driver side front. Out-of-the-ordinary damage to the rear bumper. Car went off the road, hit a field entrance road, and, from the damage, did not roll. There were no freshly made deep ruts in the ditch, but wheel marks hitting the field road near its top surface. There were no ruts or skid marks between where the car obviously hit the field road and where it was found. The car had to be driven or pushed along the field road to end up almost totally hidden from the road by the field tree line. It may have been Mrs. Hamilton who tried to drive the car after it stopped on the field road. There was blood on the car's interior. A car hitting an embankment with its front wheels should not have the extensive rear damage. That's my thought."

"Anything else? Were there any footprints or blood on the ground to indicate a direction of travel for Mrs. Hamilton?" Thomas darts for the bathroom upon hearing Johnston mention blood.

"No. Ground there is hard. The field road is hard, compacted dirt, and the highway shoulder is gravel, and footprints do not last in the un-mowed ditch grass. The only location where footprints might show up is in the cornfield, and I didn't see any."

"Is that it?" asks Johnston.

"One more thing, and please keep this under your hat—don't even tell Thomas. We found a strong smell of whiskey and an empty bottle in the car. Unusual, since I've never known either Hamilton to drink. We need to keep this detail out of any public statement."

"Thanks, Sheriff. I'll see you at your office later today."

Johnston hangs up the phone and scribbles a note to himself in his ever-present notepad. Thomas, back from the bathroom holding a towel, eagerly waits to hear what the Sheriff had to say.

"Charles, any good news?" asks Thomas.

"Well, we got news. The Sheriff found your car, damaged, and nearly in a cornfield next to the highway south of Winterville."

"And Sarah?" Thomas braces himself for the news.

"I'm sorry, she's missing. The car was empty."

"What? Where?" Wanda stands at the kitchen door. "We didn't see any car off the highway in the ditch last night."

"Don't feel bad. Sheriff said the car was off the highway almost totally hidden by a line of trees. Would have been outside a normal headlight beam. Was south of and close to Winterville."

"I'm going to call Myron and have him to take me out there. Somebody has to be looking for Mom."

"They are, young lady. Sheriff is searching himself. He'll have a deputy comb that stretch of highway. Trust me; the best thing you can do is stay home and be of as much help to your dad as you can."

"Wanda," says Thomas, "I have hope. While it's hard to accept that your mother is missing, we can pray she will be with us soon. I'm sure the Sheriff is doing everything humanly possible. We need to continue to have faith."

"I know. I know," blubbers Wanda, shedding more tears.

"Thomas, I must go. I'll stop where your car was found and maybe I can add to what has already been discovered. Sheriff didn't say, but your car should be towed to the impound lot in Winterville. We'll make sure it's returned as soon as possible."

"Charles, I wish you luck. I'll hold on the best I can. Sarah is a strong individual. I pray she will find the physical and emotional strength to survive this ordeal."

Charles puts his notepad away and, not waiting to be let out, he strides for the *Pioneer Ledger* front door.

Wanda's face is streaked with tears; eyes reddened. She knows Myron is at the elevator, but she is taking an excused work absence.

Thomas tries to read the morning newspaper. He cannot focus his eyes or his mind; the words in the paper are blurred. The fuzzy hands he sees on the kitchen wall clock appear slow to advance.

"Wanda," calls out Thomas, a half-hour after Johnston left, "I'm going next door and will lock the front door and leave the sign that indicates I will be returning shortly. You stay here. Come get me if we get another call from the Sheriff."

"Why are you going next door?" asks Wanda.

"My car was in an accident; I have no car. Even if it is drivable, the Sheriff will keep it for a few days. There is a car next door. It was Arnold Peterson's and I don't see why in this time of need I can't borrow it."

"You can use my car." Wanda rubs her eyes.

"I know that. I need to do something; even if it only means a short walk to see if the car next door still runs."

"I'll be here until you get back."

Thomas is not sure he really would drive Mr. Peterson's car, but he has to occupy his mind. He didn't want to ride his bike. He could have snuck out the backdoor, but he needed to make sure the front door of the *Pioneer Ledger* would be locked during his absence. He prays Sarah will be home safe before any gossip starts and has faith Johnston was discreet in his Clinton questioning. He steps onto the Peterson porch. It creaks even as he opens the front door. *I'm not going to do anything other than what I came here to do*, he thinks. In the kitchen, he notes Johnston decided not to put the boxes full of clothes back in the closet—they are stacked around the kitchen on the floor. He opens the door to the garage.

No car. The garage is empty.

"What is going on?" he asks the question to an empty garage. *"Who stole the car?" "Where is it?" Must stay calm*, he thinks. The overhead door is down and locked. The backdoor is locked. There are no signs of forced entry. Inside the house he checks all windows—they're all locked and intact. He quickly relocks the front door and walks around the house. No sign of any break-in. He returns to the *Pioneer Ledger*.

"Wanda," he calls out from Sarah's newspaper office, "has anybody telephoned?"

"There was a lady wanting to leave an item for Mom. I took a number and said she'd get a call back."

Thomas rotates the telephone dial in a familiar sequence. "Hello, this is Thomas Hamilton. Is George Windhurst in?"

Windhurst answers. "Hello, Thomas, what can I do for you?"

"Need your help, George. Did you take or have someone take the car from the Arnold Peterson garage?" Thomas doodles.

"No. You have my only Peterson house key."

"What about the backdoor in the garage?"

"I don't understand. The one key I gave you was for all exterior doors. That was my understanding."

"Did Arnold Peterson give you any other keys?"

"One ring had two keys for the old factory. A second ring had one key for the house which I gave to you."

"Were the two keys to the factory different or were they merely two identical keys for the same lock?"

"Different. I had to keep the house and factory keys separate to make sure I had the right one for property showings. Why all the concern? You told me you were not buying the car."

"George, Sarah is missing. Sheriff found her car with visible blood abandoned off the highway between Clinton and Winterville. Now the Peterson car is missing, too." Thomas, in Sarah's office, gazes at a photo of her holding a little girl.

"I'm sorry to hear about Sarah. That's awful. How can I help? She's more important than some old car. I'm in Winterville today. I can come to Clinton tomorrow."

"Where are those two Peterson keys you still have?"

"In my office at the bank. Top desk drawer," replies Windhurst.

"George, I'm going to call the Sheriff about the missing Peterson car. I understand he's in Winterville this morning. If he's willing to come to Clinton, would you give him the keys to your office so that he can get me the two Peterson keys you still have?"

"Sure. That's no problem. I don't see how getting the keys will help, but if you call O'Day you can tell him I'll be in my office, or my secretary will have an envelope with his name on it containing my Clinton office key. Or, would want me to call Klempler at the bank. I'm sure he would have a bank landlord office key."

"No. I'll call O'Day. The fewer people involved, the better. And, the Sheriff has to know about the missing Peterson car. If I need any other assist, George, I'll give you a call. I'm grateful for your help."

Thomas dials the Lake County Sheriff's office.

"Sheriff O'Day, please. This is Thomas Hamilton."

"Hello, Thomas. Sorry to report I have nothing new on Sarah's whereabouts. I feel really sad for you. You doing okay?"

"That's not good news Sheriff, but I got another thing. I was at the Arnold Peterson house—his car is gone. It's all very strange. The house and garage were both locked up tight. There are no signs of a broken window, jimmied lock, or any kind of forced entry. The only key I had to get into the house has been in my possession since the day I signed the lease."

"What are you asking me to do?" asks O'Day.

"Sheriff, would you go over to George Windhurst's office in Winterville and get the keys to his Clinton office? I just hung up the phone with him. He's willing to let you go into his office here to get a pair of keys received from Arnold Peterson. I think we need to know if both keys are still there. One of the keys may be for the Peterson house. May explain why the Peterson car is missing."

"Thomas, I need a report on the car. What kind is it?"

"Ford Fairlane, white. Four-door, I think. Not too new."

"Did it have a license plate?"

"I think so. I don't recall the number."

"That's okay. I'll Teletype the DMV. Give me an hour or so. You stay at the *Pioneer Ledger* and let me handle it. You hang in there. People are looking for Sarah."

"Thanks Sheriff." Thomas runs his finger over Sarah's photo.

There is a knock at the backdoor. Wanda answers it.

"Hey, Myron. What you doing here?" asks Wanda.

"I'm on lunch. Wanted to make sure you're all right."

"Wanda, who is it?" calls out Thomas.

"Myron, Dad. He is on lunch break." Thomas stays where he is.

"Wanda, did they find your mom yet?" asks Myron.

"No, but her car was found off the highway south of Winterville, back behind trees. We drove right by last night, twice. Sheriff was investigating. Dad and I are sitting here, waiting. I wanted us to go to Winterville to help search. We were told 'no' by the Sheriff."

"Your mother is a good driver. She would not cause an accident by herself. I saw the investigator talking to Mr. Oswald at the elevator this morning," says Myron. "It looked serious to me."

"Do you think it has to do with what we found at Sand Lake Saturday, or the bricks? Myron, I'm even more scared now."

"Wanda, you have to be brave. I've got to get back to the elevator. After work, I'll stop at the restaurant and bring you hamburgers and fries, enough for your Dad, too. You need a hug."

"Bye." Wanda feels a little better with Myron's words.

While Thomas waits in Clinton, Sheriff O'Day drives to the Winterville Windhurst law office. Rebecca sends in the sketchy Peterson vehicle data and gets a DMV full report. She promises a statewide all-points bulletin for the missing vehicle will be issued by the time her boss reaches Clinton.

Sheriff O'Day pulls into a vacant Clinton parking spot directly in front of the bank. He locates Windhurst's office and enters using the key in the envelope he received from Windhurst's secretary. Closing the door behind him, he searches the top drawer of Windhurst's desk—no keys. He feels awkward rummaging a second time through the drawer contents, but maybe the keys were shoved to the back.

Perhaps, he thinks, he misunderstood the drawer location. As he had driven all this way, he is sure Windhurst would not be upset if he expands his search. He checks all the desk drawers and one small unlocked cabinet, but does not find any keys.

Later, arriving at the *Pioneer Ledger*, he tells Thomas, "I checked all the drawers in Windhurst's bank office. There are no keys."

Thomas appears surprised. "That's odd." Thomas coughs. "Sheriff, can we take a ride out to Sand Lake?"

"Why, Thomas?" asks Sheriff O'Day.

"While I was waiting for you to get to Clinton, my mind was replaying over and over the events of the last three months, especially this last week. Three places are prominent: One, Clinton, obviously; two, the old factory; and three, Sand Lake. Certain people come up repeatedly: Arnold Peterson, Esther Peterson, Gordon Oswald, Myron Goostree, Father Murphy, and someone who has his or her identity scratched on that brick—the three letters. I know Charles talked to you. He said he talked to three people whose name could be connected to the letters on the brick, and the only one without a confirmed alibi was Gordon Oswald. And, he has a connection both with the old factory and Sand Lake."

"Yes, and how will that help with finding Sarah?" asks O'Day.

"The missing Peterson car struck me as strange. When I said the word 'struck' in my mind, it made sense—Sarah is a good driver. She would not run off the road. She would have had to have been pushed, or 'struck' by another vehicle—maybe on purpose. If from this town, the person or persons doing such a thing could not afford to use their own car or truck. They would have had to obtain a vehicle. How this person or person would have gotten into the Peterson garage without breaking a door or window I have not figured out, but it made good sense to me that a stolen car ran Sarah off the highway—a car stolen from the Peterson garage."

"Thomas, you make an interesting point." O'Day fiddles with a pen as Thomas watches Oscar press his face to the front window.

"Sheriff, I know you always keep certain details close to your vest. I'm not asking you to confide secrets in me, but I need your help. Wanda and Myron stopped at the old factory late last night on their way back from trying to find Sarah's car along the highway. They told me the door to the factory was locked and they could get no response to calling Sarah's name. That leaves Sand Lake. I want to have a look around."

"Thomas, I know you hurt and hurt deeply that Sarah is missing. I wish I could tell you where to find her. I find the fact that keys Windhurst said are in his office desk, were not there and the absent keys involve Old Man Peterson's property very concerning. I don't know what we'll find at Sand Lake, but I'm willing to take a ride out there to satisfy curiosity. Also, a little fresh air might make you sleepy and you look like you did not have much sleep last night."

"I haven't Sheriff. I can sleep when Sarah's home."

The official car ride to Sand Lake reveals nothing en route. Thomas spends his time trying to take in every piece of landscape he can, scanning for something, anything, that looks out of place.

"Thomas, we'll take the township road around Sand Lake's southern shore, then travel to the northern portion."

Thomas notices the two Oswald property pillars. "Can we check the Oswald driveway?" asks Thomas.

"Sure," says O'Day, turning in. There are no vehicles, no sign of any inhabitant or visitor. Backing out, the Sheriff continues on his announced route of south to north.

"Wait a minute, Sheriff. Stop!" shouts Thomas. "Look—check out that last driveway we passed here on the northern side of Sand Lake."

Slowing down, and then backing up, the sheriff notices a white Ford parked in the driveway. Turning to Thomas, the Sheriff says, "Thomas, I'm going to drive slowly down the driveway until I'm behind that white car. I want you to stay in my car. Don't get out. I'm going to switch my radio to broadcast. If need be, press this microphone button, and you'll be connected with my office. I'm getting out of the car now."

Thomas, eyes staring ahead, feels his heart pounding against his chest. He closely watches the measured steps of the Sheriff; his right hand ready to draw the revolver in his holster.

The Sheriff peers intently into the interior of the car—a white Ford Fairlane, four-door sedan. Thomas wishes he had taken note of the license plate number of the Ford he had seen in Peterson's garage. Step by step, the Sheriff reaches the front fender of the car. He looks down at the front bumper for the longest time. Finally, the Sheriff walks in hurried fashion to the front door of the property's cabin. After pounding on the door, at least twice, the Sheriff tries the door handle and finds it locked.

After satisfying himself that there is no one currently in the cabin or on the property, Sheriff O'Day returns to his car.

"What did you find?" asks Thomas.

O'Day ignores him and reaches for the radio microphone, pushes the button, and hears a female voice, "Is that you, Sheriff?"

"Yes, Rebecca. Do me a favor. Tell me the license plate number for the Peterson vehicle all-points bulletin."

"2D 7237," she quotes from a DMV sheet.

Both Thomas and the Sheriff read the same numbers on the white Ford parked in front of them.

"Thanks, Rebecca. I've located the missing car. It's here at Sand Lake, on the northern side. Sign at the front door of the cabin reads 'Welcome from the Williams Family.' See if you can track down the owner's full name and other particulars. Also, call the maintenance department and have them send a tow truck out here as soon as possible. I think the car's evidence in a hit and run. It needs to go to the impound yard not to be released without my signature. Call me if there is any problem."

"Thomas, we have to wait thirty or forty minutes for the tow truck. Come with me and let's both have another look at the front end of this Ford."

From different sides of the Sheriff's car, they walk ahead to the Ford.

"Tell me what you see," says the Sheriff.

"Looks like this bumper collided with something its entire length. There are scratch marks everywhere. I find it out of the ordinary there are dents and indentations on the front passenger side near the wheel, but no such damage on the driver's side."

"Good eye, Thomas. Reminds me of similar damage I've seen when young kids would try to run another off the road. If a full hit in the rear wouldn't cause the struck car to veer into the ditch, the car behind would race ahead and try to make the other swerve into the ditch. If the car nearest the ditch didn't swerve, the cars would collide. Do you know a Williams family that has a Sand Lake address?"

"It's such a common name. I must have a dozen subscribers named Williams. I don't remember off the top of my head."

"Just asking. I'm sure with time we'll find the driver of this car."

"Sheriff, can you check the car for keys, any keys."

"Good idea. You keep your eyes peeled and tell me if anyone comes or if you see a yellow and orange tow truck drive by. Often they don't use the radio to locate me, just drive and drive."

Sheriff O'Day undertakes an extensive search of the car's interior and trunk after putting his gloves on. "One key, Thomas," he calls out. "An ignition key placed under the front floor mat."

"That ignition key was under the front floor mat when I first found the car in Peterson's garage. I should have put it someplace else. I wasn't thinking."

"Don't worry about it. If someone was wanting to steal this car, they could have easily hotwired the ignition as used a key found under the floor mat."

"I'm happy we found the Peterson car, but we're still no closer to finding Sarah. She obviously is not here."

"Sad to say, I agree with you. I must get back to Winterville, once that tow truck arrives. I will bring Johnston up-to-date. There's the tow truck now. Get back in the car while I back out of this driveway. After I let the tow truck in, I'll give him the necessary instruction, and then we'll talk while I drive you home."

Myron is sitting with Wanda at the Hamilton kitchen table when the Sheriff drops Thomas off. He immediately leaves to go back to his office.

"Dad, did you find Mom, the car?" asks Wanda.

"The Sheriff and I found the Peterson car on the north side of Sand Lake, parked in the driveway of a cabin. A sign said home of a Williams' family. I don't know who that is."

"Mr. Hamilton, it might be Stan Williams," Myron offers. "He farms north of Winterville and has a cabin on Sand Lake. Feeds a lot of hogs. We load up bags of special piglet groomer for him about three times a year. He has told me the elevator carries the best brand. He's talked fishing with Mr. Oswald. That's the most I can tell you."

"That'll help Myron. I would have to take a look at our car, but Wanda there's more than an even chance that the Peterson car ran your mother off the highway," says her Dad. "The car had marks and dents on its front bumper and on the front passenger side, but not the driver side. If that is the case, we really need to find Sarah. I'm also missing something. The Peterson car was taken from a locked garage. I have a key to the house. And, I think Windhurst has keys, although he said he gave me the house key and the other two keys were for the old factory. He said both factory keys were in his Clinton office, but the Sheriff this afternoon could not find them where

Windhurst said they were. The Sheriff did not find them with the Peterson car at Sand Lake."

"How many keys did you say Mr. Windhurst had in his office for the old factory?" asks Myron.

"Two." Thomas takes a sip from Wanda's glass of water.

"That's not true. The old factory only has one outside lock. The second floor door only locks from the inside, and that is with a latch and a sliding bolt. The only padlock that needs a key is the first-floor sliding door."

"They could have changed that."

"No, I was told I had to be very careful with the key I had because there was only one padlock to the old factory. If I lost a key, the padlock would have to be replaced and new keys made."

"Myron, do you know how many keys there are for the old factory entrance door padlock?"

"Yes, three. Mr. Oswald has one at the elevator. I have one. Mr. Peterson as the owner had one. That was all there were. The key has 'Do Not Duplicate' stamped on it, so I'm sure no locksmith would make another," says Myron.

"From what you're telling me, Mr. Windhurst had to have Mr. Peterson's factory key, and odds are the second key on Windhurst's factory key ring was a spare for Mr. Peterson to let himself into his garage should he lose his front door key. Myron, would anybody have been at the old factory today?"

"No. This time of year only I go to the old factory. Why?"

"If the Peterson keys are missing from Windhurst's office, and I'm correct that the second key was for Peterson's house, that would allow someone to get into Peterson's garage, find the ignition key, steal the car, and lock the garage so no one would know the car was missing." Wanda leaves the table to refill her water glass.

"Mr. Hamilton, if the car was taken, then why are the keys still missing?" asks Myron.

"Either because the person still needs one of the keys, or maybe there is a plan to return the keys to Mr. Windhurst's office before they are missed, which would be next Tuesday at the earliest. There would be no need to come back to the Peterson house to return a damaged car when it would be easier to dump it at Sand Lake with a reduced chance of being caught. If dumped at Sand Lake, the person would need a getaway vehicle. Perhaps an accomplice."

Wanda is not taking part in the keys conversation, until she realizes that she and Myron had thought no one was at or had been at the old factory because they found the padlock still locked and no lights were on. They had not considered a stolen key.

"Dad, we need to check the old factory again."

"Why, Wanda?" asks Thomas.

"When Myron and I were at the old factory last night we found the first floor sliding door padlock locked as it should be. There were no lights on in the building so we came to the early conclusion that Mom had not been there. I know I said something to Myron that when I went up the stairs to the second floor there was only one light on and two were out. I was up there only a couple days before and two bulbs had been shining, only one light was out. If what Myron says is true—that no one has been in the old factory building except him and he only stays on the first floor—there should have been two lights still glowing last night. If the second had burned out, it should have popped when I turned on the switch. I don't remember any pop. And the more I think of it. When I was up there the other day, there was fertilizer dust all over the floor. My sneakers left tread imprints. Last night, I don't remember them still being there. I want to go back to the old factory. I want us to take some flashlights and really, really make sure Mom is not in that old factory."

"Wanda, are you sure," asks her father, rubbing his hands.

"Yes. We still have some daylight left to help us."

"Mr. Hamilton, you can use my car," Myron offers. "I have my factory key with me."

"You two get in Myron's car. I'll be a minute. I must leave a message for the Sheriff. Tell him what we're doing so that he doesn't call here and get nervous when no one answers the telephone."

After leaving a message with Rebecca, Thomas crawls into the back seat of Myron's car and the three of them only get more anxious on their trip to the old factory. There is still an hour of daylight left. The old factory has the forlorn look of an abandoned building.

Myron puts his key into the padlock and slides the entrance door to the left as far as it will open.

Not knowing what they might find, Thomas issues a warning to stay close together as they walk to the second floor stairs while looking every which way. Thomas takes the lead. A grackle squawks at being disturbed. Myron toggles the light switch.

At the top of the stairs, Thomas stops to look at the floor. He sees no sneaker tread imprints. Fertilizer dust is spread around as if lightly brushed by a swinging rag mop. He whispers to Myron, "which way?" Myron looks at Wanda, who points to the left.

After a few steps forward, with a turn around some piled bags of dog food, Myron stops. He points at bags in front of him as he faces the exterior wall. "Something's odd here," he says. "I was never taught to stack bags that way. There is always to be a passageway, unless the bags are up against an exterior wall." The three of them are standing close to the second floor center.

Myron walks forward, hands his flashlight back to Wanda, and grabs the top bag. Now he knows something is definitely amiss— there is no bag behind the one he has pulled down. He takes two more off the top. Suddenly, the tension is broken by his shout.

"Mr. Hamilton! Over here! It's Mrs. Hamilton!"

Thomas bolts forward, rips at two bags in his way, and leaps into the cavity created by the seed corn bags.

"Sarah! Sarah! Speak to me!" he cries, tugging at the tape across her mouth and reaching, and failing, to remove her blindfold. She offers no reaction.

"Mom!" Wanda exclaims, squeezing past Myron. Myron stands there, looking around to see if anyone else is there. Thomas lifts the bag off his wife's feet. He keeps repeating, "Sarah! Sarah, speak to me!"

"Thom … as?" she utters weakly. "Thomas, is that you?" is not audible.

Tears running down his cheeks, Thomas hugs his wife.

"Stay still," he instructs. "Sarah, thank God you're alive. We'll get you out of here. I'll get the blindfold off first. This might hurt when I pull this one end of the tape off your mouth, and from your chin."

"Ouch," cries Sarah.

"You okay Mom?" asks Wanda.

"Yes, darling," Sarah says, still barely audible.

Myron comes up behind Wanda. "Wanda," says Myron, "take my car and go home and telephone the Sheriff and ask him to send an ambulance from the Winterville Fire Department. I'll stay here to help as needed. Please, we need to get your mother to a doctor." Wanda takes the offered car keys and races back down the stairs.

"Thomas, my hands," Sarah moans. "I can't feel my hands."

"Let me see, this rope is tight. Myron, you have a knife down-stairs for working on that glider? Get it would you?"

Without a word, Myron is downstairs pawing through his tool-box for his utility knife. Once found, he brings it back upstairs.

Thomas, with the utility knife, slowly cuts through the rope strand by strand until one of Sarah's hands is free.

"Thomas! What did you do, my hand!"

"It's the blood returning, dear," he says soothingly. "One more minute and I'll have both hands free. Here, let me put my jacket around you. How are your legs? Do have pain anywhere other than your hands?"

"My head really hurts. I feel stiff and sore all over. I was ready to join Melissa."

Thomas strokes her shoulder. "We found the car that I believe ran you off the road last night."

"It was horrible. It was Klempler," whispers Sarah.

"What? How do you know?" Thomas is aghast.

"I was blindfolded but I recognized his voice, and he called his wife, Rosie. He killed Father Murphy and Esther Peterson! He told me how. It was all about gym money."

A car comes up to the factory. Thomas and Myron stiffen and then relax when they hear Wanda's voice as she shouts it is she.

"Sheriff O'Day will be here in five minutes," she calls out. "His office got him on his car radio. The fire department ambulance is also on its way."

It is exactly five minutes; the four hear the wailing of a sheriff's siren. Sheriff O'Day leaves his lights flashing as he races into the old factory. Myron rushes to the stairs and down three steps to shout for the sheriff's attention.

"Mrs. Hamilton, stay still. You're going to be okay. Thomas, you can hold Sarah, but don't move her until the medics get here. They should be here shortly. My office confirmed they're on their way. When they get here, we can step back to let them check her."

"Sheriff, Sarah tells me that Godfrey Klempler did this to her and that he killed Father Murphy *and* Esther Peterson."

"Klempler?" O'Day repeats. "From the bank?"

Sarah nods, as Thomas explains. "It all makes sense now. I don't know for sure, but I believe today the three letters on the brick were to be G-O-D—not a backwards C but the incomplete letter D."

"Well, I'll be," sighs O'Day.

"Father Murphy," Thomas speculates, "not only scratched the word 'GOD' as a dying prayer but to help identify his killer. He used the only tools he had: a brick and a nail."

Chapter Thirty-eight

Sarah rests comfortably. She has no roommate this Friday in her Winterville Community Hospital semi-private room. The on-duty emergency room doctor had declared her to be in fair condition. The prognosis was there would be no permanent circulation restriction in her hands and feet and the bruises on her throat will disappear naturally. Her head wound laceration was expected to heal and, of most concern, doctors were closely watching the pupils of her eyes for signs of recurrent intracranial bleeding.

Sarah's doctor from the Winterville Clinic had prescribed plenty of bed rest, and put a no visitor restriction on her medical chart. She did not sleep well at all Thursday night. A fluid I.V. had been dripping since her admission to safely bring her body hydration level back to normal.

Thomas, Wanda, and Myron were at the hospital overnight with Sarah, although they respected the doctor's wishes not to loiter in her room and spent most of their time walking or napping in the hospital lobby or in a small canteen area. Only Myron brought reading material having grabbed one of his sailplane books before leaving the old factory to follow Sarah and Thomas in the ambulance.

Lunch had been served and Sarah only nibbled, it's not what she would have cooked. Thomas enters her room on one of his hourly visits. His look is haggard; eyelids are at half-mast. Myron had driven him roundtrip to the *Pioneer Ledger* at four a.m. to shower and shave to be somewhat presentable for Sarah.

"How we doing, doll?" he greets her.

"I'm fine, dear. Same as last report," she answers.

"Sheriff O'Day and Investigator Johnston plan on stopping by at three p.m.," begins Thomas. He holds Sarah's hand. "They want to get a more complete report on everything that has happened. They arrested Godfrey Klempler last night. He has denied everything and said you fingered the wrong man. The Sheriff, with a search warrant for Klempler's car and house, confiscated two keys on a ring last night that did not work in any lock in his house. A deputy went to the old factory and found that one key opened the first-floor padlock and the second key operated the garage door lock of our neighboring Peterson house. Klempler obviously stole the keys from Windhurst's office, using the bank's landlord key and expecting to return them before Windhurst returned this coming Tuesday.

"When Rosie heard what had happened to you, she broke down and confessed she had lied to Charles Johnston. She was afraid Godfrey would hurt her again if she crossed him. She said she followed Godfrey in her car Wednesday evening when he drove and parked his car at Sand Lake. She claimed Godfrey told her he was selling the car to a man who had a cabin on Sand Lake. She blamed herself for telling him she had heard in Goostree's Grocery that you were investigating Father Murphy's death and asked to search for information to identify the killer." Thomas shakes his head sadly. "I was to blame myself because I vaguely remember I also, one day at the bank, made a brief remark to Klempler that you were asked by Mr. Johnston about old bake sale records.

"I'm not a legal expert but how much of what Rosie said can be used against Godfrey is problematical given that there is a testimonial privilege that a wife cannot be forced to testify against her husband.

"The evidence, while circumstantial, except for his admissions to you, points to the conclusion Klempler did in fact kill both Esther Peterson and Father Murphy. The motive was money, and bank examiners have been called in to give Klempler's money-handling actions at the bank a thorough audit. I doubt, though, that they'll find the missing money.

"Sheriff O'Day was hopeful he'll get one Klempler thumbprint off the underside of the steering wheel of Arnold Peterson's Ford Fairlane. Klempler had been careful to wear gloves—except when driving Peterson's car. However, he may have missed a print when he tried to rub the steering wheel clean. The only other possibility of real evidence to support your testimony is that Klempler had not discarded a raincoat he wore as he was most likely planning to take you from the old factory today and wear it. On the raincoat were two or three brunette wig hairs stuck to the chest by what appears to be blood. Since there were also wig hairs with blood found on the upper back of your blouse between the shoulder blades, I've made the supposition that your wig fell off after you struck your head and was lying under your shoulders when Klempler picked you up and held the top part of your back against him before he dragged you to his car. If the wig fell to the ground outside our car there is probably some raccoon now sleeping with your wig as a pillow, having scurried off with it." Sarah groans. "I'm sure you'll be happy to offer a sample of your blood for comparison purposes. The Sheriff's deputy is actually at this very moment trying to locate your wig.

"The Peterson car and your wig hairs have been the number-one item on the crime investigation priority list and the gal, excuse me, female technician who was key with the Father Murphy bones volunteered to work all last night to examine the items confiscated from Klempler and your clothes. She found your wig hairs.

"Klempler moved Father Murphy's body when he feared the grave he dug would be discovered as Esther had passed the seven-year legal time period and was eligible to be declared legally dead. It must have been dark or he had been in a great hurry to remove Father Murphy's body that he missed the pelvis bone, a forearm bone, and selected one wrong hand. He was smart enough to remove the priest's collar, but it turned out to be a mistake to weigh down his carrying sack with three of the bricks that had been in the Sand Lake grave so that the bones didn't slide back and forth while being transported in his car trunk. When he dumped Father Murphy's skeletal bones into the cistern, he apparently just turned over the sack and let everything fall in. In the process, he didn't notice the letters on the brick or the one-hand bones had feminine rings. Oscar was the one who took the bricks from the cistern and stacked them in the tunnel he discovered. He didn't think anything of the scratching. He was going to use the bricks to weight down a wooden soapbox racer he was building. He left them in the tunnel because he feared the sheriff.

"Sarah," Thomas sees Sarah's eyes close, then open. "Perhaps, when you're home and felling better, you can tell me if Klempler told you why or how two nails were in the Sand Lake grave. That remains a mystery to me. I can only guess the entombed Father Murphy took his last breath before he could make the vertical scratch to complete the backwards C into a D for the word: GOD.

"Doll, I promised the nurse on duty that I would not stay too long, and I see you may not be comprehending all of what I said. I'll come back later." He leans over to kiss Sarah.

"Thomas, I love you. Tell Wanda I love her, too. I want to get out of this place and be home."

"I know, doll. You rest. The hospital is getting so many cards, letters, and plants delivered for you. Hilda personally delivered a large mixed bouquet that I have set over by the window to let the light breeze carry its fragrance, plus others, across the room."

"Thanks dear. I'll see you later."

Thomas closes the room door as he exits.

Sarah, while physically exhausted, is able to distinguish between reality and hallucinations. Thomas' mentioning the name of her friend Hilda brought to mind what Godfrey Klempler had said to her the day before about Father Murphy's favored ladies at St. Mary's.

Klempler said Father Murphy had pleaded for Sarah's life and two others—older women who were going through a crisis in their lives. His context was that these were parish women, like her, who had been violated by Father Murphy.

Klempler mentioned his wife, Rosie, but it's unlikely, Sarah thinks, Father Murphy would have been pleading for Rosie's life to Klempler; surely the man wouldn't kill his own wife. Rosie was no threat to exposing his false bank accounts as Esther Peterson would have or had been. Rosie's death would have been too close to him.

One of the three women, Sarah decides, had to be Hilda Swanson. Hilda was one of the St. Ann Circle women who often worked late at fund-raisers. Father Murphy might have pursued Hilda simultaneous with her, or possibly after that Sunday in March 1954 when she left Father Murphy in shame and before he disappeared.

Hilda matched the profile—an older woman, who held old-fashioned values of the woman's role that conflicted with the changing expectations of society. Sarah remembers Hilda had spoken of the nude beach episode, readily admitted she had disappointed her mother, and had felt sadness for her inadequacy.

Sarah tries to imagine who the third woman could be. She thinks of several names and dismisses each one as improbable. She realizes if she was able to keep her indiscretion with Father Murphy a secret, so could other women. She may have thought Rosie was lying about the physical cause of her eye malady, but she had never connected Rosie with being violated by Father Murphy.

Her mental exercise, while frustrating in that she cannot identify the third woman, is gratifying in that she is convinced her secret remains a secret. *How has Hilda managed to overcome her admitted failure and feelings of worthlessness?* Sarah ponders. She remembers her conversation with Hilda where Hilda said no one could be perfect; all that could be expected is that one keeps trying. Hilda quoted Father Murphy as having said the same thing.

I've been trying, Sarah reflects. *Trying not to live in the past and to live in the future. Trying to forget the past.* Then she remembers what Hilda had said was similar but very different. Hilda had said she lives in the present, not yesterday, not tomorrow.

I believe that I have been shown how to live to make the most out of life. I will live each day individually and do the best I can on the day I'm in. The day that is past is past. The day ahead I will not try to get to.

My path will be the one I am on that day. Nothing else will matter or distract me. I will do the best I can each day, as that day presents itself. I will be strong for the present day, and I will love others and give myself respect.

True to his word, Thomas returns, this time ninety minutes later and asks the same question.

"How we doing, doll?"

"I'm doing better," is Sarah's new report."

Her husband smiles broadly.

"We have to be prouder than ever of Wanda," says Thomas, noting Sarah is moving her legs, being more active, and not exaggerating to make him feel better.

"It was really her observations that were pivotal in finding you when we did. Wanda was very observant about little details. She thought of light bulbs, her footprints, and realized the changes she saw could not be if no one had been at the old factory. And I got some news about Myron that also affects Wanda."

Sarah's eyes widen at his mention of Wanda's name coupled with Myron's. She squeezes his hand to emphasis her interest.

"What's this? Myron? Wanda?" she whispers.

"Well, Myron, Sr., came to the hospital last night with a letter that looked important and was addressed to Myron, Jr., from the United States government. When our Myron opened the letter he spoke out loud: 'Greetings.' Our Myron has been drafted and instructed to contact the draft board for a report date. Wanda said she's going to wait for him the two years he's in the U.S. Army. Myron lost his deferment when he dropped out of community college, and the draft board reacted."

Sarah smiles. "Thomas, I don't know what to say."

"Don't say anything. Myron said he hopes to receive military training to be a better glider pilot."

With the news of Myron being drafted, Sarah thinks there may be a chance America will revert to the days of her parents where the hardships of war are followed by prosperity, where a wife stays home to raise a family, and the husband is the breadwinner.

"Thomas, I wasn't trying to respond to Myron's being drafted. I think we need to take a vacation without Wanda for I really need to talk to you. I need to explain to you how I have to live each day and only that day. I need to tell you the values my mother taught me that I believe are so important no matter if society says I am old-fashioned, out-of-touch, and traditional. I need to share with you why so long ago I initially told you 'no' to working for the *Pioneer Ledger*.

"This trauma with Father Murphy has brought out my personal anguish. I need to talk about Melissa, my accident a decade ago, and maybe a secret that should no longer be kept by me.

"And Thomas, you're going to have to completely and without question trust me and not ask why. You must support me and give me time to find and meet with at least three other women from St. Mary's who I feel are as affected by this tragedy with Father Murphy as I am. And for reasons you would not guess in a million years, I must reach out to Rosie Klempler no matter what happens to her husband in the criminal justice system."

"We'll do that, Sarah, I promise. First, you need rest to revive your strength. Second, you must help me write our most important story in the history of the *Pioneer Ledger*. This town deserves the facts of what happened and to realize how outlandish all the harmful gossip was. And, for the first time in my newspaper career, I will ignore those prewritten national editorials and tell local voters in my own words the qualifications required in our elected public officials."

Sarah can make out from under his drooping eyelids the journalistic happiness radiating in her husband's eyes. She asks, "Are you going to call it an exclusive?"

"You bet. I'm going to use my biggest type to announce it is a story about the prettiest, most exciting, loving, and exclusively wonderful woman in my life," beams Thomas as he kisses his Sarah.

With a beginning peace in her heart, calmness in her soul, and an elfish twinkle in her eye, Sarah whispers into her husband's ear, "Wanda, our daughter, will love her exclusive as the prettiest."

-30-

(Author's note: It was a well-accepted newspaper reporter convention to add a "-30-" at the end of their stories. Thomas Hamilton of the *Pioneer Ledger*, although fictional, deserves the same respect as his real-life counterparts.)

Donan Berg likes to hear from his readers.
Write to him
c/o DOTDON Personalized Services
1800 Third Ave Ste 415
Rock Island IL 61201-8019
Or
Email him at:
mystery@abodytobones.com

If you enjoyed Donan Berg's

A BODY TO BONES

here's a sneak peek at

his next Skeleton Series novel

THE BONES DANCE FOXTROT

Scheduled to be available

in trade paperback in summer 2009!

Spirits were still high—off the charts, Jake could say, as he was "up and at 'em" after his second night in the park residence. *I need more imagination in my breakfast routine,* he thinks, *but not today.* After coffee and cold cereal—oat bits floating in milk—he greets this day with a closet full of freshly laundered clothes hanging ever so nicely on simple wire hangers.

"Life is better with choices."

"Good morning, Jake," says Ranger Scott. "You're prompt. I like that." The Lodge blueprint is still lying open on the small desk in the headquarters office. "I'll be with you in minute. Have a seat."

Jake sits down at the small desk so he can take a closer look at the Lodge blueprint. The front entrance of the thirty-by-fifty-foot rectangular two-story stone building, with full basement, faces north. Each floor is identical in outside dimensions. On the basement blueprint drawing, the entrance doors are shown on the south end. Forty-five feet straight north of the entrance doors is a concrete block wall the entire width of the basement, with a standard thirty-six-inch door opening six feet from the west wall. Entering the door, the major space is to the right, which has another door, this one steel-plated, creating a six-by-five-foot closet. Jake's eyes bug out when he sees the words "dynamite storage."

"I found indications that there's dynamite stored in the northeast corner of the Lodge basement. Is that right?" asks Jake.

"There was, until someone decided it was not safe to put dynamite a floor beneath where people meet. The dynamite we use for blasting stumps is now stored in a special shed off the beaten track, deep in the woods," replies Ranger Scott.

"Good idea." Jake flips through pages he can't understand.

The Headquarters telephone rings.

"Good morning. Ranger Scott speaking."

"Ranger Scott, this is Janet Guthrie in accounting. There is no record of any approval for masonry work at your Lodge since the building was put on its new foundation in 1955. I've checked every scrap of paper relating to Cottonwood that I could find. Stayed past quitting time to do it."

"What about an expense claim for such work?" he asks.

"Zip there, too. No person or entity has ever submitted a claim for expense reimbursement that is found in this office. I asked the person who does expense authorization, and she does not remember any. She has a good memory, too."

"To double-check, would there be any other place or agency for such records?"

"Simply, no," confirms Ms. Guthrie.

"That's what I thought. I appreciate your hard work, Janet. It really appears we've had some unauthorized work done in the basement of the Lodge. I'll have to investigate further. Bye, now. Thanks again." Ranger Scott turns his attention to Jake. "You heard half the conversation. There has been no authorization or reimbursement claimed for that blocked-in doorway."

"So, what do we do? Leave it?" asks Jake.

"No. We're going to get a sledgehammer and bring that door opening back," replies the Ranger.

"Do you think that's wise? I'm new here, but busting through concrete block seems unusual."

"Jake, don't you worry. It's my decision, not yours. Several years ago, maybe five, there was a major bank robbery down river from here. The loot was never recovered. Only one gang member out of four was captured, and he's in Stillwater Prison. I suspect he's waiting to get his share. At the time there were rumors galore on where the cash, on-demand bond certificates, and two bags of gold coins were stashed. Talk about a gold rush; none of the rumors panned out."

"You think it might be in the basement of the Lodge?"

"As good a place as any, and better than most. Relatively isolated, but still accessible. Money would be safe from rain or snow. No one—that is, except you—would feel it necessary to pace off the basement with the floor above to note the space discrepancy. The old dynamite storage area is specially built to keep contents dry."

"You got me convinced. I've never been a gold rush prospector before." Jake's heart rate quickens; his body is ready for excitement.

"You go down to the barn shed and find a sledgehammer. I forget if we have one or two. I've got to get my goggles and gloves from the truck. I'll meet you back at the Lodge basement doors."

They did rendezvous as planned.

Ranger Scott started with a twenty-pound sledge, swinging a blow near where the top of the former door should have been, explaining to Jake that the door would have been filled in from the bottom up, so the top row or two might have less mortar in the joints. The first swing only cracks a block. Six more swings, and a hole the size of one block exists. No light, only darkness behind the smashed block.

"You want to join in?" quips Ranger Scott.

"Yes, sir." Jake targets the block next to the one Scott has pulverized. Five swings later, another block is gone.

Ranger Scott shines a flashlight through the opening to see only another brick wall.

Sledge on his shoulder, Jake takes more whacks at the third brick in the same row as the demolished two. Four solid connecting swings, and one row of block is removed between what was once doorjambs.

Alternating back and forth, the two keep pounding the blocks with the sledgehammer until only two bottom rows remain. A cloud of fine particles and dust fills the basement. Sweat on both men attracts a fine concrete powder and covers all areas of exposed skin and their clothes.

Jake thinks, *Now I'm getting my arms in shape to match what Saturday's dance did to my legs. If only I'm able to lift my arms up tomorrow.*

"Let's stop for the time being," suggests Ranger Scott. "We need to go upstairs and have a drink of water while this dust settles."

Jake agrees.

Minutes later, Ranger Scott has his flashlight out again. He steps into the reopened space and startles Jake with a sudden yell. "Whoa! Whoa, Nelly!"

"What's going on?" asks Jake.

"Jake, you won't believe this."

"You found the money? The gold?"

"No, not the money or the gold. Bones. There's a skeleton on the floor."

Jake leans over into the space where Ranger Scott is standing and sees that the ranger's flashlight beam has created eerie shadows over a full-size skeleton, partially clothed. The victim is lying on his or her face. The feet are shoeless.

"Shouldn't we be careful? The bones might be booby-trapped, like I see on TV with our soldiers in Vietnam."

To be continued in "The Bones Dance Foxtrot"
Scheduled for release in summer 2009

About the Author

Donan Berg believes, first and foremost, that imagination accents the real hopes and dreams living in all of us.

Second, a glimpse of the past offers each of us a better opportunity to kindle hope in the future.

A heralded talent for storytelling, he joins with you in *A Body To Bones* to explore sharing the enjoyment of mystery and budding young love, while showcasing compassionate strength as the winner over angst, fear, and feelings of worthlessness.

His journey is as a journalist, corporate executive, and lawyer residing in America's heartland, with extended family roots in his native Ireland.

If asked, he will tell you he enjoys all kinds of reading, preferring books where one is not interrupted by modern-day computer pop-ups. The only pop-ups he enjoys are those made by batters of the opposing baseball team.

A widower, his two children are grown and pursuing their own careers, one in law and one in journalism, for as the old cliché says, "The apple does not fall far from the tree."

A Body To Bones is his debut novel. The next novel in his Skeleton Mystery Series will be *The Bones Dance Foxtrot*.

Acknowledgments

As life often demonstrates, one's path is seldom solitary.

In the preparation of the manuscript for this novel, comments were received from many. They know who they are and how much their efforts have been appreciated to finally be witnesses to this first edition. All responsibility for the end result, however, rests solely with the author.

The employees of DOTDON (pronounced in two parts: DOT, a tiny spot or mark; and DON, a nickname for Donald) hope you have enjoyed this book.

For information about this title, and to receive further information on upcoming titles, please visit our Web address at: www.abodytobones.com